FATHERS AND SINS

*Jo Bannister titles available from
Severn House Large Print*

The Tinderbox
The Fifth Cataract

FATHERS AND SINS

Jo Bannister

Severn House Large Print
London & New York

This first large print edition published 2009
in Great Britain and the USA by
SEVERN HOUSE PUBLISHERS LTD of
9-15 High Street, Sutton, Surrey, SM1 1DF.
First world regular print edition published 2008 by
Severn House Publishers Ltd., London and New York.

British Library Cataloguing in Publication Data

Bannister, Jo
    Fathers and sins. - Large print ed.
    1. Divorced men - Fiction 2. Fathers and sons - Fiction
    3. Traffic accidents - Fiction 4. Church buildings - Fires
    and fire prevention - Fiction 5. Detective and mystery
    stories 6. Large type books
    I. Title
    823.9'14[F]

ISBN-13: 978-0-7278-7770-3

Printed and bound in Great Britain by
MPG Books Ltd, Bodmin, Cornwall

One

He crouched in a corner of the burning room, too afraid even to scream. The familiar scene boiled with smoke wreathing blackly to the ceiling. He choked on acrid fumes. Flames danced before him like shimmering scarves, a living curtain between him and the rest of his life. And over all, a roar like an express train.

Beyond the roaring flame was the door, beyond the door the stairs. One deep breath would carry him through the fire, down the stairs and outside. But he couldn't find the air; or else he couldn't find the courage. So he stayed where he was, rigid with terror in his corner, waiting to die.

Educational psychologists argue about the age at which a child understands about death. Quite early he may realize that a dead pet will not rise to play again however much he shakes it; later he will know that not only his grandparents and his parents but ultimately even he himself will succumb to that same lasting stillness. But between those two moments there is a quantum leap to be made.

So educational psychologists would have been interested to know that the boy had an absolutely realistic appreciation of what death meant, both theoretically and personally. It meant he had six years behind him and just a few agonizing minutes ahead. Like all children, he'd burnt his fingers from time to time. He could guess how it would feel when his whole body burnt up – the way the *Transformers* cushion had burned, the way the bed was burning now. He shook with trepidation.

Under the ceiling the smoke was boiling over, ready to fall on him. The thunder of the flames stopped his ears. The heat of the dancing curtain closing round him seared his skin and dried his staring eyes. But he couldn't close them, or look away from the brilliant choreography of the fire. Knowing he was going to die, the exquisite triumph of those lively, leaping flames was more than he could bear. He cried out, once, almost more in rage than in terror, and then the fire flashed over.

Away from the smoke of the bustling impatient city, in a leafy landscape where the brick walls were stained only by the centuries, in a low-roofed cottage in a lane scaled for pig-carts, the man and the woman shed the present like a skin, along with their clothes, and spent more time than they had known a day could spare exploring one another's bodies with wonder, reverence and love.

In an early evening scented by camomile and lavender, the soft sweet air dyed faintly green as if the sun had drawn up the essence of an English country summer all through the long day and was giving it back now as a kind of verdant dew, they walked in the cottage garden.

Robin Firth looked at the slender girl wandering, head bowed in thought, among the sweet rockets and his chest tightened with joy. Or it may have been angina. He was a lot older than her – old enough to be her father. But there was nothing paternal in what he felt for her, nothing filial in how she treated him. He'd loved once before, so he knew the real thing when he held it.

He thought, If I were a painter I'd paint her just like this, and have her like this forever. The cap of short dark hair, the brown eyes soft with thought, their lashes hovering above cheekbones like a china doll's, her long limbs pale as ivory as they emerged from the black sheath of her ... garment. Was it a dress, or merely a vest? And he'd call this painting *Agnes in the Garden*, and if he lost her ... if he lost her...

If he lost her he'd take a sledgehammer up to his tenth-storey office and break everything he could find. Then he'd start on the office next door. And people who'd always thought him a safe pair of hands with investors' money would gather in small knots round the coffee machine to shake their heads bemusedly. Some kind of a breakdown, they'd say sadly. We should have seen it coming. So unlike Robin Firth, making a fool of himself with a girl half his age!

And this was the measure of what he felt for her, that he didn't care what a bunch of middle-aged executives in expensive suits thought. Three months ago he'd have cared. Three months ago he was one of them: a man who could see the FTSE index tattooed on the inside of his eyelids when he turned off the light to sleep. He was always good at his job. Now he'd discovered that there's more to life than professional success.

And the difference was Agnes. She was twenty-five, a dancer at Covent Garden, and they'd met in a wine bar when the people he was waiting for turned up late and the friend she was meeting never arrived at all. Neither of them cared, or even noticed. If you believed in love at first sight, maybe you'd think it was that. At least you'd have to say that whatever it was between them was there from the start.

Now, three months on, Robin couldn't imagine being without her. She filled his soul. His happiness was enough to carry a kind of government health warning: that nothing this good, this important to him, could last forever. That was the real reason for the tightness in his chest. He was afraid of what a jealous god might do to two people who worshipped one another.

As if the shadow of his fear had touched her, a cool finger in the evening sunshine, Agnes looked up and for a moment her small face was serious. Then, like the sun banishing clouds, she smiled. Her eyes danced for him, and her long pale arm reached out to him across the misty heads of the flowers.

Robin said quietly, 'I suppose you know this isn't enough for me.'

'This?'

'What my parents called a dirty weekend.' Agnes chuckled, like water running over pebbles. Robin said severely, 'It's all right for you to laugh. But I'm a man of substance, a pillar of my community. I have a position to uphold. This could ruin my reputation.'

Agnes considered. 'Or be the making of it.'

Robin gave a gruff little snort. 'Actually, you're right. I've never been gossiped about before. I'm rather enjoying it.' Once again her merry eyes had distracted him from what he was trying to say. He struggled back on track. 'Listen to me. This isn't just the wine talking. You know how I feel about you. Bizarrely enough, you seem to feel the same way. I want you. Not just in bed; not just for weekends in the country. I want you with me. I want to marry you.'

They were both in earnest now. She put her slender hand in his. 'There's no need. It won't alter anything. I love you, Robin Firth. I want the same things you do. I don't need a bit of paper to remind me what they are.'

But he shook his head. He was a big man, both tall and well built, with thick hair and a trim beard the same shade of dark auburn. People who didn't know he worked in private equity always assumed he did something rather glamorous for a living.

'You're young,' he said; and before she could accuse him of stating the fatuously obvious he forged on. 'You have the courage of youth. I had it once, but it slipped away. About the time they painted my name on a bay in the office car park, I think. Maybe I sold out. Or maybe I just paid the price for what I wanted. All I know is, mostly now I want what I'm supposed to.

'I'm sorry if that disappoints you. But I'm a conventional man these days, and I want to marry the woman I love. I'm forty-eight years old. I've lived alone for eight years. I'd

like to have a proper home again. Somewhere to share with someone I care about.'

'I'd like that,' murmured Agnes. 'But...'

He wouldn't wait for the But. 'If you won't
marry me, I'll take what I can get on whatever terms you're offering. Move in with me.
Or I'll move in with you. Or we'll carry on
the way we've been – drinks after work, a
microwave risotto and a quick tumble on
that glorified beanbag you call a bed. If that's
all I can have, I'll take it and be grateful. But
I want more. I want all of you; I want to give
you all of me. Since the word for that is
marriage, I want to marry you.'

He ran out of words, stood helpless in the
apple-green silence. For a moment Agnes
was silent too, standing bare-legged in the
grass in front of him, her head tilted to one
side like a watchful bird's, her strong slender
fingers shredding a daisy. Robin waited in an
agony of uncertainty. He'd made his best
pitch. He had no idea whether it had been
good enough.

Then Agnes said quietly, 'Have you
thought about children?'

A kind of joy washed over him. His fine
hazel eyes glowed and his lips made an idiot
smile in the frame of his beard. At least she
was considering it, considering the implications. He'd been afraid she'd dismiss his proposal out of hand.

11

So the least she deserved was an honest answer. 'I'd love a child. If it happens. If it's what you want too. But if you don't, or not for a while, that's OK too. Once I have you, anything else is icing on the cake.'

Agnes smiled. 'Plus, you already have a son.'

Robin's strong face went still. For a moment she thought she'd offended him. But in the depths of his eyes there was only a little thoughtfulness. 'That's something we need to talk about.'

Under the short dark fringe Agnes's frown was puzzled. 'I do know about them, you know. Ruth, and Matthew. You never tried to keep them secret.' Her eyes turned impish. 'You never claimed to be a virgin.'

Though Robin grinned, a shadow remained. 'No, I didn't. And most people bring some baggage to a relationship. But if we're talking like this – about marriage, about kids – maybe it's time I unpacked mine where you can see what's in there. In case it's going to be a problem.'

'You lied about the divorce?'

Robin laughed out loud. 'No. I can show you the papers. Agnes, I haven't lied about anything. I haven't misled you about anything. But it's ... complicated. The whole Mouse thing. My son is twenty – he's a grown man, you'd be entitled to expect that

12

most of my obligations to him would have ended by now. But they haven't, and they're not going to, and I owe it to you to explain why.'

He was Agnes's age when he fell in love with Ruth Pyke. They met at a wedding: he was a cousin of the bridegroom, she a friend of the bride. She was eighteen, only child of a country cleric, and the economics graduate was bowled over by her frail dark beauty. He'd never known anyone like her. Robin Firth was a city boy, at home in city streets and City finances. The quiet grace of this demure daughter of the vicarage was entirely outside his experience. He couldn't get her out of his mind. Every Friday he left work early to make the long journey to the Cotswolds.

Perhaps Ruth too was seduced by the unfamiliar: by this confident young man who talked breezily about million-dollar deals, and drove a sports car lower than the cow parsley in her lane, and took her to restaurants where they cooked half her dinner at the table. At the end of the summer they were married, in the little Norman church of St Bride's-in-Malleton where her father was incumbent.

They found a flat in London. Robin worked hard, and fortune favoured him, and when Ruth was six months pregnant they bought their first tiny house. They called their son Matthew. Robin thought he was the luckiest man on earth.

'I'm not sure why I started that far back,' he said, his brows knitting. There was a wrought-iron bench at the bottom of the garden: somewhere during the telling Robin had lowered himself on to it, Agnes sitting cross-legged in the grass at his feet. 'Perhaps because our problems may not have started with the fire at all.'

They'd talked about it endlessly afterwards, between themselves and with the child psychologists. They tried to remember anything from his first six years that suggested Matthew Firth was never going to be a perfectly normal child. They hit the usual hurdle: deciding what *is* a perfectly normal child. He was certainly distinctive. Combining his mother's lack of height with his father's breadth of shoulder, he quickly turned into the squarest toddler either of them had ever seen, with a thatch of straw-coloured hair that even love wouldn't call blond. His Terrible Twos started before he could talk and lasted till he was at school. He never cried, but if something displeased him he could stage a sit-down strike to gladden a trade unionist's heart.

'*Is* that abnormal?' wondered Robin. 'We didn't think so. Of course, he was our first –

we'd nothing to compare him with. But nobody told us we had a problem, until after the fire.'

'What happened?' asked Agnes softly.

A smell of burning, and more pain than he knew what to do with, recalled him finally from the raucous void. He'd thought it was the roar of flames, but it faded slowly as he stirred and no hungry dancing light split the darkness. So maybe it wasn't.

He thought, when he was properly awake he'd be able to move. But he couldn't. At first the pain stopped him, stabbing pains in his chest like breathing knives. But when he steeled himself against it for the few seconds it would take to map his situation, he still couldn't move. He was trapped, face down between unyielding structures.

Physically helpless, he made an effort to harness his mind – to see where he was, what had happened to him, with his mind's eye. To remember the events that had brought him here. If he couldn't see what he had to do to free himself, maybe he could work it out. He had a good brain – everybody said so. Well, some people. He cast his mind back to the last thing he could recall.

Immediately he knew this was a mistake. But even immediately was too late. The memories surged back, independent of his control, swamping him – all of them, all at once, all of them bad. Fire and smoke and heat, and more pain – different pain – and the sound of his own shriek swallowed by the roaring flames. He remembered *dying*...

Which made this forced immobility what? If hell was a bonfire and heaven was a garden – his grandfather tended to the fundamentalist wing of the Church of England – what did it mean when you were crushed into a space where you really didn't fit, and you couldn't see anything and you couldn't hear anything, but you knew you were still breathing because that's when it hurt most?

The wave of panic that had come with the memories receded a little. It wasn't helping, he was in no position to use the adrenalin it fuelled, so after a little while it began to subside. Thinking became easier.

Wherever he was, he seemed to be stuck – nailed like one of the moths in the Edwardian collector's cases in his grandfather's study. He was hurt, but – despite what he thought he remembered – he didn't think he was dying. He was puzzled by the darkness. He hadn't imagined the fire, its stench was still gripping the back of his throat, but it seemed to be out now. He couldn't believe he'd survived. Someone must have pulled him out. But what happened then? Where was he trapped, and why was he alone?

Unless...

There are times when a good brain is a bad thing. This was one of them. His mind's eye conjured a picture consistent with all the facts at his disposal. Someone *had* got him out of the fire. He was no longer in his room at home. They'd got him to hospital, and laid him on his chest because, although it was damaged, the rest of him was worse. The acrid smell in his throat was his own burnt flesh. And it was dark because his eyes were gone.

Two

Evening was drawing in. A cool breeze stroked his hair. Robin sighed.

What happened was that the family's little house in London burned down. Of course it was insured and it was rebuilt. What couldn't be repaired in the same way was his family life, which until then had seemed all but idyllic and afterwards was remorselessly crumbling.

'We never knew for sure how it started. I suppose it was Mouse – it began in his room, I suppose any six-year-old boy is a potential fire hazard, but just what he was up to we never discovered. We couldn't ask him. At least, we could ask – we just didn't get any answers. It was three years before he started speaking again. He's never spoken about the fire.'

'Was he hurt?' asked Agnes softly.

'He *was* hurt,' said Robin, 'but he didn't get the worst of it. There were burns on his arms and his face. He still has some scars, but nothing grotesque. He was lucky. Luckier...' He didn't finish the sentence, but that didn't stop Agnes hearing it. *Luckier than he deserved.*

'The real victim was Ruth. She was downstairs when it started. When she heard him yell and rushed up, the room was already ablaze. There was no time to get help, or even protect herself. She threw herself into an inferno and she stayed there until she found him. When she carried him out she had burns over thirty per cent of her body, including half her face.'

She was in hospital for five months that first time, and back there three times in the year that followed for grafts and plastic surgery. The gentle daughter of the vicarage with her frail dark beauty became a close companion of pain and despair.

'Even that wasn't the hardest part,' whispered Robin. 'I mean, at the time I thought

18

it was. My son had started a fire that maimed his mother – how were any of us going to live with that? Then I told myself, he was only six – one of us must have got careless, left something dangerous lying around. That made one of us responsible, and how were we going to live with *that*?'

He swallowed. 'The hardest part, for Ruth, was losing her son. She'd acted on deepest instinct, offered her life to save her child – but what she pulled out of the fire wasn't Matthew.' He ran his fingers distractedly through his thick hair. 'I'm not making much sense, am I? Of course it was. And of course the fire changed him. It was traumatic, there were bound to be psychological scars as well as physical ones. But it was more than that. It was more than the silence. It was like ... like the fairies had snatched our child out of the fire and left Mouse in his place. A changeling.'

As the weeks passed the experts who'd told him to be patient now began asking Robin to think back, before the fire, looking for clues that his son's development had already wandered on to paths less travelled. How had he related to his parents, to other children? How had he processed information? How confident was he with language? Had he learned from his mistakes or kept repeating them? When he was upset, did he seek solace or retreat into himself?

'What did they suspect?' asked Agnes. 'Autism?'

Robin, for whom the word had once represented the nadir of his hopes, was slightly irritated at the calm way she said it. 'That was one possibility. Dyspraxia was another; and hysterical something-or-other; and one chap in a bow tie said it could be an early manifestation of Oedipus complex and a father/son supremacy struggle. Mouse – fighting for supremacy? Mouse has trouble remembering to eat when he's hungry.'

'What did they decide?'

'They decided they didn't know. They decided he was either very bright or very stupid, and that either his condition predated the fire or was brought on by it.'

Agnes laughed out loud, confident that Robin knew her well enough to know she wasn't laughing at him or his child but at the experts at whose mercy they'd found themselves. 'What did you think?'

'I didn't know what to think,' admitted Robin. 'I was beginning to understand that the kid was in a lot of trouble. At first I told myself it was just – just! – the trauma of the fire, that as we put the episode behind us he'd gradually get back on track. But maybe I always knew there was an underlying problem.

'I know Ruth did. That was the part she couldn't bear. She'd walked through fire for him, been left with pain and disfigurement, only to find the prize she'd won had been replaced with one of lesser value. She felt – cheated. Everything she'd gone through would have been worth it to have her child safe. But what she got instead was Mouse. Mouse who didn't talk, who couldn't thank her, who withdrew into himself until his only form of communication was staring at you until you wanted to scream. Ruth hated looking at him, being with him. Everything she'd risked – everything she'd lost – and now somehow it wasn't Matthew. It looked like him, give or take the odd scar, but it wasn't him. I think if she'd had it to do again she'd have quietly shut the door behind her and called the Fire Service.'

Agnes wasn't smiling any more. But there was no censure either. 'Why do you call him Mouse?'

Robin gave an awkward grin. 'Because we couldn't keep calling him Matthew. He *was* different: we needed something else to call him. And one of the trick-cyclists was into Method acting. She wanted the kid to stamp round her office like a buffalo and then creep round it like a mouse. I knew he'd have the last word – he always did, even when he wasn't talking. He tried to run up the curtains, and since he was rather heavier than the average mouse the pole fell down. He and I laughed about it all the way home, and after that the name just ... stuck.'

Agnes pictured them together, the man and his changeling child sharing a joke at the expense of the professionals. Her eyes were warm. 'You love him, don't you?'

He was surprised. 'Of course I do. He's my son. He might not be quite the one I expected – good school, good degree, following me into business. But of course I love him. I'm proud of him. Whatever made him how he is – the fire, or something that was always in him – he's fought to have the life he wants in spite of it. He's a gardener – he has quite a thriving little business. He can drive. His speech isn't absolutely fluent – those three years when he wasn't talking left their mark – but he can make himself perfectly clear, and he understands every word that's said to him and a lot that aren't. On top of all that, I like him. He's good company. He's unlike anyone else I know – no, amend that: he's unlike anyone else – but different isn't necessarily worse. The world would be a poorer place without Mouse in it.'

From the way he'd broached the subject, Agnes knew he'd been afraid that his revelation would come between them. That she might think a man with a damaged child less

22

eligible than one whose children could be expected to grow away from him in the usual way. But he was wrong. She loved the pleasure he took in his odd son. Commitment is never the easy option. That's why it's always impressive.

But that wasn't what he'd been explaining. 'But Ruth doesn't feel the same way?' guessed Agnes.

'Ruth.' The shadows gathered again about Robin's eyes. 'No, she doesn't. She's ... reconciled to him now, I suppose. She's had fourteen years to come to terms with the situation. The scars – all the scars – are still there but they've faded a little. She never hurt him, Agnes, she was never cruel to him. I think she hated herself for being unable to love him. But the bottom line was, she no longer felt about him as a parent needs to feel about their child. All her instincts said that Matthew died in that fire, and afterwards she was fobbed off with a cheap substitute. He still needed looking after, but the love that makes you forget what hard work, and often how very annoying, kids are was gone. All he meant to her now was drudgery, and the wreck of her face.'

'She was grieving,' Agnes said softly. 'For what she'd lost. She couldn't tell you how much her beauty meant to her, it would have sounded like vanity. It was easier to be bitter.

That didn't need explaining.'

Robin looked at her with respect. 'I think you're right. And nothing that happened afterwards alters what she did for him when Matthew needed her most.' He met Agnes's gaze with piercing honesty. 'I went on loving her, you know. She wasn't easy to live with. I don't mean the scars – they never troubled me, they were proof of what she'd done. But her behaviour became quite ... challenging. Her coldness towards Mouse, her resentment. I shielded him as best I could. And in an odd way he seemed to understand. He always understood the difficult things. It was simple things like not eating toadstools to see if they're mushrooms that gave him problems.

'But a point came where we were all miserable all the time. We decided it was best if Ruth and I separated.' He gave a somewhat mirthless grin. 'At least we didn't fight over custody – I wanted Mouse and she didn't. She went back to the village where she grew up and bought a cottage across the road from her father's church.'

'Is she still there?'

'Yes.'

'Is she happy?'

Robin thought. 'I don't know. I hope she's content.'

'Who asked for the divorce?'

24

'She did,' said Robin. 'More because she thought I might want to marry again one day than because she did.'

'So she lives alone.'

'Well ... no.'

Consciousness washed around for a time like the sea at Southend – within sight, but a long way to go for a bathe. The next time the tide came in he was better equipped to deal with it.

He was pretty sure by now that he was neither dead nor dying; and notwithstanding the hot oily reek in his nostrils he didn't think he was burnt. He thought he'd broken something – possibly, several things. And he thought he'd identified what was digging into his chest. His right hand had a little movement, and his fingers had traced an arc of what he was pretty sure was a steering wheel.

Which was crazier than anything that had gone before, because at six years old he had no business being behind the wheel of a car. At six years old he couldn't have seen over the wheel of a car. At six years old there wasn't enough of him to pin to a steering wheel. He might have gone over it or under it, he might even have gone through it, but it shouldn't have cut him in half like this. Unless he'd grown. Unless he'd grown rather a lot.

His right hand, still exploring by inches, found the door handle. He pulled at it; no result; pulled harder. This time the door opened – only a fraction, even a six-year-old couldn't have crawled through the gap, but now a light clicked on. After the absolute blackness it was dazzling. He screwed up his eyes against it, but the heart leapt beneath his splintered ribs. Whatever else had happened to him, he wasn't blind. Only the dark had kept him from seeing.

As his eyes adjusted to the light he was able to view his situation for the first time. He was indeed in a car, spreadeagled over the wheel, and through the spokes he could see his legs. His jeans were torn and dark with blood. One foot was bent at an improbable angle among the pedals, and something had speared through the leather of his boot. It took him a minute to work out that it was a broken bone. He closed his eyes again for a moment, breathing lightly. Then he pressed on.

There was blood on his shirt too, either dripping down from his face or soaking through from his chest. He told himself it was just a nosebleed. A glance in the mirror would confirm it, but he'd have to tilt it first. He still wasn't sure where his left arm had got to, and moving his right across in front of him hurt quite badly, but he persevered. Still all but immobile, he cranked his head up to look.

Shock kicked all the wind out of him. He'd thought he was prepared for what he might see – blood, perhaps more bone, a broken face. The one thing he did not expect to see was a stranger's face.

He stared at the bloody mask staring back at him and tried to make sense of it. Well, the blood was obviously unfamiliar. Except at Hallowe'en, and when he was learning to ride a bicycle, he wasn't used to seeing himself gore-clad. In his mind he washed it away, and tidied up the torn and swollen flesh it issued from, and looked again for the six-year-old boy who lived in mirrors.

And he wasn't there. No part of him was there. In his place was a man.

And behind the man, sprawled in the back of what he now recognized was not a car but a van, was the body of a woman.

Mouse was twelve when his grandfather died. 'We went to the funeral,' said Robin. 'It was the first time either of us had seen Ruth for a couple of years. I think she was glad to see me. With Mouse she was ... distant but polite. Asked about school, hobbies, holidays – things you'd ask the child of a second cousin.

'The divorce had been good for her. She'd made peace with what had happened, seemed to have packed it away as something that happened long ago to someone else – the way you do with youthful indiscretions. We were married for ten years and had a child, and Ruth had written it off as a kind of protracted holiday romance, that seemed important at the time but turned out to be a mistake.'

His eyes were troubled. 'But there was something terribly sad about her. I know her father had just died, but it was more than that. He was the last family she acknowledged, now she was alone in the world. She was thirty-four, still a young woman. She should have been making a life for herself, if not with me and Mouse then with someone else. Instead of which she'd holed herself up in the back of beyond, with no friends that I could discover, her only companion an old man who'd now died. She looked tired and middle-aged, and lost. She was in the village where she was born and spent most of her life, and still she looked lost and lonely.'

Agnes had an inkling of what was coming. 'Mouse was worried about her too?'

Robin glanced at her. 'That doesn't surprise you? It surprised me. She'd saved his life, then she'd made it a misery. And he was

28

only twelve. You don't expect much insight from a twelve-year-old boy. I wouldn't have expected him to notice. I certainly wasn't expecting what happened.'

'He asked to stay with her.' It wasn't a leap of intuition. She'd known Robin Firth for three months now but all she'd known of his son was a name. If he'd stayed with his father they'd have met by now.

'Yes, he did,' agreed Robin. 'Except it was more that he informed me of his decision.'

He could see him now, the sturdy child with the thatch of straw-coloured hair, standing in front of the cottage scuffing his shoes and making no move towards the car. 'I'm staying here,' he'd said in his oddly gruff, unchildlike voice.

Robin had shaken his head. 'Sorry, Mouse, we have to get back now. I have to be at work tomorrow. We could come back for a visit in the school holidays...' He bit his tongue to stop himself adding, 'If your mother doesn't mind.'

Mouse had stayed where he was, still scuffing the black shoes that had been bought specially for the funeral until they looked like everything else he wore: older and more battered than seemed possible. His green eyes were lowered. The top of his head looked obstinate. 'I have to stay.'

Ruth was in the house. It was just the two

of them. Robin had frowned, puzzled. 'Why?'

And the boy had glanced up at him from under his tangled fringe and said, 'Lonely.' That had almost broken Robin in two. He'd thought they were doing pretty well together. He too had been lonely after Ruth left, but he'd found consolation in the company of his strange son. The idea that Mouse had been pining for the mother who rejected him, from whose anger Robin had had to shield him, went between his ribs like a sharp knife.

When Mouse saw what he was thinking, his stubborn square face softened in an expression of mingled scorn and affection. 'Not *me*. Ma.'

'He wanted to stay because Ruth would be lonely without her father,' Robin told Agnes. There was still a kind of wonder in his eyes. 'He knew she didn't want him but he thought she needed him. I couldn't talk him out of it. He was twelve years old, it wasn't his decision. But nothing would sway him, and eventually I had to go and put it to Ruth.

'I thought she'd dismiss it out of hand. She didn't. She just shrugged, as if it didn't matter to her one way or the other. I think that was when I knew she'd been right about the divorce. When I finally stopped loving her.'

He'd returned to London alone. He'd believed it was just a temporary measure – that one or other of them would phone him before the week was out and he'd have to go back for Mouse. If he hadn't believed that, he wouldn't have left him there. But the days passed, and Mouse phoned but not asking to come home, and Robin missed him more than he'd have told anyone but Agnes. And when Mouse asked for money for a new school uniform, Robin knew he'd lost him. The ache was like a hole in his heart.

Agnes reached up to hold his hand. From the way his fingers tightened on hers, it seemed nothing had come to fill the hole in the eight years since. 'He's still there?'

Robin nodded. 'I guess he was right, she needed him as much as he thought. I still see him. Sometimes he comes up to London for a holiday, sometimes I go down there. I taught him to sail, and later I taught him to drive.' He chuckled at a memory. 'Ruth thought I was crazy letting him behind the wheel of a car. She said he'd never pass his test if he lived to be ninety. She was wrong. He mastered the mechanics in a week, the road in another fortnight, and passed both the written and the practical at the first attempt.' He gave a bemused shrug.

31

'With Mouse, there's never any telling. He can surprise you both ways. He learned to drive in a month. He still has trouble telling the time.'

Agnes grinned. 'Maybe both lots of experts were right. He's both very bright *and* very stupid.'

'Actually, no.' There was that unconscious note of pride in his voice again. 'It turned out he has an IQ of 152. Just, no bloody sense. An IQ of 152, and he cuts lawns for a living!'

The story was told, and Agnes was glad to have heard it. She looked forward with interest to meeting Robin's son. 'With an IQ of 152,' she murmured, 'perhaps he's clever enough to know what he wants to do with his life.'

And Robin looked at her and smiled. 'You know it's my birthday next week?'

'No! Really?' She hadn't forgotten.

'I usually run over to the Cotswolds and take them out for a meal. Mouse and Ruth. Would it be weird to ask you to join us?'

She had to think about that. It was ... unconventional. But it was a chance to meet his son without having to make an opportunity to Meet His Son. 'How will Ruth feel about it?'

'You can never be quite sure with Ruth,' he admitted. 'I'll check with her first. But I think she'll be pleased for me. It's a long time since she claimed any proprietorial interest. She hasn't used my name for ten years.'

'OK, then,' decided Agnes. 'I'm up for weird. Let's do it.'

At half-past five in the morning the phone rang. Fingers laced in front of her eyes against the light, Agnes watched Robin's face change as he listened. He said some things she didn't understand. Then he fumbled for a pen and paper.

When he put the phone down she asked, 'What's happened?'

Robin's eyes were hollow with shock. 'It's Mouse. There's been an accident. That was the police. The hospital want me there as soon as I can make it.'

Three

Normally a train would have been faster. But there were delays due to industrial action, so they took the car. Agnes drove because Robin wasn't fit to. She didn't question him until they were on their way. Then she asked exactly what he'd been told, and by whom.

'The police, in Gloucester. They said his van went into a railway cutting. They had to cut him free. He has multiple injuries.' Robin's broad frame essayed a shrug that turned into a shudder. 'That sounds pretty bad, doesn't it? Doesn't it?'

Agnes thought so too. She thought it was the police-handbook way of describing a situation in which the body of Mouse Firth was so screwed up with a ton of steel they'd had to be forcibly separated. He could have left one or more limbs in the twisted wreckage. He could have broken his back, or his neck, or so smashed his skull that his strange, clever brain now contained nothing more than a flicker of existence. And the marvels of modern medicine were such that a body with one, or several, or all of these injuries could still be deprived of death for months or years to come.

She wasn't going to say any of this to Robin. 'It may not be as bad as it sounds. The messiest injuries aren't always the worst. With luck, we'll get there and find he's already on the mend.'

His look clawed at her with gratitude and hope and fear. 'You really think so?'

Agnes had a dancer's knowledge of medicine. She knew about strains and sprains, and where to apply a compress to limit the pain and swelling of torn muscle fibres. She knew nothing about trauma surgery. So she faked it, nodding decisively. 'He was alive when he reached the hospital, wasn't he? They'll pull him through. It's what they do.'

Robin's voice was a broken whisper. 'I couldn't bear it...'

Agnes took one hand momentarily off the wheel and laid it on top of his, lying cold and tense on his thigh. 'He's going to be all right,' she said firmly. 'Ruth didn't go through fire to save him so he could die in a wrecked van in a railway cut.'

Agnes dropped Robin at the hospital entrance, said she'd find him inside. She didn't want Mouse to die while his father was waiting for a parking space.

She caught up with him in the corridor

between A&E and the theatres. His chestnut head bowed, he was talking to a policeman. As Agnes reached them, Robin's knees buckled. She grabbed him and steered him to a chair. She thought they'd been too late. 'Mouse?'

The policeman was only young but he'd done this before, probably many times. 'And you are...?'

Robin didn't look up. He murmured, 'My...' and then stopped, not knowing how to describe her.

'Agnes Amory,' said Agnes briefly, 'Mr Firth's fiancée. Mouse ... er, Matthew. Mr Firth's son. Is he...?'

'No,' said the constable quickly. 'He's still in surgery, but they're saying he has a good chance now. Better than we thought when we hauled him out of there.'

Agnes took Robin's hand in hers. 'That's good news.'

His face was ashen. 'Yes,' he mumbled. He still looked likely to faint if he stood up.

The policeman was considering Agnes. She looked fragile, but right now she seemed stronger than the boy's father. 'Could I have a word, miss?'

They moved a little way off. 'How well do you know Matthew Firth, Miss Amory?'

'I only know what Robin's told me.'

That wasn't the answer he'd been hoping

for. 'Then you probably wouldn't know who was in the van with him.'

Agnes shook her head. 'Sorry, I don't know any of his friends. I'm not sure his father does either. Man or woman?'

'A woman.'

'And the accident was last night – Saturday night? I expect it was his girlfriend.'

'She's a lot older than him.'

Agnes bit her lip. About the only thing she knew might be the one thing that would help. 'She doesn't by any chance have scars on her face? The sort of scars you'd get from skin-grafting?'

She knew at once from the policeman's expression. 'You *do* know her, then.'

A little pang twisted in her breast. More bad news for Robin. 'No, I don't. But that sounds like Mouse's mother – Ruth Pyke, Mr Firth's first wife.' She heard herself and blushed, and mumbled a correction. 'Ex-wife. Is she all right?' But she knew, even as she said it, that if Ruth had been all right she'd have told the policeman who she was.

'I'm afraid not. She died at the scene, sometime during the night.'

He needed a formal identification, something only Robin could do, but Agnes persuaded him he didn't need it right now. She'd break the news when they were alone. But he couldn't be expected to deal with it until he knew that Mouse was safe.

The policeman nodded. 'I'll be around.'

She went back to sit with Robin, wondering how and when to broach the subject. He made it easy. 'What was he saying? There was someone else in the van?'

She clasped his hand in hers. 'Robin – it sounds like it was Ruth.'

She felt the tremor that rocked him. 'She's here too? I'd better go and see her...'

Her hand kept him in his seat. 'There's no rush. You will want to see her, and the police need someone to identify her. I'm sorry, Robin. She's dead.'

His fingers spasmed in her grasp, gripping like talons. Agnes clenched her teeth to keep from whining. She could feel his pain. Once he had loved this woman. Then he stopped loving her, and now she was dead and he'd no idea how he felt about her except that it hurt. All the help Agnes could offer him was her hand and her silence.

He wanted to get it done. Agnes went with him to the mortuary but she didn't go in. Both of them felt it was something he should do alone.

There was never a question in either of their minds about what he was going to see, and his face when he came out confirmed it. 'I'm sorry,' Agnes said again.

Robin took a deep breath. 'She wasn't

wearing a seat belt. She ended up in the back of the van. She really wasn't that badly hurt – the only significant injury was when she hit her head. But it was enough to kill her.'

Accidents, particularly road accidents, are part of everyone's experience. It remains deeply shocking when someone manages to die of an incident that should have left them with a cold compress and maybe a splint.

Agnes knew what he was thinking. 'Mouse will be all right,' she insisted. 'They'll fix his fractures and replace the blood he's lost, and a couple of days from now he'll be on the mend. He's young and strong, and you have to try very hard to die inside a modern hospital. They don't want you to. It spoils the league tables.'

Robin managed a thin half-hearted smile. He wanted to believe her. He thought he probably *did* believe her. But there are always a few that fall through the net.

Back in the waiting room, Mouse's surgeon was looking for them. The news was good. His broken ribs, broken jaw and broken foot had been repaired, the internal damage was less than they'd feared, and though he'd lost a lot of blood he was a fit young man with a fair amount to spare. He was in Recovery now, his condition was stable and there was no reason to expect further complications.

'When can I take him home?'

Though the surgeon was used to per-forming miracles, they still took a little time. 'Ask me again in forty-eight hours. Some-where between a few days and a few weeks.'

'And he's going to be all right?'

'He's going to be all right.'

'Can I see him?'

The surgeon shrugged. 'He won't know you're there. But if you want to sit with him for a while, there's no reason why not.'

Robin went where he was taken, but Agnes stopped at the door. Not because she was afraid what she might see, more because gut instinct was telling her this was no way to meet her prospective stepson. It was impor-tant, and Agnes felt it would be taking ad-vantage of Mouse's misfortune to proceed with this first encounter when only one of them could contribute to it or even remem-ber it.

But Robin paused halfway to the bed and looked back, waiting for her. 'Please.' So she came.

Fifteen hours ago Robin's son had been just a name – and not even, it turned out, the one he used. In the course of yesterday's conversation he grew into a real boy with a distinct personality and a history which defined Robin's relationship with him. Now he was before her he passed through a new stage in the acquisition of substance. There was nothing fey about him. He was as solid as she was – in fact, rather solider – real enough to dent the pillow under his battered head and hump the sheet over his damaged body. Agnes would never again think of him as *Robin's Mouse*. He became a person in his own right the moment she saw him lying unconscious in the hospital bed, his fairish head tipped to one side, his squarish face swollen shapeless.

Robin was beside him in a second, hooking a chair with his toe, bending over the bed. There were drips and oxygen tubes, and plasters and dressings, and for a moment he seemed not to know how to touch his son. Then with extraordinary gentleness one big hand stroked the slightly curly fair hair off Mouse's broad brow while the other settled lightly on his bare arm. 'Oh, Mouse,' he murmured.

Agnes stood at the bottom of the bed, watching them together. They were alike and not alike. They had the same heavy bones: somehow Robin wore them more elegantly. His chestnut beard gave a gravitas to his face, while the faint blond stubble on Mouse's looked merely unkempt. Where Robin appeared powerful, Mouse – lacking the same stature – looked merely stocky. Even unconscious his square jaw, wired in place now, had a stubborn cast, and his shut eyes were sunk and too far apart. In every particular it seemed that fate had fobbed off the son with a poor imitation of his father's advantages.

Partly, of course, it was because Robin was the one she loved. Partly it was that she wasn't seeing Mouse at his best. But mainly it was the nature of the trick played on them. Robin couldn't have denied Mouse if he'd wanted to. But Ruth, who'd borne the child twice, once in blood and once through fire, seemed to have left no mark on him. Agnes felt intuitively how that must have added to her resentment. To the feeling that she was raising her husband's bastard.

The surgeon had been right: Mouse was unaware of their presence. But he was stumbling towards the light. They could hear faint moans like half-formed words in the rhythm of his breathing. Once his eyes fell open – they were the grey-green of birds' eggs – but nothing moved in them and after a moment they shut again.

A nurse taking his readings gave them a reassuring smile. 'Why don't you get something to eat? Come back this afternoon. He'll be brighter then.'

'I want to be here when he wakes up,' said Robin, with the seeds of that stubbornness which had flowered in his child.

'OK. If he wakes up before you get back, I'll knock him out again.'

Neither of them felt like eating. But their bodies did. They found a corner café and ordered soup; but once started they didn't stop until they'd demolished three courses and a pot of coffee. To an extent it was comfort-eating. They'd been under stress since the phone went a little after dawn.

Agnes wondered if Robin would want to talk about Ruth. Over the coffee, he did. He said pensively, 'I'm glad she wasn't burned again. She might have been – they both might. There was a fire under the bonnet, but it never got into the van.'

Agnes ventured, 'It doesn't sound as if she could have known much about it.'

Robin nodded slowly. 'That's something to be grateful for. That, and the train drivers' strike.'

Agnes didn't understand.

Robin explained. 'The van ended up on the railway track. It was there most of the night. There should have been several trains through there – but nothing was moving last night because of the industrial action.'

Agnes felt the blood run chill along her spine. 'I thought he'd been lucky. I'd no idea *how* lucky!'

By the time they got back to the hospital Mouse had been moved to a side ward. The nurse pointed out the door. 'He's still asleep. But he's doing well.'

Inside the little room the floor was awash with blood.

It was impossible to know how much of it was Mouse's. The IV tube had parted and both ends were leaking. But Agnes could tell from the ashiness of the boy's cheek that some of it was his, dripping from the tube where it had fallen to the floor, and that he couldn't spare it. She gasped and froze, afraid to tread in something so precious.

Robin reacted better to the emergency. He lifted Mouse's end of the tube higher than his hand. 'Get help. Get help!' he shouted at Agnes, and she spun on her heel and ran.

Almost as quickly as the horror began it was over. Swift footsteps in the corridor, the door flung wide and the room suddenly full of professionals, trading crisp instructions and responses, knowing what to do and doing it.

As soon as she had time the nurse ushered Robin and Agnes outside. 'He'll be all right. It can only just have happened. I looked in on him ten minutes ago, and he was fine.' But the confidence she'd radiated in their earlier exchanges was gone, undermined by a crisis outside her experience.

'What happened?' demanded Robin.

'I don't know,' she admitted. 'The drip was

working fine. Everything was secure.'

'He could have bled to death!'

'I promise you, Mr Firth, I'm well aware how serious this could have been. We'll find out what went wrong.'

Mollified somewhat, he gave a little shrug. 'My son has a history of springing surprises. He must have done it himself.'

'It shouldn't be possible,' she said, but a little smile thanked him for trying. 'Will you leave it with me? I will find out what happened.'

The staff cleaned up before they asked Robin back into the room. But the sweet smell of blood still hung on the air, making Agnes light-headed. 'Go ahead. I'll be right out here.'

Already Mouse's colour had improved. He wasn't far away now. It showed in the increasingly broken rhythm of his breathing, the twitching of fingers and lips, the tiny restless movements of his head on the pillow. He was no longer sufficiently unconscious to be unaware of the damage his body had sustained. The pain was calling him back. Robin sat where he'd sat before, stroking his son's hair and arm, whispering reassurances.

News of the episode travelled down the ward like wildfire. People – some of them in hospital whites, some in pyjamas – stuck their heads round doors for a quick peek at

Agnes, withdrew as soon as she noticed them. A susurrus of whispers travelled up and down the corridor. An angular woman pushing the library cart paused at the odd sweet smell on the air, blanched and hurried away when she realized what it was.

The constable too had heard about the incident with the drip. 'Is he going to be all right?'

'They say so.' Agnes gave a helpless shrug.

'Somebody up there's got it in for him.'

'But people down here are working their socks off to help him. Even, I gather, the train drivers' union.'

The constable shook his head in wonder. 'What were the odds? Down there for five hours, he should have been dead several times over. Instead of which his mother's dead and he's going to walk away. Hardly seems fair, does it?'

Agnes didn't understand his manner. She frowned. 'He made a mistake. There isn't a driver on the road who hasn't made a mistake sometime. I have, I'm sure you have. We were lucky enough to get away with them.'

'Maybe because we hadn't downed the best part of a bottle of Scotch first,' growled the constable.

Four

In the end Mouse woke with a jerk like a startled animal. Robin felt his body lurch and then tense, as if all his instincts wanted him up and running before the hurt caught up with him.

Robin pressed him gently against the bed. 'Easy, Mouse. Lie still. You're not going anywhere.'

The grey-green eyes were wide with terror. They searched the room wildly for a moment before finding Robin's face. Even the recognition seemed to surprise him, the breath coming fast and ragged between his wired-up teeth. 'Da?'

'Right here, Mouse. You're safe. Everything's all right.'

Still Mouse seemed to see something other than what was there, as if the white room was a screen on which terrible images were projected. 'Fire! Fire, Da!'

'Not this time, son.' Robin had an arm across his shoulders, holding him, willing him back to the present.

Quite slowly the panic drained out of his eyes. For almost too long nothing came to replace it. The void, like a vacuum, seemed to suck Robin in. Oh no, he thought, not that. Anything but that...

Then Mouse blinked twice, dispelling the vacancy, and looked around the room. Then, puzzled, he looked back at Robin. 'Where...?' His voice was a hoarse whisper.

Robin breathed again and managed a smile. 'Hospital. You had an accident. You crashed the van.'

Under the fair hair Mouse's broad brow creased. 'I ... hurt.'

Robin nodded. 'You took quite a hammering. But nothing that won't mend.'

'Ma?'

Unwilling to lie to him, unready to tell him the truth, Robin evaded the question. 'What happened? Can you remember?'

'I remember fire.'

'That was after the crash. And it was only in the engine. You weren't burnt – neither of you was burnt.' He knew that would matter to Mouse as much as it mattered to him. 'Why did you leave the road? Was there another vehicle, an animal – what?'

Deep lines like an old man's wrinkles appeared between his eyebrows as Mouse tried to remember. 'What road?'

'The back road into Malleton, the one that

runs beside the railway. You didn't make the bend above the cut and you ended up down the bank. What happened?'

But try as he might, Mouse couldn't get a grip of it. Not what happened, or where, or how, or why. He tried again with the one thing he thought he remembered. 'There was a fire...'

Cold fingers stroked the back of Robin's neck as he realized they weren't talking about the same incident. 'Forget the fire, Mouse. That was years ago. What happened last night is that you crashed the van. You and Ma were in the van, and it crashed. Do you remember that?'

Slow as honey, Mouse's greenish eyes were filling up with fear once more. Not the unreasoning panic that had chased him out of oblivion into the light but the wholly rational fear of a man who doesn't understand what's happening to him. Gruffly uncomprehending he asked, 'What van?'

The nurse brought Agnes a cup of hot sweet tea. It was horrible but it helped.

'We checked the IV,' she said. 'The drip. It seems fine. All we can think is that he woke up, wanted rid of it, got as far as detaching the line and then lost consciousness again. It's a freak event.'

Agnes had no way of knowing if it was the

49

truth. Somehow, whether it was strictly true mattered less than the woman caring enough to say it. Taking the incident seriously enough to fib rather than shrug it off. 'Were you in A&E when he was brought in?'

The nurse shook her head. 'Why?'

'Something the policeman said. He said...' She didn't like saying it about someone who wasn't there to defend himself. But Robin would need to know. 'He said Mouse had been drinking.'

The other woman hesitated a moment. She must have decided she owed these people something. 'I'll find out.' She disappeared for a few minutes. When she came back her lips were pursed. 'This is unofficial. But yes.'

Agnes shut her eyes. 'Damn. Damn, damn, damn.' She stood up. 'Thanks. Listen, I'd better tell Robin before the police do. God only knows how he'll react.' But actually, Agnes had a pretty good idea too.

Before she could do anything about it Robin came out of the side ward and straight past her, addressing the nurse. 'I need to see the doctor. He can't remember. Mouse – Matthew, my son. He can't remember anything.'

A brace of doctors arrived: one tall and thin, one short and round. They talked to Robin, then they talked to Mouse, then they talked to one another. Finally they talked to

Robin and Agnes together, in the corridor. 'A certain amount of confusion is inevitable following any kind of head injury. It's not often people wake up after an accident and remember everything up to the moment they were knocked out. Sometimes they lose a few minutes, sometimes a few hours or days. Mouse – Mouse? – seems to have lost rather more than that. You'd have to say it's not so much confusion as amnesia.'

The other one, the shorter one, took over. 'Now, people hear that and think of extreme amnesia events where people can't remember who they are and don't recognize their families, and never get any better. This isn't like that. Mouse knows who he is, he knows his father, he remembers all his earlier life. He doesn't remember the last ten years. Today. By tomorrow some or all of it may be coming back. And if not tomorrow, then next week. He's had a bad concussion, there's inevitably some swelling of the brain – as that goes down his brain will start working more efficiently again.

'This is a serious development, I don't want to mislead you about that. But it isn't a life-threatening one, and it's unlikely to be permanent. He'll get better. He'll remember more as the days go on. He may end up remembering everything. We're just not going to know for a little while.'

Robin said softly, 'Fourteen years.'

The shorter doctor frowned. 'Sorry?'

'Not ten years – fourteen. He was in a fire when he was six. When he woke up he thought it had only just happened. He thought he was still a child.'

The thin doctor sucked his teeth. 'Yes. Well – what happened to him last night was a major challenge to all his systems. He was injured, he was helpless, he probably thought he was going to die. The amnesia may be a defence mechanism, giving him time to get stronger before he has to deal with the feelings that engendered.'

Agnes was stunned. 'How can he think he's six?'

The doctor shrugged. 'Brains are complicated things – there's more we don't know about them than that we do. Even him' – he nodded at his colleague – 'and he's pretty good. It's possible that, confronted with its own mortality, Mouse's brain thought back to the last time he was in this much trouble. A fire, you say? He probably thought he was going to die then, too, but he didn't. And his brain knows he didn't. Maybe it's seeking reassurance in that. Maybe as his body recovers, as he realizes he isn't going to die of this either, it'll feel safe enough to look at the time in between, and what led to this latest episode.'

'So you think his memory will come back?'

Doctors hate being pinned down. This one gave another shrug that was almost a wriggle. 'Best guess? Yes, I expect a lot of it'll come back. I can't tell you when, and I can't promise the recovery will be complete. I think if we're all patient with him, and try to help him without pushing him too hard, he'll find his way back most of the way to the present. You'll be the biggest help,' he told Robin, 'because you have shared memories. Remind him of the good times, the things worth remembering. And reassure him that he will get better. He's disorientated now, he's bound to be frightened. A familiar face, a familiar voice, will do him more good than all the medicine in our pharmacy.'

Agnes was still wrestling with it. This sturdy young man thought he was six years old. It must have been like waking up in someone else's body. If the last thing he remembered was being six, he could have no idea what had happened to him – not only to put him in hospital but to make him the person he was. All contact with himself had been severed. He had no idea who he was, only who he'd been as a young child. This man's body that had been imposed on him while he slept was as alien to him as anything in Kafka.

Even that most basic of senses which tells

a sentient being where its component parts are would be unreliable. The head would be too far from the feet, the hands too big, the voice too deep. If all his adolescence had been wiped out, what would he make of the stubble on his chin, of the hormones circulating in his bloodstream? All the learning he'd done – including how to survive in a sometimes hostile world, including how to behave – would be a yet unopened book.

And would he be able to read? Or would he still be struggling with Janet and John? Would he operate at a six-year-old's level, or a twenty-year-old's, or would he have no idea how to operate? He'd been sandbagged and shanghaied, and woken in the wrong time and the wrong place and the wrong body. He was lost in space, a scarred, scared soul drifting out of touch with anything he could recognize as reality. Weak-kneed at the thought, Agnes sat down again abruptly.

Robin was dealing with the implications rather better. 'What can I do?'

'Just be with him. Talk to him. Tell him things – not so much to jog his memory as give him a framework to hang things on. Imagine ... imagine his mind as a house, and someone's broken in and ransacked it. There maybe isn't much missing, but there's an awful lot piled in a heap on the floor. He needs to start sorting through it, deciding what belongs where. That's something you can help him with better than the rest of us put together.'

Robin nodded slowly. 'Do I tell him about his mother?'

'She died in the accident, didn't she?' The shorter doctor considered. 'At some point he'll need to mourn her, but right now he hardly knows her. All he knows about her is what he knew when he was six. I think, if you can without actually lying to him, it would be better to talk him through the relationship they had in recent years first. To tell him what he had before telling him he's lost it.'

'If you feel up to it,' said the thinner doctor. 'If it's going to upset you, leave it until he starts asking. If you'd prefer, I can tell him. Or we can tell him together.'

Robin was biting his lip. He just nodded and went back into Mouse's room.

Agnes hesitated. 'Can I help?'

The fat doctor shook his head. 'Not right now.' Then they both went away, leaving her alone in the empty corridor.

For a little while she just sat there, quiet and very still, swamped by a loneliness that was partly her own – excluded from all the useful activities of the hospital, even from those which most closely concerned her – and partly intuitive, sharing in the feelings of Robin's son, the broken man-child lost and afraid behind the closed door.

Then she stood up, and she did what she always did with emotions that were more than she could contain. Alone in the empty corridor, in a quiet broken only by the occasional distant voice, slipping off her shoes and with the music only in her head, she danced.

Inside, they'd reached the new millennium. 'The next year we went to Dorset.' Robin was watching for a response. 'Near Bournemouth – little place, castle on a hill ... I can't remember the name. Hell's bells, my memory's worse than yours!'

'Corfe,' said Mouse.

Robin's hazel eyes smiled. 'That's right, Corfe. You must have been about fourteen. We took the caravan. We had a puncture on the M5, and left the jack on the hard shoulder. It took a twenty-mile round trip to pick it up again.'

'Was Ma there?'

'Not that time. We didn't have a holiday together after your mother went back to Malleton.'

'She was glad to get rid of me,' said the boy, without much reproach.

Robin didn't argue. It was the truth, and he wasn't going to take advantage of Mouse's condition to edit the past. 'She was glad to get rid of me, too.'

'Yes. Why?'

Robin considered. 'Because your Ma wanted a nice, simple, straightforward family life, and what she got instead was us. We were better apart than we were together.'

'Where is she? Ma? Wouldn't she come?'

For all his attempts to shield him, Robin's son had grown up knowing that his mother didn't much care for him. Presumably they'd found some kind of accommodation in the last eight years or they wouldn't have remained in the same house, but Robin had never understood what Mouse got out of the deal. Board and lodgings – which is maybe enough when you're twenty but not when you're twelve. Yet the boy had remained adamant that his mother's house was where he belonged, and the fact that he was missed and wanted in London never swayed him. Nor did he succumb to a resentment of his own, accepting that this was his choice and his mother's coolness was the price he paid for it. It was hard for Robin to know whether that hurt him – where Mouse was concerned, none of the normal standards quite applied – or whether he was content, even happy. For all their fondness, in some ways Mouse was a closed book even to his father. But he could have changed the situation simply by asking, and he never did.

All the same, Robin felt it as a physical pang that the boy had no expectations of his mother's concern. Today she had an excuse for neglecting him, but Mouse didn't know that. Still he was unsurprised that she hadn't bothered to visit him in hospital.

He'd known the moment would come when he'd have to tell Mouse what had happened. It had come now; it would do neither of them any favours to avoid it. He took a deep enough breath to get it said in one go. 'She couldn't come, Mouse. She was with you in the van when you had the accident.'

The boy's eyes stretched, their grey-green hollowing like a trough of the sea. His lips parted, showing the wires. 'She's hurt?'

'Not any more.'

Watching him, Robin thought the information wasn't falling into an absolute vacuum. That somewhere in the depths of his occulted memory Mouse already knew. His plain, strong-boned face was still but not stunned; his eyes filled enough to make him blink but no tears fell. Not for the first time, Robin wished he could cry properly and let himself be comforted. But they'd never had that kind of relationship. They were close, and affectionate, and he'd never doubted his own love for his son or Mouse's for him. But it would have been as easy to hug Animal Earnshaw who, besides being a merchant banker, was prop forward for the Barbican Barbarians.

'Was it my fault?'

Robin blinked away a tear of his own. 'It was an accident, Mouse. Accidents happen. Maybe you misjudged the corner, or maybe there was something on the road. We'll probably never know. She wasn't wearing a seat belt. That was pretty stupid, but it didn't cause the accident. It was just ... bad luck.'

'I was driving. I was responsible.' Robin heard his voice waver as he tried it out for size.

And he couldn't actually argue with that, so he skirted round it. 'I'm sorry about Ma, Mouse. But most of all I'm glad you're going to be all right.'

A little while later he said, 'There's someone I'd like you to meet. I told you about Agnes, didn't I...?' The blankness of expression, the tiny frown between the eyebrows, reminded Robin that nothing he'd told Mouse recently was accessible. Which made it both harder and easier. The details of his middle-aged father's relationship with a young dancer could wait until he was stronger. 'Sorry. Well, Agnes is a friend of mine. She drove me up here. She's been wanting to meet you. Can I bring her in?'

It would have been awkward in more normal circumstances, introducing his son to the woman he intended to replace his mother. Again, Mouse's amnesia simplified matters. He had known about Agnes, but now he knew nothing. He might never have heard her name.

Again she felt uneasy about editing the truth when Mouse had no way of knowing. Perhaps he would be hurt to learn, the day his mother died, that his father was planning to marry again. But Agnes felt instinctively that he was entitled to the knowledge, and to whatever pain went with it. She couldn't see how he could be helped to remember if important matters were going to be kept from him.

The other thing that troubled her was that, over the last couple of days, she'd learned so much about him. She'd seen him before, lying unconscious in this bed. Dear God, she'd smelled his blood! And he knew nothing about her.

But right now Robin's feelings were more important than hers. She followed him into the room and stood at the foot of the bed, her hands folded behind her. She said quietly, 'Hello, Mouse.'

Conscious, he looked not only stronger but bigger. The grey-green eyes contained surprising depths. Robin had said he was smart, but Agnes hadn't altogether believed it until now. His eyes convinced her. Steady and timeless, they were the key to his ambivalent personality. They said that it was strength, not weakness, that had sent him marching after his different drummer. That he could have bowed to the pressure to conform but chose not to.

Agnes began to understand how Robin loved him because of what he was and not in spite of it; and also how he'd irritated his mother beyond endurance.

'Agnes, this is my son Matthew. Mouse – my friend Agnes Amory. She's a dancer, Mouse.'

'It was you, then.' Mouse's voice was low and husky, which might have been a consequence of the accident but in fact was not. 'Outside. Dancing.'

Agnes nodded. 'That's right. I dance when I can't think what else to do. How did you know?'

'I heard you.'

That surprised her. 'You have good ears.'

'Like a mouse,' said Mouse, and smiled gingerly through the wires.

She pulled up a chair. His eyes followed her. She said, 'How are you feeling now?'

The smile fell off his face as if she'd kicked it. His eyes fell too. 'Not great.'

'I'm sorry about your mother,' Agnes said softly.

'My fault. My fault...'

'It was an accident,' Robin said firmly. 'We

61

don't know what happened.'

Agnes said nothing and didn't look at them.

The long day was wearing down. Mouse looked exhausted. Robin stood up. 'Right now you need sleep more than you need company. Come on, Agnes, let's leave him in peace. I'll call tonight, Mouse, but if you're resting I won't come. We'll see you tomorrow. Try to get some sleep. And try not to worry.'

Mouse fought to stay awake a minute longer. 'Will you feed the cat? He must be hungry by now.'

Agnes nodded. 'What's his name?'

The boy looked faintly puzzled. 'Cat.'

Robin chuckled. 'OK. We'll stay at your house for a few days. Then you – and the cat – can come home with me. All right?' Agnes liked that, that he'd ask permission before going into his son's house.

Mouse nodded fractionally, his eyelids already drooping again. He was asleep before they left the room.

The police had Mouse's possessions, and Ruth's. Robin asked for a set of keys to gain access to the house. There was a slight delay, then he was taken to an interview room at the police station and the duty sergeant came to talk to him. He put a plastic bag containing Mouse's belongings on the table between them.

'I'm glad you called in, sir, there's a couple of points I want to clarify with you. I understand you and Mrs Firth were divorced?'

'That's right. Ten years ago. Nearer twelve since we separated.'

'She lived alone?'

'My son lived with her. I don't think she had a partner, if that's what you mean.'

'Any other relatives?'

Robin shook his head. 'No one close. Her father died a few years ago. I suppose Mouse is her next-of-kin now.'

'Yes.' He sighed. 'Well, I have to inform you that we'll be referring your son's case to the Crown Prosecution Service for a decision on charges. Dangerous driving causing death, and driving while under the influence of alcohol.'

If he'd accused Mouse of unlawful possession of a haddock, Robin could not have been more astonished. He felt his jaw drop. 'Don't be absurd!'

The sergeant blinked. 'Mr Firth, I'm absolutely serious. Matthew Firth was drunk, he was driving and Ruth Pyke is dead. However sorry we might feel for him, that's not something we can ignore.'

Robin shook his head in absolute confidence. 'Someone's made a mistake. Mouse doesn't drink. Mouse never drinks. Mouse is weird enough sober!'

The sergeant said nothing more. He considered for a moment, then reached for the bag. 'I shouldn't be doing this,' he observed, half to himself. Then he opened the seal.

The pungent sourness of stale alcohol filled the room.

Five

Robin drove in a kind of savage silence, and he took the main road that was further and faster and didn't pass the railway embankment. They reached Malleton as the slow summer evening gave way to a reluctant dusk.

The village was tiny, much smaller than Agnes had expected: three streets of stone houses the colour of buttermilk, with a square-towered little church at one end and a rill – not even a brook – flowing through the middle so that the front doors on one side were reached by a succession of footbridges. Trees were everywhere: big ones behind the cottages, their high rounded heads visible over the ridge tiles, and smaller fruit trees in the front gardens. At the end of the main street, trees and flowering shrubs filled the churchyard so that the tower and the high-pitched roof seemed to float like a galleon on a green sea flecked with a foam of blossom.

Agnes had kept a diplomatic quiet most of the way from Gloucester. She wasn't afraid of Robin's anger; but the longer he had to come to terms with this latest development, the less likely he was to say something he'd regret later. Also, it was none of her business. It was a family tragedy, but Mouse and Ruth weren't her family and wouldn't be even when she and Robin were married. Her lips twitched a secret grin about how much easier it was becoming to think in those terms. Some day – some better day, but some day soon – she must let Robin know that his proposal had been accepted.

In front of the little Norman church the rill bent to the left and the road, bending to the right, crossed it on the low span of a single-arched bridge made of the same sunshine-coloured stone and continued roughly north. But Robin turned into a lane over-hung on both sides by fuchsia hedges and immediately pulled in. Ruth's cottage had diamond-paned windows and a wooden porch around the front door where a tiger-striped cat was waiting, impassive as a Staffordshire ornament, tail curled neatly round its paws.

Agnes was glad to be out of the car, breaking the tension that had been growing for an hour. While Robin picked through Mouse's key ring, she stroked the cat. It arched upward into her hand. Inside the house she located the kitchen, the can opener and the cat food, and was rewarded with a sound like a very small motorbike.

She heard a banging through the house as Robin moved from room to room. If he was looking for something, she didn't think he knew what. By the time the cat was fed he'd banged and stamped his way back to her, glowering through the kitchen door, filling the cramped space with anger and grief.

It burst from him all at once. 'How could he do that, Agnes? How could he be so stupid – so criminally, irresponsibly stupid? He can't *afford* to drink. He knows that. I mean, nobody can afford to drink and drive, but nobody as strange as Mouse can afford to drink at all! He swore to me – he *swore* to me – he'd stay away from alcohol. That was the deal: I'd teach him to drive, and he'd never, ever drink. And now it turns out it was just an easy lie – keep the old man happy, tell him what he wants to hear. And his mother's dead because of it.'

She didn't know how to comfort him. 'We all do stupid things sometimes.'

Robin shook his head fiercely. 'That wasn't a momentary lapse, or a bit of bad judgement. At the point he was opening the bottle he had a choice. He chose to drink. And then he chose to drive the van. That's not a mistake, it's a decision.'

In fact Agnes agreed with him. There were no mitigating circumstances. But somehow they were all going to have to live with this, and not letting Robin tear his son's throat out seemed a good place to start. 'And he'll have to pay for it. But Robin, that's the job of the courts. Can't we just...?'

'Forgive and forget?' he spat, as if she were the transgressor.

'I wasn't going to say that,' she said quietly. 'Look, I know this is hard. On everyone, but maybe most on you. You've lost someone you used to love. But Mouse survived, and I think that right now supporting him, helping him through this, is more important than laying blame. Particularly if he doesn't remember doing what he's being blamed for.'

'*If* he doesn't remember,' Robin echoed bitterly. 'If it isn't just an act, to get him off the hook.'

She didn't think he believed that. But he was entitled to his anger. 'Let's at least make sure you and I don't fall out over this.'

He needed to hold her. But he couldn't let go of the rage for long enough. 'He'd achieved so much. None of those doctors thought he had much of a future. But he made a life for himself. And now he's thrown it all away, for a bottle of whisky! Maybe the doctors were right all along; maybe Ruth was. Maybe I should never have taught him to drive. I should have known he wasn't responsible enough to be in charge of something that can kill people.'

Still trying to mollify him, Agnes said, 'We don't really know what happened...'

The auburn beard jutted aggressively as Robin's chin came up. 'His clothes stank of alcohol, and he left the road on a corner a milk-tanker could take flat out. He must have been out of his skull. I wish...'

Agnes recoiled as if he'd slapped her. He'd managed to stop short of saying it but he couldn't keep it out of his eyes. He wished his son was dead and the woman whose place he'd asked her to take was still alive.

She swallowed, fought for calm. His emotions were in turmoil, he wasn't altogether responsible for what he was saying. 'Why was Ruth with him?'

He stared angrily at her. 'How should I know?'

Agnes persevered. 'It seems ... unlikely, somehow. It was late Saturday night and he'd been drinking. If it had been a girl in the van, or a couple of other guys, it would have made perfect sense. But his mother? Nobody goes out to paint the town red with their mother!'

She wasn't sure why she was standing up for Mouse. She didn't know him, didn't know what he was capable of. And the last thing she wanted was for these events to come between her and Robin. But that was the danger. Robin's response to what had happened, the strength of feelings it had revealed, threatened their relationship in a way that Ruth alive and well and living in Malleton could never have done. Agnes had no intention of competing with a martyr's memory.

Robin Firth was a good man. But he was also, at this moment, a man under considerable stress. One of his less attractive traits was a somewhat viperous tongue. He knew it, and controlled it so well that people who'd known him for years had never heard it. But today his control was minimal, and he said something that if he'd waited a moment longer he would not have said, because while it vented his feelings it did not accurately reflect them. 'You're only defending him because you're glad she's dead.'

Agnes stared at him in hurt disbelief. She knew him well enough not to think he meant that. But she was stunned to the soles of her soft shoes that he should say it.

She did what he should have done – waited until the first flood of emotion had washed over her and she knew what would come out when she opened her mouth. By then Robin too had had time to think about what he'd said, and his strong face was flushed with regret.

Agnes said quietly, 'Your ex-wife and your son are nothing to do with me. Not alive and not dead. If they're a problem, they're your problem – you find a way of dealing with them. But don't expect me to nod enthusiastically any time you open your mouth. If you don't want my opinion, keep your problems to yourself.'

This time he managed to control his tongue. 'I'm sorry, Agnes, that was out of order.' He shook his maned head in helpless despair. 'I don't know what I'm saying. I can't get my head round it – the sheer blatant irresponsibility! All the time I was with him I kept saying, It was an accident ... accidents happen, they're nobody's fault ... you're not to blame. And then I find that this one only happened because he was drunk. It *was* his fault. He couldn't have been any more to blame if he'd hit his mother over the head with the bottle! And I don't know how to handle that.'

Agnes was not a vindictive woman: he had only to ask her forgiveness to have it. She

70

could see what this was doing to him. She went on point to kiss him. 'We have to be gentle with one another for a while. We're all in shock – we're *going* to say stupid things. Let's have an early night. Things will look better in the morning. Then we can go back and talk to Mouse again.'

But Robin couldn't look at her. His voice was low. 'Agnes ... I don't want to. I don't have anything to say to him. Right now I feel like I never want to see him again.'

There wasn't a double bed in the house. Robin slept in Ruth's room, Agnes in Mouse's.

It smelled of earth and of books. There was a small wardrobe, the bed and a rather battered desk, and everywhere else was books. In cases, on shelves, in piles. They filled every available space and kept the door from opening fully. Agnes turned her head sideways to read the titles. Many were on horticulture, but the rest were so eclectic a mix she couldn't imagine how he'd chosen them.

It had been a long day. She climbed between Mouse's sheets and hoped for a dreamless sleep.

She didn't dream, but she didn't get much sleep either. Robin barely dented Ruth's pillow. All night he paced the room, or the landing, or up and down the narrow creaking stairs. Agnes could see him padding restlessly, shoulders hunched, eyes turned inward to the tumult in his soul, as clearly as if the cottage walls were glass. Her heart filled for him, but she couldn't help him. This was something he had to find his own way through. Towards dawn she finally slept.

In the morning she wasn't sure if he was calmer or just exhausted. Agnes made a point of not quizzing him. But in the hospital corridor outside Mouse's room she said, 'You should see him alone. And Robin ... gently?'

He nodded briefly and went inside.

He was ready to make his peace with Mouse. To offer not forgiveness but acceptance. Through the long, wakeful night he'd done battle with the demons of fury and by and large he'd won. If Mouse was responsible for his mother's death, he'd pay – not just in court but every day for the rest of his life. He didn't need any more punishment. And Robin didn't need to salve his own pain by adding to his son's. They were the only family either of them had left. He just wanted to get through the next hour without saying anything unpardonable.

Mouse was in the middle of a liquid breakfast – purée, not alcohol – his clamped jaw frustrating his desire for bacon and eggs. He was mending fast. Robin tried to take pleasure in that. But all he felt at the sight of Mouse's wire-framed grin was anger. Cold, remorseless anger. He wanted to knock the smile off his stupid face.

And he succeeded. Mouse saw the bitterness smouldering in his father's eyes, the rigidity of his big frame, and his grin of welcome faltered and died. His eyebrows tugged together in a troubled frown. 'Da?'

Robin had wondered how to broach the subject. In the event it was easy. 'You were drunk.' The tone of his voice took the comment beyond the realm of explanation.

Mouse's eyes saucered. For some seconds he neither blinked nor spoke. Then he shook his head. 'No.'

'You were drunk,' Robin said again. 'Your clothes stink of it. That's why you ran off the road. Your mother's dead because you couldn't keep clear what little brain you've got.'

'That's not true,' Mouse said, very clearly. 'Who told you that? It's not true.'

'What, memory come back now, has it?' asked Robin nastily. He wasn't shouting, not yet, but there was real venom behind the words.

'No. But...' Mouse sounded breathless, as if his cracked ribs couldn't hold enough air. 'I don't drink. You know that.'

'I know what you tell me,' retorted Robin.

'I also know what I smelled when the policeman opened the evidence bag. It wasn't fishmeal fertilizer, Mouse. It was whisky.'

Mouse was white – hardly less white than when they found him bleeding. His eyes were shocked, but there was a characteristic stubbornness in the jut of the square jaw. 'No. It's a mistake. They opened the wrong bag. Someone else's clothes...'

'Someone else's clothes but your keys? If you're looking for a get-out clause, Mouse, you'll have to do better than that. And better than amnesia. They don't need you to remember anything. They can prove what you did. You killed your mother. She walked through fire for you, and you couldn't stay sober for her.'

'Da...' The gruff voice was wrung with pain.

This was the last thing Robin had wanted to say when he opened that door. Somehow he couldn't stop himself. His soul revolted at what his child had done. He could accept it no more than he could forgive.

Agonizing outside the door, Agnes was about to go inside and try to broker a truce when Robin stormed out. He didn't stop but caught her elbow in passing, towing her along with him. 'We're going home.'

She twisted out of his grip and stood her ground, trembling with indignation. 'Leaving? Of course we're not leaving. Whatever he's done, he needs you now like never before. You can't walk away.'

'Watch me,' he snarled, and turned his back and stalked away down the corridor.

Right up to the point where he turned the corner Agnes thought he'd relent, stop and come back. Until the moment he entered the lift Robin expected to hear Agnes's light steps running after him. But when the lift descended Agnes was still standing, astonished, outside Mouse's door. 'Oh shit,' she said shakily.

Six

In spite of his many virtues, one of which was the ability to be virtuous without annoying people, the vicar of St Bride's-in-Malleton was not usually mistaken for a fairy godmother. Partly because he was six foot two in his bare feet, partly because he broke his nose falling off an Alp once and returned to the piste instead of having it set, and partly because St Bride's was a conventional parish not yet ready for a pastor in a chiffon tutu.

Mostly it was a matter of timing. If he'd arrived at the hospital half an hour earlier or later, Agnes would have had to fall back on her own resources and they'd never have met. Without the means of returning to Malleton – for she thought Robin had returned to London, though in fact he was waiting shame-faced in the car park watching for her – she'd have taken a taxi to the station and made her own way home; and after that any kind of reconciliation would have been almost impossible. She'd have learned about developments in the tiny Cotswold village the way the general public did, in the newspapers.

But the vicar had been in Gloucester talking to a contractor about his church roof, and he thought he'd pop in to see Mouse while he was handy. In so doing he walked in on just about the loudest silence he'd heard since his Mothers' Union debated the ordination of women. Mouse, in bed, was looking at the dark girl by the window, and the girl was looking at Mouse, and neither of them looked at the vicar even when he bade them a cheerful, 'Hello.' He winced. He wasn't sure what he'd interrupted but it was pretty clear they both wanted him to leave.

But sometimes a cleric's job is to do not

what's wanted but what's needed, and this one thought it just possible that he was needed here. So instead of excusing himself and backing out he stepped quietly into the little room and said, 'I hope I'm not intruding.'

Mouse said, 'Yes,' gruffly, and Agnes said, 'Of course not, Mr ... er...'

'Parsons.'

She blinked. 'OK. Of course not, Parson.'

He grinned. This happened at least once a month, but he went on finding it funny. 'Peter Parsons. The world's stupidest name for a vicar.'

Agnes smiled too. She had been desperate to complete this difficult conversation with Robin's son and go home. But now she was glad of the interruption of this big fair Viking of a cleric. If she left Mouse with him, she wouldn't be abandoning him. 'The only real drawback with Agnes Amory,' she said, 'is the initials.'

The vicar's grin broadened. 'You're a friend of Mouse's?'

'Of Da's,' said Mouse. His green eyes never shifted a millimetre from her face.

Parsons looked round hopefully. 'Your father's here?'

'No,' Mouse said tightly.

Agnes felt the need to explain. 'He was upset. He left. I suppose you heard about...?'

She hoped he had, because she didn't want to have to finish the sentence.

Mouse didn't share her reticence. 'Ma's dead.' There was a tiny crack in his voice. 'She was in the van. Don't know why. Don't know why *I* was in the van. Don't know what happened. But I know what didn't happen. I wasn't drunk. I didn't crash the van because I was drunk.'

Already Parsons had a hand on his shoulder. 'Mouse, I believe you. You don't have to convince me.' He looked at Agnes. 'Is that what the police think?'

She could have said more. She just shrugged. 'Apparently.'

'That's crazy. I've never known Mouse to drink, even when he wasn't driving. Someone needs to tell them.' A thought occurred to him. 'Is that where your father's gone?'

It's hard to snort mirthlessly with a break in your jaw and a crack in your heart. But Mouse managed. 'Fat chance!'

Now Parsons understood that painful silence. 'He didn't believe you?' He looked Agnes in the eye. 'I've known Mouse for four years – for three of them he's worked for me. Malleton's a small village, a long way from anywhere else, so we make a lot of our own entertainment – which means I also see him socially. Yes, I've seen him with mates in the pub. He drinks cola. To the best of my knowledge, I've never seen him drink alcohol.'

Agnes sighed. 'I wish you'd been here ten minutes ago.'

What Parsons had intended as a flying visit stretched in the end to over an hour. Not because he'd nothing else to do but because he had nothing better to do. No one he knew needed him as much as a boy being blamed by his father for the death of his mother.

Mouse didn't court sympathy. Whatever hurting he did, he did on the inside – you had to know him to see it through the sullen mask he hid behind. At the same time, it didn't take a clairvoyant to guess how he must be feeling. He'd lost his mother. Maybe they hadn't enjoyed the perfect family relationship, but the ties had been strong enough to keep them together when it would have been so much easier to part. Now she was dead, suddenly and violently, and people were telling Mouse it was his fault, and he didn't believe them but he couldn't actually remember. And the one person who might have been expected to stand by him regardless had stormed out. Behind the stony mask, Mouse Firth was in agony.

But he wasn't alone. Standing between him and the abyss were a slender girl and a large young vicar; and if he couldn't tell them what that meant to him, still both of them somehow knew. It's why they remained for an hour after there was nothing much left to say. Their company was balm for Mouse's fire-licked soul. By the time the nurse threw them out, some sense of perspective was seeping back. Their only thanks was in his eyes, but his eyes were eloquent.

'Are you coming back to Malleton?' asked Parsons. 'I can give you a lift. Or if you want to get home I'll drop you at the station.'

Agnes had no idea what to do next. Robin had gone – in fact he'd waited for almost an hour before deciding he must have missed her – taking with him the keys to Mouse's cottage. But getting on a train and creeping home with her tail between her legs wasn't her style. She wasn't sure what she could do for Mouse if she stayed, but leaving would certainly accomplish nothing. 'I'll come with you.'

His car was an elderly 4x4, equally suitable for visiting outlying parishioners and snowy Cairngorms. They took the main road south into the Cotswold Hills. But after about half an hour Peter Parsons slowed down, watching Agnes sideways. 'Would it upset you if we turned off up the old road? Where the accident happened? I don't understand what went wrong. I'd like to take a look.'

Agnes contemplated visiting the spot where Ruth Pyke had died and found, somewhat to her surprise, that it didn't trouble her. What troubled her was that she was already clearing an emotional no-man's-land between herself and the man she'd planned to marry.

She said none of this to Parsons. 'Dancers only look delicate – actually we're as tough as old boots. Look at Salome.'

The old road was a way of meadowsweet and cow parsley, and bends that respected the lie of ancient fields. The fields were turning from green to gold with the alchemy of the sun. Five miles short of Malleton the railway line strode out of the hilly wooded distance and the country road fell into step with it. When another of these copse-crowned hills came towards them, the road bent again to skirt it while a black mouth opened to swallow the line. As the road climbed the shoulder of the hill, a deep cut ran down to the track.

On the far side of the hill, where the track reappeared, there were tyre marks on the grass.

Parsons parked well past the bend and walked back. Almost without hesitation, Agnes followed him.

The van was gone, removed by lifting equipment, but scuffed ground, shards of windscreen and one burnt spot showed where it had straddled the line. But for the train drivers' strike, Mouse Firth would have died with his mother, and people on the train could have died too.

For half a minute neither of them spoke. The crushed grass and the glass sequins sparkling in the sunshine brought home the enormity of the episode as even Mouse's broken body had not. Then Peter Parsons offered up a simple prayer.

He thought Agnes was staring at him. 'I'm a vicar,' he shrugged. 'It's what I do when nothing else seems enough.'

She flicked him a quick smile. 'I dance.' But it wasn't him she'd been staring at. It was the bank. 'Remind me: what's supposed to have happened here?'

'Mouse took the corner too fast, and the van left the road and ended up in the cut.'

She didn't respond immediately. She looked up the road towards Malleton and back the way they'd come; and she looked down into the cut and then at the tyre marks. A frown gathered across the bridge of her nose. 'Then why are these tracks straight?'

Parsons didn't follow. 'Sorry?'

Movement is something dancers understand instinctively. 'If he lost it on the corner and skidded off the road, the van should have been going more or less sideways when it hit the bank. It would have turned over and rolled down the slope.' She looked him in the face and her dark eyes were stunned. 'It didn't roll, and these tracks are straight, because he didn't skid off the road at all. He drove off it.'

Robin's car was parked outside the cottage. Parsons discreetly excused himself. 'I'll be over there if you're looking for me.' He pointed at the church tower, the width of the lane and the churchyard away.

Agnes paused in the porch, wondering if she should knock. But she had Mouse's permission to be here, she didn't need his father's, so she lifted the latch and walked in.

In the living room Robin lurched to his feet, his big body unaccustomedly clumsy. Their eyes met briefly, then Agnes went through to the kitchen. Robin hurried after her. 'I'm sorry. All right? – I'm sorry.'

Until he spoke she hadn't realized how angry she was. 'Yes?' she said coolly. 'That's all right then, is it?'

'I shouldn't have left you there. I waited for you outside, but...'

She didn't carry a handbag. Her purse was slung over her shoulder on a long thong: she took it off and hung it behind the kitchen door, mostly to give her time to calm down. Then she turned to face him. 'I don't want your apologies, Robin. I don't need them.

I've got home from stranger places than that when someone's let me down. It's not important. What's important is that a few miles up the road there's a sick boy who thinks that the only person in the world who matters to him wishes he was dead.'

Robin's green-flecked eyes burned with outrage. 'I did not say that!'

'You didn't say anything to stop him thinking it, either.' Agnes knew her voice was rising and didn't care. 'Mouse is your son! He's hurt, and he's frightened, and he's lost his mother and his memory both, and all you can offer him is a homily on the perils of drunk driving! He needed his father more today than at any time in his life, and you let him down. I can always get a lift. But Mouse can't just stick his thumb out and stop someone who'll hold him till the pain goes away.'

But Robin was hurting too. Perhaps she wasn't making enough allowance for that. There was a turmoil in his eyes, a whine in his voice. 'He killed her, Agnes. He killed Ruth. And it wasn't an accident – it was deliberate, criminal irresponsibility. How can I forgive that? How could anyone?'

Agnes remembered the tyre marks on the bank. And pushed the memory down hard, out of sight. If Robin for a moment suspected what she suspected ... Her voice was timbred with challenge. 'Robin, *this isn't about you!* What if he did kill her? What if he drank himself stupid, and that's why he tried to cross the railway line where there's no bridge? It's somebody's job to find out if that's what happened, and make him pay if it is, but it's not yours. Your job is to be his father. Whatever he's done. You don't have to forgive him. You don't have to pretend it was just bad luck and could have happened to anyone. But you do have to stand by him. You have to help him through this. *That's* your job.'

His eyes were anguished. He had trouble finding the words. 'From the moment he was born, Agnes, I loved him more than anything in the world. I loved him after he burned my house down. I went on loving him through three years of silence, and after that when he seemed to be getting odder every day. He was always a challenge, but I never wished he wasn't my son. I thought, after what we've been through, nothing could ever come between us.

'But now ... I don't know what to say to him. A rage boils up inside me when I look at him. I think, You *killed* her! After everything she did for you, you got drunk and you killed her. And I want him to pay for that. I want him to go on paying for the rest of his rotten life.' Bitter, ashamed and obstinate, he let his gaze fall.

Agnes felt torn in half. She wanted to comfort him; she also wanted to slap his face. 'You owe him better,' she hissed. 'You owe me better, too.'

She'd managed to surprise him. 'You?'

Agnes breathed heavily at him. 'Yes, me. How do you think it makes me feel, when one day you ask me to marry you and the next you make it crystal-clear you're still in love with Ruth? You need to work out your priorities, Robin. I can cope with a stepson who's not so much colourful as hand-knitted, but I draw the line at sharing our bed with the ghost of your ex-wife!'

Soon after that he left. He'd have stayed if she'd asked him, but she didn't. She hoped he was going back to the hospital to see Mouse. But he said he was going home and would call her from London.

Seven

'You can't believe it was a suicide pact. You can't.'

Peter Parsons had waited a diplomatic half-hour after Robin left before checking that Agnes was all right. He'd have settled for a quick word, but she waved him inside and told him everything that had passed between her and Mouse's father.

Parsons found this happened a lot. People he didn't know, people who weren't parishioners or even churchgoers, confided in him details they'd have kept from close family. Mostly he found that just listening to them made them feel better. But sometimes it took more.

Agnes was bitterly disappointed at Robin's reaction to the crisis, but that wasn't what she wanted to talk about. She wanted to talk about the tyre tracks on the bank at the Mile End Cut. 'All right then, not a pact. Maybe it was a spur-of-the-moment thing. Maybe they were arguing. Ruth was telling him off about his drinking...'

'So he thought he'd shut her up once and for all?' Parsons's voice soared like organ music. 'I'm sorry but it's nonsense. When you've known Mouse for a week you'll know it's nonsense. He's not crazy. People will tell you he's unpredictable, but he isn't that either. He's ... different. Things matter to him that don't matter to everyone, and things that rule most people's lives leave him unmoved. He wrong-foots you sometimes. There's something childlike in the way he interacts with the world. And sometimes you forget this is an intelligent young man, and talk to him as you might to a child.

'But he's not remotely unstable. He doesn't do angst or self-loathing. His eccentricities may trouble other people but Mouse is quite comfortable with who he is. I think he's happy with his life. Off hand, Miss Amory, I can't think of anyone less likely to commit suicide.'

'Then how do you explain the tyre tracks?'

He had no answer.

'Maybe the happy savage is just an act,' suggested Agnes. 'Camouflage. Someone said that most men lead lives of quiet desperation' – it was Thoreau, but Agnes wasn't a great reader – 'well, maybe Mouse was doing too. He grew up apart from the father who loves him and with a mother who didn't; and though he has the kind of brain that designs nuclear power plants, what he was doing with it was cutting lawns. If he was out on a Saturday night with his mother, I'm guessing he doesn't have a girlfriend. That doesn't sound like a very rich life, Mr Parsons. I'm left wondering if you know him quite as well as you think. After all, you thought he didn't drink...'

'All right,' said Parsons shortly. 'I never claimed to be infallible – that's the other guy. Maybe knowing Mouse and his mother for four years doesn't make me privy to their innermost thoughts and feelings. But you're asking me to believe he'd sunk into a state of murderous despair and I never noticed. And I can't. I don't.'

The last thing Agnes wanted was another argument. Perhaps she should have kept her suspicions to herself. She'd hoped the vicar might shoot them down, save her having to worry any more, at least about that. But nothing he'd said seemed as convincing as the silent testimony of the flattened grass above the railway line.

'Well, you know Mouse a lot better than I do,' she said wearily. 'Maybe you can judge what he is and isn't capable of. But if the scene looks suspicious to me, you can bet the police have been crawling all over it with tape measures, and if it wasn't an accident they'll prove it. Maybe Robin's right. Maybe the amnesia is a last-ditch attempt to shirk responsibility for what he did. And I don't mean drunken driving.'

Parsons shook his head angrily. 'You think he wanted Ruth dead? Enough to risk his own life doing it? *Why?* If she was making him miserable, all he had to do was leave.

'It's true that Ruth wasn't the easiest person in the world to like. She was critical, impatient, intolerant. She found it hard to make friends, harder to keep them. She was an intelligent woman stagnating in a rural backwater, and it may have been her choice but it became her prison. She wasn't happy. But Mouse was. All the time I knew them, it was as if she was the restless teenager and he the long-suffering adult. He cared for her; he looked after her. I cannot conceive of the circumstances in which he would deliberately put either of them in front of a train.'

Agnes shrugged. 'How can anyone know what happens inside a mind like Mouse's? Maybe he snapped. Maybe the stress of being *that* different finally got to him. And that's why, when he woke up in the hospital and realized he was still alive, the first thing he did was try to finish the job by breaking the IV.'

Parsons had no more arguments, remained unconvinced. 'There has to be another explanation. The police will find it. Or else he'll remember, and be able to tell us what happened.'

Agnes thought he was fooling himself. She changed the subject. 'So tell me, Vicar – how's your church-roof fund?'

He knew what she was doing. But he too wanted to end the dispute. He managed a smile. 'Surprisingly healthy, in fact. That's why I was in Gloucester. I've got an anonymous benefactor. A *generous* anonymous benefactor. I went in to see the contractor, plan a schedule of works. For the first time in decades we have the funds to do more than just paper over the cracks.'

'Is it an old church?' asked Agnes politely.

'The present building's Norman, with later additions.' From the glow in his face he might have been talking about his mistress. 'But there was a Saxon church on the same site in 900 AD. St Bride's-in-Malleton is over a thousand years old – and now we can do something about assuring her future. I wish I knew who I had to thank.'

'That's kind of the point with anonymous benefactors,' said Agnes. 'Though if it was a cheque...'

'He's doing it through the bank. And the bank won't tell me – I've already asked. Some local worthy, I suppose. I thought about the Freyns – they've probably got the deepest pockets around here – but charity isn't really Nick's style. He's a businessman: if he'd wanted to give money to the church he'd have told me to my face. But only after he'd told the media.'

Agnes grinned. That was what Robin would have done too. 'A *modest* anonymous benefactor. Even rarer!'

'Couldn't have come at a better time,' said Parsons fervently. 'We had to do something by winter or the roof would have been more than just iffy, it would have been dangerous. Without this donation I'd have had to sell my relic.'

'Relic?' Agnes was glad of something safe to talk about. 'What relic?'

'It's not a proper relic,' admitted Parsons. 'The Anglican Church doesn't much go in for holy bones and fragments of the one true cross. It's more an artefact. But it's jolly old and jolly interesting, and I'm jolly glad to be keeping it.'

When Agnes pressed him to explain, he offered to show her. They crossed the road and entered the churchyard by the lychgate. 'It's what's left of a Crusader banner. It went to Jerusalem with Richard the Lionheart and spent the next eight hundred years working its way back. We're terribly lucky to have it. Freyn brought it back from the Middle East.'

'Nick Freyn?' Agnes was wondering why

the name sounded familiar to her.

'No, his father. Stuart.' Parsons opened the black oak door under its round-headed arch and stooped under the low lintel. 'He was in the army. In Aden.'

Agnes knew nothing about churches. She'd seen some of the grander cathedrals, usually on wet days on family holidays. This tiny rural church was nothing like that. Its size gave it a kind of intimacy, and the fact that there wasn't much of a budget for maintenance meant that it felt its age. There were dark marks on the walls where oil lamps and, earlier, rushlights had lit the space. Three lancet windows, jewel-like with bright medieval glass, pierced the end wall and painted the sanctuary.

'It isn't all Norman,' said Parsons. 'The chancel was added a hundred years later, and the tower a hundred years after that.' Halfway down the nave he stopped and pointed upwards. 'There.'

Agnes peered into the gloom above the arch and could see almost nothing. 'Why did you put it up there?'

The vicar shrugged. 'It was there when I arrived. I think my predecessor was afraid it might distract the worshippers if they could actually see it. I did ask Colonel Freyn if he'd like it moving somewhere a bit more visible, but he said to leave it there. I think he quite likes being one of the few people who've seen it up close. It was put up there almost forty years ago, and nobody's been up there since except Mouse and *his* predecessors.'

'Mouse?' Agnes hadn't seen him as a prayerful man.

'Someone has to dust the thing, and you can't present your cleaner with a ten-metre ladder. Mouse is our handyman as well as our gardener.'

She made admiring noises, though all she could see was something pale in a sturdy dark frame, then she left Peter Parsons in his church and walked back to the cottage. When she got there the phone was ringing. She hoped it was Robin, but it was his son.

'Hi, Mouse. Everything OK?'

It was a stupid thing to say to a young man accused of killing his mother, but Mouse grunted affirmatively. 'Do something for me? Call my clients, let them know what's happened. Tell them I'll be back in a couple of weeks.'

It was absurdly optimistic. But Agnes wasn't going to argue with him. 'Who should I call?'

'There's a diary on my desk. The list's at the back.'

'I'll get on to it. Anything else you need?'

'I need to get my head straight,' growled

Mouse ungratefully, and rang off.

The diary surprised her. Knowing his history, knowing Mouse a little now, Agnes expected his methodology to be chaotic and his handwriting illegible. But the large green desk diary was a model of concise orderliness, the entries – made in a strong blunt hand – detailing where he was to work on what days and what he wanted to achieve there. At the back was a list, in alphabetical order, of some thirty names, addresses and phone numbers.

Intrigued, she explored further. On the shelves above the desk she found box-files, also arranged alphabetically, containing folders corresponding to the names in the diary. Each included a ground plan, a history of work done and plantings made, a note of clients' individual likes and hopes, and an outline of future works. Another file recorded financial transactions.

Agnes put them all away carefully as she'd found them. She was impressed. Mouse Firth might be odd but he was nobody's fool. His mind was not a floss of cotton wool but an organized and efficient work-space.

She had a promise to fulfil. The diary told her who was expecting him immediately and she started with them. There'd be time to contact the others later.

One name on the list gave her pause. She

passed it and went back at the end. Still she didn't dial. Her delicate features arranged themselves in the impish smile of someone who knows she's behaving badly but also that the grown-ups are out of earshot. As local gentry, surely Colonel Freyn was entitled to be notified in person of his gardener's indisposition.

She asked at the village shop for directions to The Nail. The Freyns' house was a mile out of Malleton but Agnes was ready for some exercise. When she wasn't working she always found herself with more energy than she knew what to do with.

She'd hoped for a Tudor manor, more of the buttermilk local stone or perhaps some rosy bricks. What she got was a Victorian villa, perhaps not a pile but definitely a heap, made of slightly metallic dark bricks and rising out of a thick planting of trees. The drive was guarded by high wrought-iron gates pinned back into the rhododendrons.

Although The Nail was a house in a garden rather than a mansion in a park, the drive was long enough for Agnes to start feeling conspicuous as she approached. But she had business here so she pressed on.

The tall woman who answered the door might have been family or staff. Agnes gave a bright, all-purpose smile. 'I'm Agnes Amory. Mouse Firth asked me to call on

Colonel Freyn.' Which was approximately if not scrupulously true.

The woman beckoned her inside. 'How is Mouse? We heard about the accident. Have you seen him? Is he all right?'

'Not bad, considering,' said Agnes. 'He's got some nasty injuries but he's on the mend now. He phoned me this morning. He wanted me to tell his clients he'll be out of action for a while.'

'We guessed that much.' She smiled suddenly. 'I'm Frances Freyn, by the way – Colonel Freyn is my father. He's down the garden somewhere – we won't see him till teatime. But he'll be glad to hear Mouse is going to be all right.' She cleared her throat. 'Has he been able to tell you what happened?'

Agnes shook her head. 'He doesn't remember. Not just the accident – he doesn't remember anything that's happened for months. It'll come back, of course. When he first woke up he'd lost fourteen years.'

Frances Freyn gave a sympathetic scowl. 'Poor Mouse! Does he know about Ruth?'

'His father told him. I'm sorry,' said Agnes, 'I'm being very rude. I came down with Robin when we heard about the accident. He and I are...' And there she stopped. What she'd had no difficulty in saying at the hospital, suddenly she felt reticent about repeating. As if the events of the intervening hours cast a shadow of doubt over their precise relationship. 'Friends. I'm staying at the cottage for a few days.'

'I see,' said Frances, as if she didn't. 'So Mouse's father's in Malleton.'

'Actually, no. He had to go back to London.'

'Yes?' said Frances.

'And I didn't. So I'm trying to sort out Mouse's affairs for him.' Agnes wondered how to say this politely. 'Is it OK if I go down and speak to Colonel Freyn? I promised Mouse I would. He's a bit strung out, he doesn't want to upset his best client.' Sometimes she impressed even herself with the ease of her lying.

Frances pointed the way. 'Head for that big willow. He's cleaning out the pond. He's not really up to it, but with Mouse out of commission he felt he ought to try. If Mouse is laid up for too long this garden will revert to jungle and we may never see my father again.'

Agnes found the old man sitting on the edge of his pond, legs cased in waders dangling in the water. He looked up at her approach. He had his daughter's tall, narrow build and fine grey eyes, and a white moustache still trimmed to precise Sandhurst specification. Agnes put him in his seventies.

98

Which didn't stop his face brightening at the approach of a pretty girl.

She told him why she'd come, then sat on the grass beside him and nodded at the pond. 'If Mouse knew you were doing this he'd be round here tomorrow, plaster cast and all.'

Colonel Freyn was unoffended. 'Don't worry about me, Miss Amory. I have a keen awareness of my own limitations. I garden for pleasure, not to get things done. But I feel less guilty about sitting here doing nothing if I have the pond-rake by my side.'

Agnes smiled, liking him. 'I was in the church earlier. Peter Parsons showed me the banner. I wished I could see it better.'

Freyn's eyes twinkled. 'No, high up is the perfect place for it. If you could peer through the glass all you'd see would be a scrap of old silk. But while it's thirty feet above the aisle, anyone can look up and see a Crusader banner.'

Agnes nodded appreciatively. 'So proof denies faith but mystery restores it.'

Though Freyn raised an eyebrow, he seemed pleased. 'It's hardly a matter of faith. The thing has no religious significance. But yes, even in a pragmatic world – perhaps especially in a pragmatic world – you have to leave a little room for wonder.'

'How did you come by it?'

The old man's smile turned sly. 'Didn't the vicar tell you?'

'Only that you were in Aden.'

He nodded, stirring the water with his feet. 'At the time of the Arab revolt. It was a bribe.' He chuckled at Agnes's expression. 'I was new to the Arab world, I didn't realize until too late that this was how things got done. He was a Turkish merchant, a respectable member of the local community, and when he asked my advice about obtaining some permits I told him what I knew. It never occurred to me that when he got his damned permits he'd think I'd pulled strings for him.

'Even when the case arrived with a thank-you note, I didn't suspect. He knew I was interested in antiquities, he said he'd found this bit of medieval cloth in a bazaar and hoped it would amuse me. In my youthful innocence I assumed such things must be as common in the Middle East as Roman potsherds are in England – interesting but of no great value. I thanked him, and packed it away with my dress uniform. That was in 1967, and soon afterwards we left Aden.'

'When did you find out what it was?'

'A couple of years later. I had a junior officer with me who'd read archaeology at Durham – I thought he'd be interested so I got the banner out for him. The jaw nearly fell out of his face. He couldn't believe it had spent two years under my bed. He reckoned any decent museum would give their second-best torque for it. When I asked how much a second-best torque might be worth, *my* jaw bounced off my belt buckle. I knew then the merchant hadn't picked it up for a song in a bazaar. He'd paid serious money for it, thinking it would put me in his pocket. I don't doubt that if we'd stayed in Aden, sooner or later he'd have come back to me to reap what he'd sown.

'I should have despatched the banner to the Foreign Office with an explanatory note, and let them do with it what they would. But I was worried how it would look on my record. Either I'd been corrupt or naive, and neither was a passport to promotion! So on my next home leave I gave it to my parish church. It seemed fitting, somehow, and less likely to rebound on me than giving it to a museum.'

He looked at Agnes and his eyes were merry. 'Now I can laugh about it. At the time I thought I was facing a court martial. When Dr Pyke decided the thing might distract worshippers and should be stuck as high up the wall as a ladder could reach, I was in absolute agreement. I was convinced that one day the entire General Staff would want to visit St Bride's-in-Malleton, and my only chance of avoiding disgrace was if they couldn't make out what the damned thing was.'

Eight

She stayed a few more days. But there was nothing more she could usefully do in Malleton, and sooner or later she'd have to go home and deal with Robin face to face.

All they'd managed so far were a couple of guarded phone calls. Agnes had made one, Robin the other. They'd stuck to the safety of facts rather than venturing into the quicksand of emotions. He hadn't asked how Mouse was progressing, but he'd let her tell him. He'd told her about the mountain of work waiting when he got back to the office, and in that she heard the echo of an unspoken apology for leaving her.

She took the opportunity to check another fact with him. 'The Freyns, up at the big house – is that the same Freyns you know?'

Business was the ultimate safe ground for him. She heard him relax a little. 'Yes. We bumped into Nick Freyn and his wife at The

Brewery one night, remember? He's CEO at Suleiman Freyn – they specialize in the Persian Gulf. He's Stuart's son. I wouldn't say I know him. It came out at some corporate shindig that my son cuts his father's grass, which occasioned a certain hilarity.' A week ago he'd have been grinning as he said that. Agnes could tell that now his lips were tight.

'Does he live at The Nail?'

'No, they have a place in Docklands. They visit Malleton during school holidays, when Nick isn't in the Gulf. Why?'

She explained that she'd been to The Nail. 'I couldn't think where I knew the name from.'

'You'll have heard me talk about him. We're not usually in direct competition, but it has happened.'

'Who won?'

'He did,' said Robin without hesitation. 'He's good. He's also pretty ruthless. He does things I think about doing, and don't do for fear of what people might think.'

Agnes hadn't realized he cared what people thought. She'd assumed all businessmen were ruthless. But Nick Freyn struck other businessmen as a tough operator.

She changed the subject. 'I don't suppose you could get back here?'

'No. I'm sorry.' At least he didn't lie. The pressure of work was always an issue, but it wasn't what was keeping him in town and both of them knew it.

'Robin, sooner or later...'

'No,' he said again, tersely. 'He got himself into this, he can get himself out. Or not.'

One day, Agnes told herself, they'd broach this subject and the anger would be gone. But not yet. 'Robin – don't cut yourself off from him. Or...' But he grunted something about being wanted on the other line and rang off, leaving her gazing unhappily at her phone. She finished the sentence anyway. 'Me,' she murmured.

The next morning, which was Friday, Agnes put her few belongings into a bag and phoned for the times of the London trains. She was almost out of the door when the hospital called.

Her heart turned over before she realized it wasn't bad news; or only in a way. They wanted to know if she was staying on at the cottage for a week or so.

'Er...' Another second and she'd have said no, and that would have been the end of it. But she hesitated, so the voice at the other end explained.

'Mouse is desperate to get home. And it might help his memory to be surrounded by familiar things. But he couldn't manage on his own just yet. He's fairly mobile on his crutches, he doesn't need heavy nursing, but he does need someone to look out for him still. He said you'd be there. Before discharging him, we wanted to be sure he was right.'

Agnes felt as if she'd got as far as the prison gate only to have it slam in her face. She could of course say she had to get home – no one would reproach her, except maybe Mouse in the redoubt of his private thoughts, and it might show in his eyes but she never had to see him again. It might be the wisest thing to do.

Because she was conscious it wasn't just her time that was being asked of her. The last woman who shared a house with Mouse died in unexplained circumstances. Maybe it was an accident. But if it wasn't, behind that stony facade Mouse Firth was dangerously out of control. There was no unavoidable reason for Agnes to risk being the next person who got in his way.

On the other hand, she was a dancer and he was on crutches – she ought to be able to stay two steps ahead of him. And maybe she was reading way too much into some marks on the grass at the Mile End Cut. Maybe he fell asleep at the wheel and missed the turn altogether – which was criminally stupid but didn't make him dangerous to be around, unless she let him drive.

He wasn't her responsibility. She wasn't his stepmother now, and quite possibly never would be. If even his father had washed his hands of Mouse, Agnes could go home with a clear conscience. It was probably the sensible thing to do.

She sighed. 'I'll borrow a car and come for him.'

The Technicolor bruises were fading now. But instead of looking better Mouse looked pale and strained, waiting in reception with his left leg plastered from knee to toes. His jaw was still clamped by the wires but his lips were drawn tight by illness and worry. Agnes thought he was as anxious about going home as she was about taking him.

'You're sure this is what you want to do?' she asked softly; and he just nodded, mutely, without meeting her gaze.

The features that made the vicar's car suitable for skiing trips also equipped it to carry someone with a broken leg and crutches. Agnes headed for the main road.

For the first few miles she made an effort to talk to him. But his responses were monosyllabic and she gave up. They passed the rest of the journey in silence, until about five miles short of Malleton when Mouse pointed to an upcoming intersection. 'Turn off here.'

Agnes recognized where they were. 'Later, Mouse. When you're stronger.'

He was insistent. 'Now. I have to see.

Where Ma...'

'The Cut'll still be there in a day or two.'

'Now, Agnes. Please.'

So she turned off, drove to the point where the tunnel spat out the railway line and stopped the car. He couldn't get out alone and she wouldn't help him so he just sat there, looking and saying nothing.

When she saw tears on his cheek she started the engine again. 'Can we go now?'

Mouse nodded, and she drove him home.

That night the church burned down.

Agnes made up a bed on the living-room sofa, and when Mouse was too tired to stay awake any longer she got him into it.

She checked at about midnight and found him sleeping, his face white between the fading bruises and slack despite the wires. The living-room curtains didn't quite meet and a band of moonlight lay across his throat as if to restrain him. Then she went to bed.

Three hours later she woke to a hot, thick stillness in the bedroom and an unholy flickering across the walls. For long seconds she couldn't work out what it was, or even if she was awake or dreaming. Then suddenly she knew. She knew that she was wide awake, that there was a fire, and even where the fire had to be. When she threw back the rosy flickering curtain, flames filled the sky.

Her first instinct was to rouse Mouse. But actually there was no point. The cottage was in no danger, and if he woke he'd want to go out there. On crutches he could be no help, just a hindrance to others and a danger to himself. So Agnes called the Fire and Rescue Service, then pulled on shoes and a minimum of clothes and ran into the road.

The red glow from the church lit the whole village. The row of little windows high above the pews that normally let the daylight in now let out a ruby belligerence, blinking balefully as the smoke wreathed across them. The medieval stained glass behind the altar was already history: gouts of flame belched from the lancets and licked the pointed gable. The tower funnelled smoke like a squat chimney.

Fire has a sound all its own. A snapping like hounds' jaws, a cracking like bones, all against a rushing roar like nothing else on earth. A primitive sound buried in the soul of mankind.

Through the sound came the crash of beams as the blaze found the weaknesses in Peter Parsons's roof and brought down an eight-metre section of it. Flames leapt through the gap.

With no clear idea what she could do there, Agnes hurried across the road to the churchyard. Horrified and fascinated, she stared up at the mad-eyed ghost of the pretty little church and thought it would burn to the foundations before anything would stop it.

She'd thought she was the first one there. But there was someone standing closer than her, closer than was wise, and as she tried to make out who it was the figure dropped to its knees. She ran and grabbed him by the sleeve, tugging him back. 'Come away, Peter. There's nothing we can do. The fire engines will be here soon.'

He went with her but reluctantly, as if he was leaving a friend to burn. The firelight glinted off a wetness on his cheeks. 'Oh, Agnes.' It was all he could say.

Other people began arriving. Within minutes the entire village was gathered there, but there seemed no point collecting buckets. Diverting the rill down the aisle wouldn't have stopped the fire then.

Agnes glimpsed an awkward movement in the crowd and trotted towards it. *'Mouse?* What are *you* doing here?'

Hunched on his crutches like Quasimodo, his face lurid with firelight, he grinned manically up at her. 'Same as everyone. Best free show in town.'

She frowned reprovingly. 'Don't let Peter hear you. He's terribly upset.'

Mouse shrugged. 'I didn't start it.'

'No one said you did!' said Agnes, startled.

'Might as well enjoy it then.' And the boy lurched off into the crowd, leaving her staring after him.

The Fire Service did their best, but dawn revealed the extent of the damage. Most of the roof was gone. The tower still stood against the pale sky, so did the gable walls, but nothing connected them except a few charred beams like the stumps of teeth in a rotten mouth. Only the stones had endured. It looked more like a wrecked ship than a building.

Around seven o'clock two policemen came to the cottage. 'Is Matthew Firth here?'

He'd gone back to bed after they returned from the church. The last time Agnes looked he was asleep. 'I don't think he's up yet.'

'Then get him up. Please?'

Agnes was puzzled by their attitude. 'You know he's not well? He should still be in the hospital, by rights.'

One of the policemen said, 'Yes,' rather forcefully, and the other said, 'Just show us where to go, miss.' So she took them to the living room.

The sound of voices had roused him. He was sitting on the sofa, fully dressed, with the quilt around him like a bag-lady. His face was pinched with tiredness. 'Who...?' Then he saw.

'What can you tell us about the fire, Mr Firth?'

Mouse didn't even try. 'Nothing.'

'You were there.'

'Everyone was there.'

'And we're going to talk to everyone. What time did you get there?'

Mouse only shrugged. 'Dunno.'

The policemen turned to Agnes. 'You were there too, miss.'

She nodded. 'I think I was the first there, apart from the vicar. The fire woke me, I called the Fire Service, then I went across. A few minutes after three, I think.'

'You went together?'

'No. Mouse wasn't there till later.'

'Do you know that for sure?'

That wasn't a routine question. But she saw no alternative to answering it. 'Well, no. He was sleeping in here, I've got a room upstairs. I tried not to wake him.'

One of the policemen indicated the crutches. 'Do you need those things?'

Mouse's green eyes were insolent. 'No. They're just for decoration.'

'Of course he needs them,' Agnes said quickly, 'his ankle's smashed.'

The officer nodded. It was impossible to tell if he was satisfied. 'We'll have to take them, I'm afraid. For forensic examination.'

Agnes was indignant. 'That's crazy! Why

111

would Mouse burn the church down? Why would anyone? It'll be an electrical fault. The place is a thousand years old, and the wiring's not much younger...'

'That may be exactly what happened,' said the policeman. But he took the crutches anyway and bagged them carefully. 'The fire investigators will be able to tell us. Till then, though, we have a job to do and this is part of it.'

They also wanted Mouse's boots. Agnes found him another pair. To the policeman who went with her she said, 'You know this isn't fair. Everyone in Malleton was the same place Mouse was last night. But I don't see you collecting boots from all of them.'

'Most of them don't have a history of setting fires, miss.'

Agnes stared at him in astonishment. 'He was six years old! *Every* six-year-old boy is a fire hazard, by definition.'

'True enough. But most of them grow up to be normal, reliable members of society. That's where we hit a problem with young Firth. And it would have been a problem even before...'

Agnes wouldn't let him finish. 'That was an accident!' Even if she didn't believe it herself, some primitive clannishness made her take Mouse's part in front of strangers.

'Another one? Maybe it was. And maybe it

was an accident when his IV came apart in the hospital. But you see where I'm going with this, miss? If we couldn't see a pattern in that little lot, we wouldn't be doing our job. Put at its mildest, an awful lot of accidents are happening around young Firth.' He paused, wondering whether to say more. In the end he decided he had to. 'You're staying here? Are you sure that's wise?'

'He can hardly move!' she exclaimed. 'What possible danger can he be, to me or anyone else? Without crutches he's confined to the sofa. If you're keeping them, send him some more.'

She saw them to the door, for the satisfaction of shutting it behind them. But even as the policemen left, another visitor approached. The scale, mainly, identified it as Peter Parsons. Everything else, including a most ambivalent expression, was visible only through smuts of wet ash.

'Come with me,' he said without preamble. 'I've something to show you.'

They went to the ruined church. The firemen had finished their work and left. The sightseers had gone too, and the contractors who would make the place safe had not yet arrived. The churchyard was deserted.

Inside, the devastation was absolute. The wreck of the roof filled the nave to shoulder height, char-blackened spars projecting at odd angles like the yards of ghost ships. It was impossible to progress more than a few metres into the building. Stopped by the debris, Parsons looked up and pointed.

For a moment, in all the surrounding chaos Agnes didn't see it. 'What?' Then: 'Good God!'

'Quite,' said the vicar quietly.

'How...?'

'I don't know.'

Their eyes were glued to the transverse wall, high up where the Crusader banner in its sturdy ornate cabinet had been hung. The whole wall was stained now with great black tongues where the fire had licked it. Detritus piled head-high under the great arch.

What held them transfixed was the fact that, where the banner had always hung, despite the devastation all around, there it hung still.

Nine

The media called it the Malleton Miracle. Photographers and film crews gathered in the churchyard, looking for the angle which would give them the best shot of the improbable survivor. Since there were only a couple of safe spots the banner could be seen from, most of the pictures looked exactly the same. They showed a heavy rosewood cabinet mounted high on a smoke-blackened wall, the glass front cracked but unbroken, stained with soot but still clear enough to show the ancient, delicate fabric somehow preserved within.

Peter Parsons, who refused to call the banner a relic, was horrified to hear it referred to as a miracle. He explained to the reporters that while the artefact was of archaeological interest it had no religious significance, but that only made them worse. *Flag of King Richard wins battle with flames*, they hazarded. *Holy Crusade echoes across centuries.* Or how about: *Undefeated by Saracens, Undefeated by Vandals?*

'We don't know it was vandalism,' growled the vicar. 'It may have been the electrics.'

'OK,' they said. 'Then how about: *The Power v The Glory?*'

The lunchtime news confirmed Parsons's worst fears. His heart sank as he speculated on the likely consequences of such sensationalism. Nor was he kept waiting long. The first twitchers arrived mid-afternoon.

Bird-watching twitchers favour olive-drab cagoules, lace-up boots and pom-pom hats. Mysteries attract, on the whole, a more colourful following. By teatime Malleton was awash with a kind of people never seen there before: young people in sandals and long loose clothes, either very bright or very dark, with hats woven from yak wool and mango-wood crosses dangling from one ear. The women dressed much the same. They laughed like silver bells, then fell silent for no obvious reason, and the sheep-farmers of Malleton could hardly have looked more shell-shocked if Martians had landed in the churchyard of St Bride's.

By suppertime there were forty cars and as many tents in the field behind the church where the annual fête was held. They emptied the village shop of wholemeal bread, then asked Parsons for a service of thanksgiving. When Parsons – who felt he had very little to be thankful for – refused they produced a homespun version of their own, full of chanting and spontaneous expressions of religious fervour.

Parsons consulted his bishop. He pointed out that, with modern long-haul flights, there's never a time of year when you *can't* go skiing. The bishop told him sternly to stay where he was and keep control of the situation. A burned church was a misfortune, he said, but a miracle was a disaster.

At first Agnes was amused, then slightly disturbed by the invasion. 'Where have they all come from? What are they looking for?'

'Portents and wonders,' declared the vicar, spreading his palms evangelically. 'The word of the Lord as revealed in the pattern of the flame.' He sounded bitter.

'They are harmless, aren't they?' She was thinking of Mouse.

'Not really,' said Parsons grimly. 'I don't think they're a danger to life and limb. But they're a threat to the Church – my Church, what I believe in. They're looking for magic tricks. They want the walking on the water, not the daily commitment of responsible Christian living. They call themselves pilgrims: actually they'd follow any Pied Piper with a catchy new tune. That's not religion. It's the same urge that makes people buy lottery scratch cards. They want something for nothing. What my Church offers is something for something.'

It was the first time Agnes had heard him talk seriously about his job, and it altered her perception of him. She'd thought that he was a vicar by profession, as other people were dentists and lawyers and postal workers. But it wasn't like that. It was a vocation for him, as dancing was for her. This miracle nonsense offended him as a pantomime *Swan Lake* would have offended her.

'Don't worry,' she said. 'The next crying statue and they'll all move on.'

He grinned at that; for a moment, before growing serious again. 'Until then, we should keep Mouse out of their way. The recurring theme of religious zeal is that it can't wait to find someone to martyr. If they learn he's being blamed for the fire...'

That startled her. 'The police said that?'

Parsons shook his head. 'No. But this is a small village. Everyone knows they took his boots and his crutches away. Well, that's all right – the locals know Mouse, they'll give him the benefit of the doubt, wait and see what the police can prove. Those people out there...' He waved a helpless hand at the field. 'I don't know. And I don't want to find out.'

'I'll keep him indoors,' Agnes reassured him. 'Shouldn't be too difficult. At least till the police bring his crutches back.'

She was walking back across the church-yard when someone fell into step beside her. After another step or two Agnes paused and looked round. 'Can I help you?'

It was one of the invaders. At least, she was fairly sure it *wasn't* one of the sheep-farmers. But there was something a little stylized – even stylish – about his unkemptness that didn't quite fit. The green combats and the knee-length shirt he wore over them looked at a distance like those of the others; but close up Agnes could see that the labels were on the outside, and they weren't Army & Navy Stores. The sandals were Italian. And he was too clean to be living in a bender and travelling in a superannuated VW.

He smiled. The dentistry was pretty good, too. She put him in his mid-thirties. 'I'm Flanagan.'

Agnes blinked. 'Just that?'

The handsome smile broadened. 'Just that. I'm the seventh son of a seventh son.'

Agnes frowned. 'And ... what? They'd run out of Christian names by the time they reached you?'

Flanagan laughed out loud. 'Sorry. I'm spending too much time with...' A not en-tirely respectful thumb indicated the field filling up behind him. 'They think it's signifi-cant. I don't usually have to explain.'

Agnes smiled at him. 'Do you know what,

Mr Flanagan? You don't have to explain this time either.' And she turned away and resumed walking.

She was a dancer: she could make her body do things most people couldn't. One thing she could do was walk very fast without appearing to hurry. Flanagan had to jog to catch up with her. 'Please wait. I think we may be able to help one another.'

'Really? I wasn't aware of needing any help.' But she slowed to a more normal pace.

'You're something to do with the church, yes?'

'No.'

The handsome smile wavered round the edges. He wasn't used to things being this hard. 'But you know the vicar.'

'Yes, I know the vicar.'

'I need to talk to him.'

Agnes turned round and pointed. 'That's him, over there. The one in the dog collar.'

Flanagan wasn't the only one puzzled by her manner. Agnes wasn't sure why she was reacting like a cat stroked the wrong way.

'Will you introduce us?'

'I don't know you,' she said; but her tone left a little room for manoeuvre.

'I'm Flanagan,' he said again. 'I'm...'

'Yes,' she sighed. 'Oh, come on then. If it'll get you out of my hair.'

She could have done it and walked away.

But she stayed with them, curious despite herself to know what the strange man had to say.

He came straight to the point. 'I think there could be trouble here if we don't work together.'

Peter Parsons bristled. 'More trouble than having my church burn down, you mean?'

'I suppose that depends on your point of view,' conceded Flanagan. 'It must have been a lovely building, I'm sure you're devastated to lose it. But I don't think it would make you feel any better if people got hurt.'

The vicar drew himself up to his full, considerable height. 'Are you threatening me, Mr Flanagan?'

The visitor just wasn't used to life being this difficult. 'Jesus! – what *is* it with you people? I'm trying to help here. And she' – the thumb jabbing now at Agnes – 'thinks I'm trying to pick her up, and you think I'm trying to put the frighteners on you! Can we start again? I'm Flanagan, I'm the seventh son of a seventh son. I'm a healer. It's kind of an inheritance, where I come from.

'I'm not responsible for these people.' This time he afforded the gathering a whole hand gesture. 'But they do rather follow me around. So I know them; and I know when the fervour level is getting too high for comfort. What's happened here *is* extraordinary – maybe you don't consider it miraculous but these people do. And they're hoping this is just the start. They think if they stay here they're going to see wonderful things.'

'They are,' agreed Parsons. 'If they stay till tomorrow they're going to see me conducting open-air services. A pleasant enough departure, though most people wouldn't sleep in a field in order to see it.'

Flanagan ploughed on doggedly. 'And at some point they'll get tired of waiting. It would be smart to know what you're going to do then. I suggest you go along with it. Give them their thanksgiving service. Let them sit out here among the tombstones and look at their relic, and give thanks for the fact that nobody got hurt in the fire. They'll be happy with that. And I can't see why it would give you a problem.'

'Do you think they'll move on afterwards?' asked Agnes.

Flanagan considered. 'Maybe.'

'Maybe?' echoed Parsons, with the opposite inflection.

The healer gave an elegant shrug. 'I told you, I'm not responsible for them – they do what they want. What they want now is some kind of a ... punctuation mark. Something to draw the story of the Malleton Miracle to a close. With luck, a service will do it. Then I'll move on somewhere *my* services will be more welcome, and with luck they'll follow me. What do you think?'

'A service,' said Parsons warily.

Flanagan nodded soothingly. 'A nice, healing service.'

It turned out he meant *A nice healing service.*

It wasn't going badly. Unable to use the church, on Sunday morning Parsons set up shop in front of the ruined porch from where the more supple of his congregation could crane a sideways glimpse of the scorched cabinet high on the blackened wall. With hardly a hint of irony he adapted a form of service usually used for blessing parishioners' pets. And indeed, the hundred or so newcomers were almost as well behaved as its regular beneficiaries, with the added bonus that he didn't have to tidy up after them with a shovel and a wheelbarrow.

If he wasn't entirely comfortable with the situation, he conceded it was probably for the best. And any churchman has to enjoy a congregation three times what he's used to, especially one focused on his every word and movement.

The finishing line was in sight. He was about to dismiss them in the time-honoured fashion, and invite any who were still here next week to join the locals in their regular worship, and to apologize silently to his God for hoping none of them would take up the offer, when Flanagan moved quietly beside him, graciously thanked him for his ministry, and took over. Took over the congregation, took over the service. Turned it from something you'd have been happy taking your cat and your children's pony to, into something that made Malleton families, who did the church thing on Sundays mainly because they always had, feel deeply uncomfortable.

You couldn't have said it was sacrilegious because it wasn't. No one in the congregation, nor Flanagan himself, said or did anything overtly objectionable. But it was disturbing. There's a point at which belief turns to fanaticism, and this little tribe of miracle-hunters wavered perilously on the nexus. And while Flanagan's words were in no way inflammatory, there was something in his manner which seemed almost calculated to excite. Parsons knew what was coming next – and so did Agnes, who'd been on more foreign holidays than she'd attended church services. The suggestion didn't come from Flanagan but from one of his acolytes, but when he was asked to do a healing he demurred so unconvincingly that the whole gypsy band took it up as a chant.

Parsons had his mouth open to forbid it. But Flanagan said softly, 'They need this.

Give me ten minutes, then they'll disperse. Turn them away now and I don't know what they'll do.'

It wasn't the stagiest bit of healing ever performed. Old men weren't throwing away their Zimmer frames to tap-dance among the gravestones; young women with up-turned eyes weren't reaching out to touch the hem of his shirt and falling in a dead faint at his feet. He moved among them quietly, holding a hand here, touching a head there, speaking softly and smiling gently – and that other gentle cleric Peter Parsons wanted to hit him with a brick.

Agnes saw, and edged round quickly to where he was standing, and put her hand on his arm and drew him away. 'He's right,' she whispered. 'Make a scene now and someone will get hurt. Let it go. It's childish, it's foolish, but it's not doing any harm. Let them watch the magic show if they'll go quietly off to bed afterwards.'

He knew she was right. At least, he thought she was probably right; and he knew that if she was wrong, his God and his Church would survive. Still his soul rebelled to think that all of them, and probably the excitable congregation too, were being used by this man Flanagan.

But he was as good as his word. Ten minutes later he had the churchyard cleared and the faithful back in their field, and he shook Parsons's hand as if they were partners in the enterprise. Then he turned and followed his flock – or drove them – leaving Agnes and vicar alone among the tombstones.

Not, however, for long. Before they'd worked out what to think of the absurd episode, another was unfolding.

A long dark car, not at all like the daisy-painted VWs in the field, pulled up at the lychgate and a man in a suit walked up the path. 'Mr Parsons?'

Since Parsons was in what he thought of as his dress uniform, there was no point denying it. 'I'm Peter Parsons. How can I help you?'

The man in the suit introduced himself as Albert Archer, of Archer, Archer & Smedley, solicitors to the Freyn family. He produced a piece of paper which he gave to Parsons. 'It concerns the artefact lent to St Bride's by Colonel Stuart Freyn. My client is anxious that in the present circumstances the church is no longer in a position to safeguard the item. He considers the presence of so many strangers in the village, and particularly in the church grounds, as a threat to its security. Consequently, he would like to have custody of the item returned to him until such time as St Bride's may be restored or alternative, more fitting arrangements be made for its conservation and display.'

He said all this with one breath, then did the smile again. 'Accordingly, I have made arrangements for the cabinet containing the banner to be removed from St Bride's and taken to The Nail where it will remain until further notice. That is a receipt for your records. I hope your current difficulties will soon be resolved. Good day.'

Before Parsons had got his mouth shut, a white van had pulled in behind the dark car and two men unloaded a ladder.

Something made them stay until the van, the car, the cabinet and the banner had all departed. Then Agnes steered Parsons across the road to the cottage. She thought if she left him in the churchyard he'd still be there in the morning, staring bemusedly at the bare spot on the burnt wall. He looked as if he'd been mugged.

'I didn't know what to say,' he confessed, hands clasped round a mug of coffee in Mouse's kitchen. 'I don't know if I've been robbed or not. I mean, it wasn't a loan, it was a gift – it belongs to the church. I was going to sell it to repair the roof – I couldn't have done that if it had been a loan. It wasn't – it was always meant as a gift. It says so in the church guide. There's a brass plaque on the cabinet saying it was given by Colonel Stuart Freyn. Nothing else makes any sense. He couldn't have salved his conscience about the thing merely by lending it to St Bride's.'

He appealed to Mouse, hunched over his own mug at the end of the table so that only the top of his head showed. 'You must have seen it. The plaque. I'm not imagining this, am I? It says it was a gift.'

Mouse nodded. 'A gift.'

'So he's not free to take it back.' Parsons gave a helpless shrug. 'So what am I supposed to do? Accuse him of theft?'

'Why not?' growled Mouse. 'People get accused of worse things.'

Agnes ignored him. 'You do what everyone does in these situations – you pass the buck. You tell your bishop. He'll tell his solicitor, and his solicitor will tell Freyn's solicitor, and Freyn's solicitor will tell Freyn. And you'll get a little note saying there seems to have been some misunderstanding, Freyn was only offering to look after it until the church can be made secure – of course it belongs to St Bride's, it was never his intention to suggest otherwise. Problem solved, embarrassment largely avoided.'

Parsons looked relieved. 'Yes, that's good. That'll work.' Then he frowned. 'It's still a funny kind of stunt for a man in his position.'

'Funny kind of man,' grunted Mouse.

Agnes had found him rather charming, in a crumbly sort of way. 'Why do you say that?'

Mouse thought for a moment, his broad brow creased. 'You know how some people can't tell left from right? And some can't tell red from green? Stuart Freyn can't tell the difference between right and wrong.'

Agnes thought she understood. 'You mean, like the business with the merchant in Aden – he should have realized he was being bribed?'

Mouse shook his straw-coloured head. 'More like the business with the daffodils.'

He'd lost her. 'Daffodils?'

'Spring show.'

He had this intensely annoying way of starting a story, then leaving the other party to winkle the rest of it out of him. Agnes turned to Peter Parsons. 'Do you know what he's talking about?'

It seemed Stuart Freyn had set his heart on winning the Daffodil Cup at the Malleton Horticultural Society's spring show. Most of Mouse's endeavours at The Nail had been directed to that end from the previous year. They'd tended and nurtured the bulbs through the growing stage, protecting them from the excesses of rain that might rot them and drought that might parch them. They'd sheltered them from the winds that might stunt them, and shaded the ones that looked like peaking too soon, and on the morning of the show they went round the beds together, hand-picking the best of the blooms, sorting them in bunches of six and making them comfortable in the back of Freyn's car for the short journey to the village hall.

All of which seemed to Agnes a bit excessive for a few daffs. But keen gardeners wouldn't understand the time she put into practising at the barre. 'And did it pay off?'

'He won the cup,' said Mouse.

Agnes gritted her teeth. 'He must have been pleased.'

'He was. He gave me a bonus.'

'Mouse – is there a point to this story at all? Or is it just going to go on until one of us dies?'

'They weren't his daffodils. I went to the show, I saw what he'd won with. They weren't the ones we picked in his garden that morning. He'd gone somewhere and bought better ones.'

Ten

It happened more or less as Agnes had predicted, except that it wasn't a solicitor's note that came to the vicarage, it was Nick Freyn.

Two days later Agnes saw his car arrive – long and silver this time – and scrambled for an excuse to go across the road. With longer to think she'd have done better, but needs must when the Devil drives. 'Peter, you don't have a screwdriver? I need to shorten these new crutches of Mouse's. Oh ... you've got company.'

They were still standing in the hall, the tall burly cleric and a smaller, older, greyer man in a grey suit, the quality of which she would never have appreciated before knowing Robin. They were talking earnestly rather than aggressively. There was a hint of apology and a hint of exasperation in the visitor's body language.

'Er ... yes,' said Parsons. 'Can it wait a moment? I'll pop over with it.'

'Of course. Sorry to interrupt.' But actually she made no move to leave. 'Excuse me, but ... it's Mr Freyn, isn't it? We met at The Brewery a couple of months ago. A DETI do. I'm Agnes Amory – Robin Firth's fiancée.' She was starting to notice, and not much like, the way she put on and took off the metaphorical engagement ring depending on circumstances.

'Miss Amory. Of course.' She wouldn't have recognized him if they'd met in Tesco's, and it was clear he didn't remember her. But studying him she could see elements of both his father and sister. He was shorter than either of them but had the same narrow, rangy build and radiated the same kind of energy. In the Colonel it was muted now: in Nick Freyn it hummed like an electricity substation. Because he'd gone into business rather than the army he'd made money rather than collecting medals, but the same urge to succeed marked both of them. They were a high-achieving family.

And they weren't used to being put on the back foot by country clerics. He'd wanted to have the last word, but Agnes's arrival had rather spoiled his timing. He looked at her coolly. 'Good to see you again. How is Robin?' Then, remembering: 'Oh – yes. A difficult time. Give him my sympathy...' The sentence foundered on the rocks of propriety. *Can* you ask someone's next wife to convey condolences on the death of their last one?

Uncertainty, something he hadn't much experience of, made him forgo his parting shot and reach for the door. 'Don't go, Mr Parsons and I are finished.' He returned his attention to the vicar. 'I'm sorry about the misunderstanding, Peter. It was thoughtless. We were just trying to help – thought it would be one thing less for you to worry about. But of course we should have discussed it with you first. You must have wondered what the hell was happening.'

Parsons was magnanimous in victory. 'Just a little puzzled. I thought we needed to clarify the situation. But if you're willing to keep it at The Nail until I have a church to display it in again, that seems the ideal solution.'

On that they agreed, and parted. The silver car whispered away.

'You let him flannel you,' said Agnes critically.

Parsons was indignant. 'I did not!'

'You let him flannel you. He wanted the banner where no one was going to see it, and you went along with it.'

'He agreed that the thing is Church property! He's just looking after it for me.'

'It was never about who owned it,' she said patiently. 'It's about keeping it out of sight. High on a church wall above a congregation of twenty myopic pensioners, it was. As the centre of a news story and the object of veneration by a band of New Age hippies, it isn't. The thing's an embarrassment to him. He doesn't want people looking at it. He's afraid what they might see.'

Parsons's eyebrows arched like a couple of Early English lancets. 'Like what? It is what it is – a bit of twelfth-century silk that travelled to the Holy Land and then travelled back again. It's interesting, it's historic, but it hasn't any real importance. It can't have. It's been up on that wall for almost forty years, and no one's even asked for a closer look.'

'And now it isn't, and people are getting a closer look, and Nick Freyn doesn't like it. If everything his father says is true, why's he so twitchy? Forty years is forty years, Colonel Freyn is retired – and that was in another country and besides, the merchant's probably dead.' Agnes was better on theatre than literature. 'This long after, who gives a shit?'

Parsons blinked. People never expected her to swear. They thought decorum was part of the ballet-dancer package. Margot Fonteyn, she thought darkly, had a lot to answer for. Aloud, she said, 'Have you ever had it valued?'

'Of course not. It was a gift. And the guy who gave it lives just up the road!'

'But you thought of selling it.'

'As an alternative to having my roof fall in,' admitted Parsons. 'Fortunately it wasn't necessary. And now we've been rather overtaken by events.'

As well as being a decent and personable human being, he was an obviously intelligent one. Agnes couldn't think why he was being so dim. She cut it up into small manageable chunks for him, like feeding a toddler. 'For forty years the thing was mounted high up on your wall and everyone was happy. Then your roof started leaking and you asked yourself what you could sell. Did you talk to Freyn about it?'

'No.' Then, remembering: 'I kind of sounded him out. Not Nick – his father. It seemed only polite.'

'And you are a polite man,' nodded Agnes approvingly, 'and no doubt your mother's pride and joy. And – stop me if I'm wrong – within a few days, bless me if you haven't got an anonymous benefactor begging to be allowed to fix your roof!'

Even the vicar could spot irony when it was laid on with a trowel. 'You think ... the Freyns?'

'They have the money. And they obviously still have an interest in the banner. If that's what it is.'

Parsons frowned. 'What do you mean? What else?'

'Well, if you've never had an expert look at it, all you know is what Stuart Freyn told Dr Pyke. It could be a Crusader banner. It could be the Virgin Mary's nightie. Or it could just be an excuse to put something where it wouldn't be touched for forty years. It's a damn big cabinet for a glorified silk hankie! There could be *anything* in there with it – wads of cash, a Nazi art collection, a murder weapon – anything.'

Peter Parsons's jaw had dropped on his chest. And she'd seemed such a nice, gentle little soul! A dancer. What was she doing harbouring these suspicions?

What she was doing was sharing them. Suspicion is contagious: it passes from one person to another. Parsons could have served all his ministry here and never had an unkind thought about the Freyns or their banner. But now she'd put the thoughts in his head they were going to be hard to shift. 'Maybe we should get an expert up to The Nail to take a proper look at it,' he said slowly.

Agnes was dismissive. 'You'll never get an expert near it. The Freyns will burn it themselves first. Maybe they'll burn it anyway, just in case. You know – another accident? If you want to know what this is all about, Peter, it's up to you and me and a digital camera.'

His jaw dropped again, and further. '*Burglary?*'

'Of course not burglary,' she said briskly. 'Surely you can find some pretext to go up there? We distract them, you whip out your Swiss Army knife, and...' Even to herself this was beginning to sound like fantasy. 'Or we could ask Mouse.'

Her thought-processes were just too fast for Parsons. 'Mouse?' he echoed weakly.

'He's the one who goes up the ten-metre ladder, isn't he? To dust it, to check that the woodworm aren't winning?' Parsons nodded. 'Then he's probably seen more of it than anyone else in the last forty years. Maybe he can tell us what's in that cabinet.'

Parsons was afraid she'd overlooked something. 'But Mouse...'

'Can't remember,' said Mouse succinctly.

Agnes breathed heavily at him. It might be true. Or it might be an easy way to avoid thinking about things that were painful and difficult. 'What can't you remember?'

He shrugged. They were back round the kitchen table in Ruth's cottage. Mouse had his arms folded on the scrubbed deal, and when he lowered his head to look at her from under his tangled straw-coloured fringe he looked as stubborn as a three-year-old faced with a plate of greens.

'All right then, tell me what you *do* remember. You remember cutting the grass in the churchyard?'

'When?'

'Any time.'

He shrugged again. 'Sure.'

'Do you remember doing work inside the church? Repairs, maybe a bit of painting, things like that.'

He thought a moment longer, then nodded.

'What about the long ladder? Do you remember being up the long ladder?'

Another nod. 'Light bulbs.'

Parsons translated. 'We change all the light bulbs once a year. It saves having to get the ladder out every couple of weeks because another one's blown.'

'When did you do it last?'

'Not long ago.'

'About six weeks ago,' volunteered the vicar.

'While you were at it I bet you dusted that cabinet. You'd change all the bulbs, then before you put the ladder away you'd have a glance round to see what else needed doing. And you'd think, There's that cabinet with the banner in. I'll give it a quick dust, polish the glass, make sure the fixings are still sound. Did you, Mouse? Can you remember doing that?'

Six weeks ago was palpably close to the point where his memory failed. He didn't remember everything before that; he remembered almost nothing after it. But at least he was trying. Agnes saw the effort in his eyes like broken seas in a rip tide. 'Maybe...'

She didn't want him to give up in disgust and frustration. 'OK. Maybe will do for now. Because I expect you did pretty much the same things every time you went up there. After three years you must have worked up a bit of a routine. That's a long ladder, you wouldn't want to be up and down it half a dozen times. What do you do, take a bag of the things you're going to need? A duster, polish, glass cleaner, a screwdriver and some spare screws in case you notice any problems...'

Mouse's troubled grey-green eyes, that had been narrowed with effort, suddenly widened. 'Two sizes, two kinds. Slot-head and cross-head.'

Agnes smiled in triumph. 'Good. Good, Mouse. That's something you couldn't guess – you remember it. You were up with the cabinet, and you were close enough to see what kind of screws were holding it together. Now: what else could you see?'

Uncertain, Mouse glanced at Parsons. 'The banner.'

'Yes,' said Agnes. 'But I haven't seen it, have I? Tell me what it looks like.'

'It's just a bit of cloth.' There was a kind of shrug in his oddly gruff voice.

She persevered. 'What colour? What's it made of? Is it embroidered or painted? Spread out or folded up? When you're close enough to polish the glass, *what can you see?*'

He was out of patience – with her, or with his own frailty. 'I told you. It's just a bit of cloth. It's pretty much the same as the bit of cloth I polish the glass with! I can't make it more interesting to please you!'

Immediately she backed off. That stubborn look of his, filtered by his fringe, told her that if she lost him she'd never get him back. And in an odd way it was starting to matter to her, that they solve the mystery of the banner. Why it was making respectable people behave irrationally. If she couldn't get the information out of Mouse's addled brain, she was horribly afraid she was going to end up breaking into The Nail herself.

'All right,' she conceded. 'So it's not the banner itself. So maybe there's something hidden behind it. That's a big lump of a case – there's plenty of room. What about it, Mouse? Any sign of anything else in there?'

But he was sulking now and wouldn't, or possibly couldn't, say.

Agnes saw the vicar as far as Ruth's gate,

only the width of a narrow road from his own. She thought that was why she was starting to think of him as a close friend. She said something of the kind, with a grin, and was surprised when Parsons didn't grin back but excused himself with a mumble and hurried back to the safety of the vicarage.

Agnes was puzzling over it as she walked back to the cottage. When, as she closed the door behind her, she realized what was going through his upright, clerical but still male mind her grin only broadened.

More midnight alarums. Not a fire this time, thank God, though it might have been from the clumsy urgency of feet – or rather, one foot and two crutches – on the wooden stairs and the unceremonious way he threw open the door she was sleeping behind.

She hadn't thought she was in much danger from him. But Mouse was becoming increasingly agile on those crutches, and his unexpected arrival in her bedroom in the middle of the night jerked Agnes awake with the heart already thumping in her chest. She fumbled wildly for the bedside light. 'Mouse? What the hell are you *doing*?' Her voice soared in mingled indignation and, yes, fear.

His eyes were wild, his straw-coloured hair more than usually unkempt. He leaned swaying on the crutches. She could knock him over with one hand. Her heart steadied. In his distress he stumbled over the words. 'I ... remember. Something. Like you said. Up the ladder. I remember!'

'OK.' She drew herself up in the bed, keeping the light quilt around her, and patted the vacant end. 'Sit down before you fall down, and tell me what.'

'The banner. The case.'

She'd got that much. 'You remember cleaning it? Six weeks ago?'

He nodded, emphatically.

But doing a bit of housework, even at the top of a ten-metre ladder, hadn't got him this worked up. 'What do you remember, Mouse? Did something happen? Did you see something?'

More nodding; urgent, agitated. 'Agnes – I saw a face!'

Eleven

It was late; from his more than usually rumpled appearance it was clear he'd been sleeping. 'Mouse – you had a dream.'

'No.' He shook his head insistently. 'Not a dream. A memory. A face in the cabinet.'

Agnes thought she understood. She smiled. 'Your face. You polished the glass until you could see your face in it.'

His look was withering. She had to keep reminding herself that, however he looked, however he behaved, whatever he might or might not have done and whatever damage his brain had sustained, this was a highly intelligent young man. Speaking to him as if he was a child was guaranteed to anger him.

Distinctly, pronouncing each word precisely, as if Agnes was the idiot child, he said, 'Not in the glass. On the banner. There's a face on the banner.'

Now she thought about it, it didn't seem improbable. What she knew about medieval textiles you could put in your eye without blinking, but if the features of saints and

143

kings could grace stained-glass windows she supposed they could also figure on flags. When few people could read there was no point putting up a notice: if you wanted troops to know where their command post was, putting a likeness of their commander on a flag was an effective way of doing it.

'OK,' she said again. 'That's interesting. Just not quite interesting enough for' – she glanced at her watch – 'four in the morning. Can we talk about it at breakfast?'

He clambered to his feet and turned his back on her, just slowly enough for her to glimpse the curl of his lip. He'd brought her significant news. He'd remembered something important. And she'd rather sleep. She was a disappointment to him. Agnes had to keep reminding herself that he wasn't her responsibility. Not a relative, not a friend. He was nothing to her.

But then, Mouse was used to that. He was nothing much to his own mother. Agnes wasn't sure why that thought slid under her ribs like a knife, but it did. She wondered if she should call him back. But she very much doubted he'd come.

In the morning she found the kitchen table set with cutlery, crockery, a steaming pot of coffee and a large book open like a place mat where she sat. 'Mouse?'

He waved a hand without looking round

from the hob. 'Bacon and eggs. Almost ready.'

She had her mouth open to say she didn't eat cooked breakfasts. She stopped herself just in time. He didn't know that because this was the first time he'd been able to make breakfast for her instead of her making it for him. 'What's the book?'

'Ma's.'

His verbal shorthand was growing tiresome. It was as if he considered people owed it to him to work out what he was thinking.

Agnes declined to play. 'Ma's?' she echoed woodenly.

He turned round at that. Then he brought the pan over and served her carefully, and then he sat down to his own plate. With a precise enunciation that would have brought tears of joy to Henry Higgins's eyes he said: 'The book belonged to my mother. It is a history book. There are illustrations of medieval banners in it. They do not have faces on them.'

Agnes chuckled; and through his glowering she sensed Mouse was not displeased. She looked at the book.

And he was right. There were golden lions on a scarlet ground, thin as alley-cats and facing uniformly left. This was the standard of King Richard, Cœur de Lion. A little later, when Edward III advanced his claim

145

on France, the lions were joined by fleur-de-lys worked on a royal-blue ground. The standards, and banners, and a dozen lesser flags with half-forgotten names – pennants and cressets and gonfalons – gleamed on the pages in front of her, brilliant in primary colours. Of course, the illustrations depicted how they would have looked fluttering over the war tents of the period and took no account of the eight centuries since.

Keeping the page with her finger, Agnes looked at the front of the book. 'Was your mother interested in medieval textiles?'

'She typed,' said Mouse gnomically. Agnes, wise to his game now, kept a stony silence until he elaborated. 'That's what she did for a living – she typed manuscripts. For academics, mostly. Brains the size of planets, but they can't spell and they can't punctuate. They sent her hundreds of sheets of handwritten scrawl, and she sent them back a typescript and a computer disc. When the book was published, they signed a copy for her.'

Which explained the eclectic mix of reading matter on the shelves upstairs. Agnes looked at the publication history inside the front of the book. 'This one's ten years old.'

'It's about medieval heraldry. What's another ten years?'

She flicked through a few more pages, then

closed the book and nodded. 'OK, no faces. Where does that get us?'

'Whatever it is that's been up on the wall of St Bride's for the last forty years, it isn't a Crusader banner.'

She thought that was a leap too far. 'This book's talking about royal standards and the banners of famous commanders. Maybe not everyone was so showy.'

His eyelids dipped, conceding the point. 'But it doesn't look anything like these. You'd expect even a second-class banner to try a bit harder to look like what the A-team were using. Without the gold thread, maybe paint instead of embroidery, but the same idea. And colour was everything. So why's our banner white?'

'Is it?'

'Except for the face.'

'Which is?'

'Fawn,' said Mouse. His grey-green eyes never left hers. He was deciding whether to trust her.

'Some fading is probably inevitable in eight hundred years,' she hazarded.

'Probably. Enough to turn it white?'

Agnes didn't think so either. 'Maybe it was the banner of a notable coward – whichever side was winning, he hoped they'd respect a flag of truce.'

Mouse rewarded her with a gruff little

chuckle. 'Or it's something else.'

'Why would Colonel Freyn say it's a Crusader banner if it isn't?'

'Why would he say he'd grown some prize-winning daffodils when he hadn't? He enjoys ... admiration.'

Agnes had sensed that. 'Still, it's an elaborate story if none of it's true. If he was caught out in a fib, all he had to say was that the merchant lied. Smirks, chuckles all round, a cheque for the church-restoration fund and honour unimpeached. Why involve solicitors and workmen and the whole Freyn family to keep the secret that the thing in the cabinet is probably worth rather less than the cabinet itself?'

It was a puzzle. Whatever Mouse had seen from atop the long ladder, events since the fire indicated a mystery of sorts. And the rest of a long hot summer stretched ahead of her, and Agnes was missing Robin and wanted a distraction. 'I'm going to try to get a look at it. See if I can see the face too.'

She debated – with herself: she didn't entirely trust Mouse's judgement, and she thought Peter Parsons would try to stop her – the best approach. She thought there was a good chance that if she batted her eyelashes at the Colonel he'd show her the banner. What stopped her was the possibility that the secret was more important than that, and by the time she realized he wasn't going to help, Freyn would know she was taking an unhealthy interest in the thing. So, subterfuge. Well, a dancer is also an actor – she could lie with the best of them. She just had to come up with a plausible scenario.

In the event, a plausible scenario came knocking at her door barely an hour later.

It was Flanagan, and he looked worried. 'I'm not sure if I'm talking to the right person. But there's going to be trouble here if we're not careful, and everyone but you seems to have vested interests to protect. The vicar's pissed off with me, he's not going to listen, and I can't see the Freyns welcoming me with open arms either. But you know them, don't you? You could introduce us.'

'Flanagan, I've been here a few days longer than you have! I don't know anyone in Malleton. I've met the Freyns, but the sum total of my conversations with the entire family wouldn't fill a postcard. They're not going to help you because I ask them to.' Belatedly she realized that in refusing him she was also missing the opportunity to use him. She back-pedalled gracefully. 'Which doesn't mean we can't try. The old man's a bit of a Lothario – he might see us if I ask nicely.'

Healing was doing more than just paying the rent. The leather seats of Flanagan's sports car enfolded her. As he drove she quizzed him. 'What sort of trouble? What are you afraid of?'

He glanced at her sharply but didn't contest the word. 'I told you the people in the field aren't my responsibility, but maybe that's a bit disingenuous. We're more than fellow-travellers. They regard me as some kind of figurehead; and that suits me fine because people would rather join a congregation than begin one. Half the places I pitch my tent, nobody'd notice if it wasn't for these people coming in as soon as I open the flap.'

'Nothing worse than an empty front row,' agreed Agnes.

Flanagan frowned, unsure how to take her. 'The problem is, there's nothing cynical about it. They really do believe. Not just in me – they believe in *everything*. Right now they believe in that banner. They believe it has real religious significance. It came unscathed through a fire that destroyed a thousand-year-old church: they don't believe that's a coincidence. They think it has a purpose here, and it's their job to bear witness. And to protect it.'

'From what?'

'From whatever! They don't think the fire was accidental. They think someone's trying to destroy it. And they've heard about the police coming here, and leaving with your friend's crutches; and they're not stupid, they can put two and two together.'

Agnes felt herself go still. 'Are you saying Mouse is in danger from these people?'

He shook his head. 'No. At least, I don't think so. Not yet. But you see, they were watching over it. As long as they could see it they knew it was safe. But now it's gone. Someone came with a screwdriver and took it away, and they can't be sure it's safe any more.

'They started off upset about that, but now they're getting angry. I'm afraid that if they can't be sure where the banner is they'll want to make damn sure they know where the boy is. We need to get it put back in the church, where they can see it's safe. Then they'll calm down. If the Freyns insist on hanging on to it, tempers are going to escalate.'

'Two screwdrivers,' said Agnes, absent-mindedly. 'Slot-head and cross-head.'

Flanagan looked at her again, bewildered. He'd no idea what she was talking about; but he knew she held him in contempt, and he wasn't used to that and he didn't like it. 'You think I'm a fake, don't you?' he said in a low voice. 'You're wrong. It isn't just a snake-oil show. I am what I claim to be.'

'The seventh son of a...'

'A healer. I can't prove it. People don't throw away their crutches and run out the door after I touch them. I can't perform miracles. But people tell me I make them feel better.'

'Anything that makes people feel better is worth doing,' said Agnes tactfully.

'You don't believe in it, though, do you? You think it's all in the mind.'

'I think it would still be worth doing if it *was* all in the mind. I'm not sure I'd call it healing.'

'It's what it is,' he insisted. 'I don't know how it works. I only know what people tell me. They tell me they feel better, stronger, in less pain. I know, those are subjective assessments. But why would they say it if it wasn't true? Why would they come, and keep coming? Why would they give me money?'

Agnes gave a delicate little shrug. 'Because the more desperate people are, the more off-the-wall things they're willing to try. You say to them what you've just said to me and it becomes a matter of belief – a self-fulfilling prophecy. If they believe they feel better, they do. I'm not saying you're making it up. I'm saying that as long as it's something you can't measure, there'll always be a psychological element. And sick people who desperately want to believe they're improving will see some improvement. I think you're wise to ask how they're feeling after a session. If you asked what they could do now that they couldn't do last week, you'd never see them again.'

Her honest opinion unsettled him more than her mockery. But he didn't pursue the argument, only asked, 'Is this it?' when they reached the gates of The Nail.

Frances Freyn answered the door again, the unmarried daughter cast – willingly or otherwise – in the housekeeper's rôle. Agnes introduced Flanagan by the only name she had for him, and asked if the Colonel was at home.

Frances's brows gathered in a protective frown. 'I think he's resting.'

As if determined to make a liar of her, the old man appeared round the corner of his house, edging shears in one hand. There was still something military in the scope of his long-legged stride, and his face brightened at the sight of the visitors. 'Miss Amory – what a pleasant surprise. Has Mouse sent you to check up on me? Worried I'm weeding wrong?'

Agnes shook her head. She wondered how to explain about her companion, decided she wouldn't even try and waved an airy hand. 'Over to you, Mr Flanagan.'

The odd thing to her mind was not that Freyn decided not to help. It was *when* he decided not to help. Because Agnes already knew what Flanagan wanted to say, she could watch the pair of them, see how they related to one another, without being distracted by the words. The old man was untroubled by the appearance of his visitor, seemed only amused when Flanagan explained his relationship to the travellers. But shutters fell behind his eyes when Flanagan spoke of the banner.

'I know you're trying to protect it. But I'm concerned you're putting yourself at risk having it here. I really think, in everyone's interests, it would be better to return it to the church. Cover it with a tarpaulin – shrink-wrap it in plastic if you want – but put it back where it belongs.'

Stuart Freyn's expression had gone from merry to guarded to hostile in the space of two or three sentences. His voice was cold. 'Mr Flanagan, if you suspect that your friends are going to break into my house, it isn't me you should be talking to, it's the police.'

Flanagan shook his head. His dark hair was longer than was fashionable – longer even than Mouse's, though better groomed. 'Nobody's saying that. But ... Look, I know these people. I consider them friends. They're nice people: if you were in trouble and needed help there's no one likelier to give it.

'But they have weaknesses as well as strengths, and one of them is a tendency for common sense to go AWOL when their emotions are involved. They think that if something matters to them, that's enough to make it important. They've decided your banner is important – special – and telling them they're wrong won't make any difference. Threatening them with the police won't make any difference. Putting it back on the church wall will. And in another few days they'll hear about some new marvel somewhere, and you'll wake up next morning to an empty field. It'll be as if they were never there. Then you can bring the thing back here, and look after it until the church is renovated, and no harm will have been done.'

'You think not?' said the Colonel icily. 'A gang of leftover Flower Children dictating to me what I may and may not do with my own property in my own house? And you're telling me they'll storm the place if I don't comply, and involving the police will only make things worse ... and you think no harm's being done? Mr Flanagan, what you're describing is mob rule. I've fought that all my life. I spent a lot of my career fighting it. I don't propose to give in to it now.'

Flanagan wiped a hand across his mouth.

His lack of composure surprised Agnes. 'I'm not doing this very well,' he mumbled. 'It's not something I've had to deal with before. I'm not threatening you with anything. And I may be wrong. But I hear people talking, and what's being said, and how they're talking, worries me. If they keep working themselves up like this, sooner or later they'll do something stupid.

'And yes, the police will sort it out. Some of them will get fines they can't pay, and others will do time, but it'll be too late to do any good. Your property will have been damaged and your family frightened or, God forbid, even hurt by then. All because you don't want to be pushed around.

'Well, right now they don't know I'm talking to you. They won't know, if you put the banner back, that it was anything to do with them. They'll just think, *Great guy*, and go back to gazing reverently at it – and if I get on the Internet tonight I can find another miracle for them to go and be pilgrims at, and then they'll be out of your hair and so will I. After that you can do anything you want with the damn thing. All I'm trying to do is stop anyone getting hurt.'

Agnes believed him. She thought that explained that uncharacteristic diffidence: he wasn't accustomed to acting selflessly. Or maybe it wasn't entirely selfless. If there was

156

trouble here it would cast a shadow to the next place he wanted to pitch his tent.

Colonel Freyn didn't believe him. Or maybe he believed him but it didn't make any difference. 'Well, thank you for coming, Mr ... Flanagan.' He managed to say it as if he didn't quite accept it was a name. 'I'm afraid I shan't be doing as you ask. If you have any influence with your friends, your time might be better spent advising them to respect the law. The banner will be returned to St Bride's in due course, when the church is in a condition to receive it. At that time anyone who wants to gawp at it will be able to. Until then it will remain here, and will not be on public display. Good day.'

Agnes said, 'Before we go, could I have a gawp?'

She'd managed to catch Freyn completely off guard. 'You?'

'I haven't seen it,' she said, in a kind of apologetic whine. 'Everyone's talking about it. Even Mouse, who can't string three words together. And I never got to see it. Could I sneak a quick look? Please?'

He had two problems, and Agnes was well aware of both of them. The first was that it was a modest enough request from someone he knew, if only a little, and who wasn't threatening him with anything. And the other was that he was, and had always been,

157

the sort of man who finds it difficult to refuse a pretty girl anything. He wavered.

Another day, perhaps even a few more hours, and he'd have found somewhere to put it that wouldn't have been in full view of anyone entering his house. An attic, a cellar or one of the bedrooms would have sufficed. Then he could have said it was away being cleaned, or he'd deposited it in the bank for safe keeping, or that he'd put it in the hands of the Church Commissioners. Anything that would leave the earnest enquirer with only two choices: to leave quietly, or to call him a liar.

But he hadn't got round to it. The cabinet needed two people to carry it, and when the workmen asked where he wanted it he hadn't had an answer ready. He'd indicated the heavy wooden coffer that served the household as a hall table, and that's where it remained.

And while he wavered, Agnes headed that way as if his consent was a formality. Before Freyn had decided what to do she was standing in front of it, peering down with unconcealed curiosity. He said, 'Er ... of course.'

This was a view that, in the last forty years, only Mouse Firth and earlier handymen at St Bride's had enjoyed. Peter Parsons had looked at it through binoculars but never tackled the climb, and though most of his parishioners were just about aware of the heavy dark cabinet mounted high above their heads they had scant knowledge of what it contained and not enough interest to ask.

This close, the overwhelming impression was of age. The fabric was so fine, so pale, it was almost translucent – only the fact that it was folded on itself again and again stopped her seeing right through to the back of the cabinet.

Or, just possibly, to whatever else the cabinet contained.

There was no embroidery. There were no blazing medieval colours, or even the pastel remnants to which eight hundred years might have reduced them. There were no traces of pigment that Agnes could see. There was, perhaps, a slight staining which – caught in the right light – might have looked like a face, in the same way that people claim to see a man in the moon.

She stepped back with a smile. 'So that's a Crusader banner. Amazing, isn't it? You can see how a castle could survive, but something that fragile? It's a wonderful thing to have. Thank you for showing us.' And she linked her arm through Flanagan's and headed for the door.

Twelve

'I don't know what it is,' she said to Peter Parsons half an hour later. 'But I do know it isn't a Crusader banner. It isn't silk. It could be cotton, but I think it's a very fine linen. Very worn and a bit stained. But it could never have been a banner. There's nothing on it to tell you whose army was meant to rally round it.'

Parsons didn't know what to say to her. This was at least in part because of things going on at the back of his own mind. He felt she was doing something she shouldn't, though she'd hardly broken into The Nail and mugged the Colonel to get a look at the banner. He felt she was in danger, though there seemed scant likelihood of the Colonel mugging her. He even felt that by being seen with Flanagan she was laying herself open to gossip. This thought bothered him, if anything, more than the others. Because it wasn't Robin Firth's feelings he was worrying about.

If he'd taken them out and examined them,

he'd have realized there was nothing wrong with how he felt about Agnes. He was a single man, she was an unmarried woman if not an entirely unattached one. Agnes herself was unsure whether she was currently in a relationship or not. Many men would have considered her fair game for a speculative approach. She was well capable of deflecting him amiably if she wanted to give Robin Firth another chance.

But though Parsons had always assumed he'd marry one day, a wife being an indispensable accoutrement to an Anglican vicar, he'd never done much about it. He'd thrown himself into his vocation, and devoted such time as it left him to the pursuit of the perfect piste, with the result that he could talk to archbishops about religious philosophy, to ladies in hats about flower arranging and to chalet girls about black runs with equal ease. But he'd never had a serious girlfriend and wasn't sure how you set about acquiring one. He had the sneaking suspicion that not sleeping in a T-shirt printed with the legend *Skiers do it with their knees together* might be a good start.

He managed to drag his mind back to the problem at hand. 'Agnes – what exactly are you trying to achieve?'

She raised perfectly arched eyebrows. 'Me? Nothing.'

'That's not how it seems. Are you helping Flanagan? Using him? Either way, why?'

She hadn't heard that note of censure in his voice before. He'd bent over backwards to give Mouse the benefit of any doubt going; and though he'd been very angry about the healer's behaviour at the church, even then he'd managed to bridle his tongue. She was taken aback that he felt justified in criticizing her. 'I took Flanagan up to The Nail because he asked me to. Colonel Freyn showed me the banner because I asked him to. What's your problem with that?'

Parsons flushed. 'You know this is a sensitive issue. Why are you so determined to get involved?'

'To poke my oar in, you mean,' she retorted. 'Because it's ... a puzzle. I'm curious why the Freyns are so embarrassed by the thing – whatever it is – that they'd lie about it. That may make me a nosy cow but I don't know why it would bother you. Anyone would think you'd something to hide too.'

And of course he had, and he wasn't prepared to tell her what it was. So he snorted derisively. 'The Freyns have nothing to hide! They're embarrassed because something they gave to St Bride's in good faith has become a cause célèbre to the last kind of people they'd want to encourage. I'm with them. I don't think Flanagan and his entourage are doing anything here except causing disorder and a mildly threatening atmosphere. I'm surprised you'd want to be associated with that.'

'Peter, you haven't even *begun* being surprised by me! Don't tell me who to associate with. And don't be such a...' She stopped short of saying it.

He wanted to hear it. 'Such a what?'

'Such a lapdog,' said Agnes hotly. 'You don't owe the Freyns anything. This isn't the eighteenth century – the family in the big house don't get to say who keeps his job. You can afford to look at what they've said and what they've done, and recognize the fact that they're telling porkies. That artefact is not what Stuart Freyn said it was. And if it isn't what he says it is, maybe he didn't come by it how he said either. That's why they're worried, and why they don't want people looking too closely at it. As much as the people in the field, they think the thing exerts some kind of power. The Freyns are afraid that, even after forty years, it has the power to hurt them.'

'You're making this up as you go along!' snapped Parsons. 'Let it go, Agnes. So what if Stuart Freyn did something foolish forty years ago? It's history.'

'And those who can't remember the past are condemned to repeat it,' she shot back.

'And why do you think you can tell me what to do?'

'I ... I don't want...'

'*What?*' she yelled, irritated beyond endurance.

'I don't want you getting hurt!'

They stared at one another, frozen by the words. It was hard to judge which of them was the most startled. Neither of them had been expecting what came out when Peter Parsons opened his mouth.

He tried, unconvincingly, to back-pedal. 'I've had my church burn down. I've had one of the Lost Tribes of Israel camp in my back field. I don't need to be explaining to Robin Firth how you broke your ankle falling off a high windowsill while trying to spy on a bit of medieval cloth!'

'Peter...'

'Don't...'

Agnes cleared her throat. 'I'm sorry. I didn't realize I was giving you grief. I'll stay out of your way.'

His eyes pleaded with her. 'Don't do that. I didn't mean to shout. It's been a trying week. I'm glad you've been here. If you hadn't been willing to look after Mouse, that's something else I'd have had to cope with.'

'All the same, it's probably time I was getting home. I think he can manage now. If you'd look in on him every couple of days, make sure he has something in the house to eat...'

Defeated, Parsons took a step back. 'Yes, I can do that. And if you'll leave me Robin's number, I'll make sure he knows of any developments...'

Back at the cottage she wrote it down for him. Then she sat for a while looking at it. And then she dialled it.

He didn't answer. He may have been in a meeting. Or just possibly, Agnes thought, he didn't want to speak to her. She gave a sort of mental shrug. If so, the sooner she knew that the better. She waited to see how long it would take him to call back; and indeed, if he would.

He called back almost immediately. 'I'm sorry, I had some people with me. Where are you? Are you all right?'

'I'm still at Ruth's. And yes, I'm all right.' And she waited.

He hesitated a moment longer, then he said it. 'And Mouse?'

'Mouse is mending. He's home now, hobbling round on crutches like a cross between Quasimodo and Richard the Third.'

She thought she heard a grim chuckle. 'Any more from the police?'

Agnes gave a gusty sigh. 'Oh yes. Not about the accident.' If that's the right word, she added silently. '*Now* they think he burned the church down.'

She told him everything that had happened. She had no idea how he'd respond – if some lingering instinct of parenthood would make him leap to Mouse's defence, or if this new challenge would finally break the overstretched ties between them. Almost, she was past caring. She didn't know if Mouse had done all, or any, or some of the things he was suspected of. She was no longer even sure that Robin was wrong to leave when he had.

Time is a great healer, but so is distance – oddly enough, it makes things look clearer. Peter Parsons was right: she was too keen to stick her oar in. Robin's relationship with his difficult son was something for them to work out. Deep-rooted feelings – emanating, possibly, from her womb – were telling her a man should love his son even when he couldn't excuse what he'd done; but if that was true, wasn't there a similar kind of duty on her? She'd been ready to marry this man. If his response to a family tragedy had been less dignified than she might have hoped, was that reason enough to stop loving him?

And did it make it easier or harder, that she had options she had not until half an hour ago been aware of?

'Is there any evidence?' Robin asked when

she'd finished.

'I don't think so. He was in the churchyard the night of the fire, but so was I – so was the rest of the village. The police took his things for analysis. I think if they found paraffin they'd have been back by now.'

'Then they were just flying a kite.'

'Probably.' She bit her lip. 'They know about the fire at your house.'

'Ah.' He considered. 'I suppose it's their job to.' Another pause. 'Are you staying on for a while?'

She'd phoned to tell him she was on her way home. Now she found she couldn't. 'I think I have to, at least until things settle down here. It's not the police I'm worried about – there's no point, if they charge him with something he'll have to deal with it. The pilgrims are another matter.'

'Pilgrims?' Robin sounded puzzled.

'The weirdos camped in the field behind the church. They think it's all some kind of mystical happening – the fire, the banner coming through unscathed, now the banner's been taken away and they want it bringing back. Flanagan thinks they'll turn nasty if it isn't returned soon – and it won't be, because the Freyns don't want anyone looking at it, and that's *another* puzzle! And I'm just scared that at some point the Living Dead' – Agnes *liked* weirdos: the situation must have been very tense to make her talk like this – 'will look round for someone to blame for the loss of their treasure and settle on Mouse. I'm going to stay until either he's cleared by the police or the circus moves on.'

It wasn't a deliberate pitch for sympathy. But that was how it came out, and Agnes was anxious enough not to care too much how she got his help. If she got it. She waited.

The silence coming down the phone stretched until it groaned. Then she felt the tiny tremble in the ground that heralded the bursting of the dam. Robin gave a weary sigh. 'All right. This has gone on long enough. Get packed, Agnes, and pack some things for Mouse too. I'll pick you up tonight.

'And find a cardboard box for the god-damned cat. I don't want it boking in my car.'

Thirteen

Mouse wouldn't leave. His square face, across which had flitted the shadows of a dozen expressions as Agnes talked, finally settled on stubborn. 'I'm going nowhere. Why should I? I haven't done anything.'

Agnes had been so relieved to see Robin's attitude softening that she hadn't noticed Mouse gearing up for a rebellion. When she realized with astonishment that he wasn't going to accept his father's olive branch, a wave of frustration that Ruth would have recognized swept over her. Disabled, vulnerable, the butt of official suspicion and unspoken menace, Mouse was in no position to reject any help he was offered. He was doing so anyway. Agnes felt like kicking his broken ankle.

She clung on to her temper. 'Mouse, we have to be practical. I know you'd sooner stay here. But I'll be honest with you: the people out there scare me. While they're here I don't feel safe.'

'Then you run away.'

169

Her eyes spat fire at him. 'Listen, sonny, I don't *have* to run away – I can turn my back and walk. And it isn't your overwhelming charm and good nature that have kept me from doing it before now.'

'What, then?' The green eyes were a challenge. He was daring her to say, *Nothing at all*, and do what everyone else in his life had done, sooner or later – give up on him. It wasn't what he wanted. He needed her to stay. But it was what he expected, and he seemed to find it easier on his pride to push Agnes away than to wait for her to go.

She declined to play his unhappy game. 'Only the fact that you need help. You're right – it shouldn't be me. It should be your father. We both know that, just for a time, he couldn't cope with the situation. Well, now he's pulled himself together and it's time you did the same.'

'I don't need help,' the boy said sullenly.

'No? I must have been fetching and carrying for someone else, then, these last few days,' exclaimed Agnes. 'Someone else whose crutches split up and hide when he isn't looking. Someone else who can hardly move first thing each morning until I've poured hot coffee down his throat and massaged half a pint of horse liniment into his shoulders!'

Mouse had the grace to shift his ground

rather than deny it. 'I can't leave the house empty. The God-botherers'll burn it down.'

'Better to burn it empty than with you inside,' said Agnes shortly. 'Mouse, like it or not, you owe me something for the last ten days. Well, this is it. If you won't leave Malleton for a couple of weeks for your own sake, do it for your father. He doesn't find it any easier to bend than you do. It took guts for him to say he'd come for us. Refuse to go with him and you might as well kick him in the teeth.'

He looked away. 'Da doesn't want me in London. He wants *you* in London, and he thinks that's the only way you'll go.'

'He's worried about you.'

'He's worried,' growled Mouse, 'that I've let him down again. He thinks I got drunk, and Ma's dead because of it. He's never going to forgive that. However much I deny it, he's never going to believe me. OK, he's made a gesture. But better all round if I don't hold him to it.'

Agnes was watching him with mounting compassion. The stony impassivity he wore like a shield was barely skin-deep. Underneath it he was as hurt and as frightened as anyone else would have been.

'Listen to me,' she said; and her voice was gentle but also firm, because he needed support more than he needed sympathy. 'You're

171

not a child and you're not a fool. You know how upset he was. He and Ruth were together a long time, and they went through a lot together. A part of him still loved her; the *rest* of him still cared about her. He lost her, and he nearly lost you, and on top of that the police were telling him it wasn't' – she picked her words carefully – 'just an accident. Of course he was upset. And people say things they don't mean when they're upset. If I know he didn't mean it then you do too, which makes it pretty cruel to pretend otherwise.'

He opened his mouth to reply but she wasn't ready to let him. 'None of us really knows what happened that night. You might remember in time, you might not. The police may come to a conclusion, but we'll never know for sure if they're right. And in one way it hardly matters. Whether it was an accident, stupidity or something else, somehow both you and Robin have to come to terms with it. He's trying, Mouse. Won't you meet him halfway?'

'What – about Oxford?' Agnes grinned, and for a moment Mouse's grey-green eyes smiled with her and she thought she had him. But the moment passed and he shook his head. 'It's not that simple. Yes, I could go to London. Today, tomorrow – yesterday. He's my da. He's wrong about this – about me – but there's no point loving someone if you can't forgive them. One way or another, we could work it out.

'That's not the problem. The problem's not going to London, it's leaving here. Running away.'

She thought he was still worrying about the house. 'We'll tell the police what we're doing. Where we're going, and why, and how to get in touch with us if they need to. It's their job to protect people's property. Let's let them do it.'

But she'd misunderstood. He tried to explain. 'I don't want to lose this house. It was Ma's home, everything I have of her is here. All the same, there's nothing worth risking my neck for.'

'Then why?'

'Because I've more to lose than bricks and mortar. More even than memories. If I leave now it'll look as if I'm running away. As if I've something to run *from*. These people are my friends, the only ones I have – this is pretty much the only place I know. But if I leave now, like this, they'll think the police are right. That Ma's dead because of me, and the church is in ashes because of me. Because of me.'

He swallowed. 'I don't know what's going to happen. To me. I could go to prison over this. If I was drunk and that's why I crashed the van. If I was sleepwalking and burned the church without knowing it. Even if I didn't, but a court decides I did. I could go to *prison*. For years. Agnes – I get stir-crazy if a wet afternoon keeps me indoors. How am I going to survive in prison?'

There was very little comfort she could offer him without actually lying. 'Try not to look too far ahead. Let's deal with the problems we have now. Let's get you and your da back on speaking terms. Then we'll be stronger to tackle whatever lies ahead.'

It didn't escape his notice that she was saying *we* when she could have said *you*. He wished he was better at gratitude. He felt it: he was just very bad at showing it. He stumbled on. 'Even if nothing's proved, I'd never be able to come back here. People would always think I'd got away with it. They'd think I ran home to Da so he could get me off with his high-priced lawyers. They've lost their church and a member of their community: if they decide that was my doing I might as well go to prison because I'll never be welcome back here again.'

He gave a tight little smile that broke her heart. 'If I start running, I'll never to able to stop.'

When the going gets tough, the tough get sneaky.

174

Agnes phoned Robin and put him off. She lied about the reason. 'The police might want to interview Mouse again before the weekend. Why don't you come down on Saturday? With luck we'll all be ready to leave by then.' *Three days to talk some sense into him,* she thought in the privacy of her own head. *And if that doesn't work, I'll tie him in a sack and throw him in the boot myself.*

There was nothing she could do about what happened at the Mile End Cut. The facts were clear: there was enough alcohol in Mouse's bloodstream to have compromised his ability to deal with a crisis. It might have been an animal on the road, or a drunk stumbling home who didn't even know, once he'd sobered up, that someone had driven into the cut to avoid him. Legally, Mouse shouldn't have been behind the wheel of a vehicle, and that was something he'd have to pay for.

If only that was the worst they faced. But what if Mouse, who said he never drank, whose father and vicar had both thought he never drank, had needed Dutch courage to be on that back road late at night? The tracks on the bank haunted Agnes. Before she knew Mouse their message had seemed clear enough. Now she knew him, a little, she longed for an alternative scenario. Not because she thought him incapable of suicide.

As he opened up to her, she'd seen how close he teetered to the brink of undoing. But almost against her better judgement she'd begun to care about this strange, sullen, intelligent young man. At first she'd hoped he'd regain his memory so matters could be resolved and she could wash her hands of him. Now she was beginning to think it might be better if he never remembered.

What she could maybe do something about was the reason Mouse was reluctant to leave and in danger if he stayed. Agnes saw no reason to blame him for the fire at St Bride's. But stone churches don't combust spontaneously, and a combination of circumstances made Mouse an easy suspect. The police were looking for evidence: the motley crew in the back field couldn't be counted on to be that meticulous. Even Flanagan, who knew them best, was nervous about how they'd react if provoked. And one thing Mouse was *good* at was provoking people.

It occurred to her, thinking it through as she lay sleepless in the quiet hours of the night, that what Mouse needed was for someone else to take a share of the suspicion. For the police to question someone else about the fire. Even if it came to nothing, it might stop people thinking the result of the inquiry was a foregone conclusion. If the muttering ceased, perhaps Mouse could be persuaded to come to London.

What she needed was an alternative suspect. She was quite ruthless about it. She wasn't worried about finding who actually did it, only someone who might have done. She was perfectly happy to sow the seeds of doubt that would give people another name to conjure with. There was nothing personal in it, she told herself, it wasn't malice. It was just, if there was unsupported speculation going round, she didn't see why Mouse should bear all of it. She just wanted people to realize there could be other culprits with other motives.

Lying in the dark room hours after the rest of Malleton was asleep she realized she already had three-quarters of a perfectly feasible story to offer as an alternative to that odd boy of Ruth Pyke's being responsible for this too.

It was only five in the morning: she might arrive with Peter Parsons's milk, she couldn't for shame cross the road any sooner. But nor could she sleep. And in the hours of thinking, her plausible scenario hardened from something she hoped people might believe could have happened to something she at least half-believed *had* happened.

The vicar opened his front door to find

Agnes Amory presenting him with a milk bottle. 'Peter, I need to talk to you.' She blinked. 'Nice T-shirt.'

While he was dressing, she made the coffee. Then she laid out the ground rules. 'Can we not talk about this until I've got it all said? It's going to sound crazy, you're going to want to tell me I'm imagining things. Try not to. We can discuss the details afterwards. If you're still sure I'm talking out of my left ear, I'll shut up and go away.'

He nodded solemnly. 'All right.'

'Go back,' said Agnes, 'to the point at which all you had to worry about was your roof. But it was a major worry. It was going to need a lot of money to put it right, and church-restoration funds work better in parishes where the average congregation reaches double figures.'

Parsons refrained from correcting her. In principle she was right. A hundred thousand pounds is a lot of money for even twenty-five people to find.

'You had one thing which might have paid the bill. You didn't want to sell it, not least because the guy who gave it to the church was still around. So I'm guessing you dropped a lot of hints and made a lot of appeals, and maybe you got an extra tenner in the collection plate every week but it wasn't enough and it was never going to be enough.

178

The Crusader banner was going to have to go.

'Being a considerate sort of guy, you didn't just advertise it on eBay. You went round to Stuart Freyn first, to explain that you had no choice and that people would never forget that his gift had made it possible to preserve St Bride's for future generations. And though he didn't seem very happy, he didn't raise any outright objections. So you consulted your bishop and he agreed. You decided to call in an expert and get it valued.

'But before you could do that, why goodness me, another miracle! An anonymous benefactor put up the cash to repair the roof. You could keep your banner *and* keep the weather out. Peter, you know as well as I do who it was. The Freyns are the only people you know who could *afford* to be that generous.'

He couldn't argue with that. 'OK, maybe it was the Freyns. Why not? Like you say, they can afford it. The Colonel was unhappy about his gift being sold off, however good the cause, so Nick dipped into his pocket for the solution. Happy smiles all round. What's *wrong* with that?'

'Nothing, if that's the whole story. I still don't know why he'd want to stay anonymous. If his father gave you the banner, and he gave you the means to keep it, why would

Nick Freyn want to keep quiet about that? He's a businessman, and that's exactly the kind of publicity he should relish.'

That puzzled Parsons too. But he was religious: he was used to things passing all understanding. 'What do you mean, the whole story? What else could there be?'

'Peter, I don't know,' said Agnes honestly. 'But events continued as *if* there was something else. I don't know where the fire fits in. We don't even know if it was arson or some kind of a freak accident. But either way, it drew attention to the banner. There it was, virtually unscathed up on its smoke-blackened wall, and outside was a growing crowd of gullible but also rather threatening people determined to get a closer look.

'Which is when Freyn pulled his next stunt – having the thing taken up to The Nail.' She cut off the vicar's protests. 'I know: it's all been sorted out, we've agreed to call it a misunderstanding. But once again it's the Freyns doing something unexpected to keep that banner out of the public gaze.

'And why? Because it isn't what it's supposed to be, Peter. It's no more a Crusader banner than ... than...' She picked up the tea towel and waved it at him. 'I've seen pictures of Crusader banners. They're bright and colourful, and even if it had faded it wouldn't have faded to plain off-white. That is not a Crusader banner.

'And that means Stuart Freyn lied. If it isn't what he says it is, he didn't come by it the way he claims he did. So what is it? What's its story? Why did he want to give it to the church but lie about what it was, and why is he so scared he's going to be found out forty years later?'

Peter Parsons hardly knew what to say. 'Well – so far as I know, the Crown Jewels are still in the Tower of London! Agnes ... don't you think you're reading too much into an act of kindness that backfired a bit? The Colonel was bothered by the thought of me selling his gift, and his son stepped in so it wouldn't be necessary. He made the donation anonymously so it wouldn't look like he was muscling in on the gift.'

'Why do you call him that?' asked Agnes. 'Why does everybody call him that?'

'The Colonel? Because that's what he was.'

'*Was* being the operative word. You stop dancing, you no longer describe yourself as a dancer. You stop cleaning windows, you no longer describe yourself as a window-cleaner. It must be a quarter of a century since Stuart Freyn was in the army. Why do you still use his rank as a title, and why does he let you?'

He didn't understand the point she was making. 'It's traditional.'

'Maybe. But to me that's a man clinging desperately to the ghosts of past achievements. Those were his glory days, and he doesn't want anyone to forget it. Whatever the banner is and however he came by it, he's afraid the truth will make people think less of him.'

'I don't know what you're accusing him of,' said Parsons shortly. 'Theft? False pretences? Why the hell would he have given the thing to St Bride's if he wanted to keep quiet about it? If he stole it, either he'd have sold it or he'd have kept it for himself. Why the hell would he have given it away?' He heard himself shouting and pulled up short. 'Sorry. But it doesn't make any sense. He could have kept it at The Nail all these years and none of us would have been any the wiser. If he had something to hide, that's what he'd do.'

'That is a problem,' admitted Agnes. 'I don't know why he'd take that risk. But suppose he had his reasons, and that's exactly what he did. And for forty years the thing was safe. Then it wasn't, so Nick dipped into the family coffers to ensure it could stay at St Bride's after all.'

She took a deep breath. The hardest part was still to come. 'So the money's there to fix the roof. But that means removing from the church anything that could get damaged, including the banner, and that's the last thing Stuart Freyn wants. Once it's down, someone with an interest in medieval textiles will ask to examine the thing. Someone who knows exactly what a twelfth-century banner should look like will hear that St Bride's is being restored and realize this is the most accessible the artefact has been in a generation. When they see the thing is a fraud, *they* won't be concerned with sparing Freyn's blushes. They'll tell the world what he's done.

'But what can he do to protect himself? He can't ask for the banner back. When his little secret becomes public knowledge he can whistle goodbye to the respect he's enjoyed all his adult life. All that Colonel business will end right there. I don't suppose it'll do Nick's credibility a lot of good either. I know it's traditional for financiers to tread a thin line between profit and legality. But they're not supposed to cross that line; and if they do, they're definitely not supposed to be caught. I wonder how many working breakfasts he'll be invited to after the tabloids have had a field day with his father's reputation?'

'All right,' said Parsons unhappily. 'Suppose – just suppose – you're right. What do they do about it?'

She regarded him levelly. She knew that he

genuinely had no idea what she was about to say. 'The only thing they can do. Destroy it. Even if that means destroying St Bride's as well.'

Fourteen

'Don't be absurd!' Parsons couldn't have been more outraged if she'd expectorated in his font.

Agnes had had hours to think about this. She knew he needed more time. 'Peter,' she said patiently, 'I'm not making this up. I may be wrong, but it's not idle speculation. I think this, or something like this, is what happened. I think Stuart Freyn has been lying about that piece of cloth, what it is and where he got it, for forty years, and he couldn't face the truth coming out. I think he may have decided anything was better than that.'

She gave a wry little chuckle. 'What he never guessed was that he was going to make things worse for himself. That the church would burn back to the stones but the banner would survive untouched – and that would attract more attention than he'd imagined in his worst nightmares. It's now being venerated by the kind of worshippers that gave the Inquisition a bad name, and even though he's got it out of sight there's a real danger they'll storm The Nail unless he sends it back.

'None of which will have escaped the notice of the reporters. They probably don't think it's holy but hey, this is the silly season, they've nothing better to fill their pages. They'll throw paraffin on the fire just for the fun of it. By the weekend there'll be a queue of archaeologists knocking at Stuart Freyn's front door asking very politely to examine his banner.'

Parsons was still staring at her in affronted disbelief. But somewhere in the backs of his eyes she could see the worm of doubt. He didn't think she'd got this right. He couldn't believe she'd got this anywhere near right. But he was beginning to see that something didn't add up. That the story he'd got from his predecessor and passed on without much thought didn't stand up to close scrutiny. He said slowly, 'You've seen pictures? Of how it should look?'

It felt like a chord played on her heartstrings. The beginnings of belief. 'One of the books Ruth worked on. She had a whole library, on every subject under the sun. One of them was on heraldry.'

'Show me.'

Agnes filled in the background as they crossed the road. 'Apparently the Crusaders were the first English knights to use banners. They got the idea from the Saracens. But while the Saracens went for plain flags in bright colours, the English decorated theirs with symbols to say who they were. Richard the Lionheart had three golden lions on a crimson background. He stuck that in the dust outside his tent, and that little patch of desert became royal palace, seat of government and army headquarters all rolled into one. Subtle was never going to cut the mustard.'

She said nothing more until he'd had a chance to look at Ruth's book, study the pictures and read the words. A couple of times he looked up at her, his face troubled. 'I've been the vicar here for four years and I've never made the effort to have a proper look at it. You saw it close to?'

'As close as I am to you.'

'And that's all it is – just plain cloth? No decoration?'

Agnes rocked a hand. 'Mouse thinks he saw a face in it. I couldn't see that. There were some stains but they didn't look like anything to me. Maybe you have to have the light just right.'

'So what do you suppose it is?'

'I have no idea what it is,' said Agnes honestly. 'I'm not sure it matters *what* it is. I think the significant thing is that it's *not* what Freyn claimed. It's probably some cheap souvenir from a Yemeni souk, only it made a better story if he called it a Crusader banner. He lied. Everyone he knows is going to know he lied. That he gave a bit of cheap tat to his local church and pretended it was valuable.'

'That was reason enough to burn the church down?'

Agnes too thought it was a touch of over-kill. 'He's a proud man. He's used to respect. The respect of his men and his neighbours. Would I burn a church down rather than admit to telling fibs? – No. Would Stuart Freyn? – I don't know. Maybe.'

They hadn't realized they were no longer alone. But this was Mouse's house, and as the days passed he was less noisy as he moved around it. He was standing in the doorway. Agnes had no idea how long he'd been there.

'He did *what*?'

Agnes found herself back-pedalling away from Mouse's lowering brow as she had not from Peter Parsons's righteous outrage. 'I don't know. I'm not saying he burned the church – I don't know that. I'm just trying to make sense of what's going on.'

'You think that makes sense? That Stuart

Freyn set fire to St Bride's because he wanted to get rid of what's in the cabinet?'

'I know it sounds unlikely. He's – what? – seventy-odd, and a pillar of the community. And why give the thing to the church if he didn't want anyone to see it? I'm probably wrong, Mouse. We were just talking through some possibilities.'

'Keep talking,' rumbled Mouse.

'Maybe we shouldn't,' said Parsons uneasily. 'I mean, this is pure conjecture. We've no evidence. There could be any number of better explanations for what's happened.'

'Yeah,' growled Mouse. 'Like, I burned the church. That's much easier to believe, isn't it? The police can't prove I did it, but I can't prove I didn't. And I've got form. I burned my house down with my mother in it! And now Ma's dead, and I was driving, and *another* fire's destroyed the church where I worked, only a quick hobble across the road from where I live. It's enough to make anyone suspicious. Hell, *I'd* suspect me if I didn't know better!

'Only now you're saying someone else might have had a motive. That the banner got to be such an embarrassment to Stuart Freyn that he was ready to destroy it. Yes, it's pretty off-the-wall. But keep talking. Work it out. This matters to me. If someone else had a reason to burn St Bride's, maybe I'm not

188

going to prison for something I didn't do.'

When he had his stubborn face on, it was easy to forget that Mouse Firth was still very young and rather vulnerable. He'd just lost his mother, and everyone – including his father, and a bunch of people whose actions were unpredictable even to someone who knew them well – was angry with him. He had reason to be.

The vicar said quietly, 'I don't know what the police are thinking. I know they're definitely treating it as arson now – the fire investigators found traces of an accelerant. But Mouse, I never thought you burned our church.'

'I was pretty ... upset,' muttered Mouse. 'After Ma died. I said some things...'

'Did you?' Parsons chuckled. 'I forgive you.'

'Not about you.' The green gaze was scathing. 'About God.'

The vicar didn't laugh again, but he did smile. 'I'm pretty sure He'll have forgiven you too.'

But that, Agnes realized, wasn't quite the point. 'You mean ... someone could have heard you sounding off, and told the police you had a grudge against God? Against the church?'

Mouse shrugged, embarrassed. 'I don't know. Maybe.'

'Who?'

He looked at his feet. 'Frances Freyn, for one.'

'Freyn's daughter?' Agnes heard her voice climb. 'How come?'

'She was doing the books at the hospital.'

Agnes gave this some thought, but it really didn't help. 'She's an accountant?'

Parsons had had more practice with Mouse's shorthand. 'She's a hospital volunteer. She does visiting, takes flowers, that kind of thing. Sometimes she takes round the cart with the library books in it. Did she pop in to see you, Mouse?'

He nodded. 'I was pretty...'

'Upset,' repeated Agnes, and he nodded again. 'She'd understand. She wouldn't take anything you said in that state as being meaningful. And if she'd said anything to the police, they'd have questioned you about it. You were ill, you were on drugs and you'd just been bereaved. No one would hold you responsible for anything you said at a time like that.'

Mouse looked to Parsons for confirmation, a tiny hope glimmering through the fear in his eyes.

'I told you,' the vicar said softly. 'You have more friends than you think.' The vicar flicked a shy grin at the ceiling. 'Someone up there has a lot of time for you, too.'

190

'Yeah? Well, God help me if I ever get on His wrong side!'

'What do we do, Peter?' asked Agnes. 'Who do we tell? Do we tell anyone?'

'*What* do we tell them?' countered Parsons. 'That we're trying to keep Mouse out of jail, and the only substitute we can find is Colonel Freyn? I think we're better saying nothing than that. Before we say anything, we need some kind of evidence.'

'There's the banner.' They didn't know what else to call it.

'We don't even know what it is, let alone what it proves. I know this isn't what you want to hear, Mouse, but I think we should keep this to ourselves for now. Wait to see what happens. If Agnes is right, the banner will have another nasty accident. And if you stay well away from The Nail, no one will be able to blame it on you.'

'But by then it'll be gone, and we'll never know what it was all about!' objected Agnes. 'Sorry, Mouse – of course it matters that you're in the clear. But it's also important to know why any of this happened. At least, it is to me.'

'Oh, me too,' agreed Parsons in a low voice. 'In fact, the only thing I can think of that's more important is keeping you safe.'

Agnes stared at him. 'You don't think Freyn would try to shut us up?'

'No, of course not.' But once he'd said it Parsons found himself wondering. 'Let's just be careful, all right? Whoever's behind this, it was damned convenient when Mouse was a credible suspect for just about everything that happened. Maybe he was safer as the prime suspect than if we start saying we think he's innocent and we're going to prove it.'

'You want us to keep quiet about this? He burned your church down – all right,' she amended before he could object to that, '*may* have burned your church down. And you want us to let people go on thinking it was Mouse?'

'Agnes, I can't tell you what to do,' said Peter Parsons quietly. 'I hope you think of me as your friend – I know you *don't* think of me as your priest ... and all I can say is what I think would be best. I think we should say nothing about our suspicions until either we have some evidence or the police charge Mouse with arson.'

Agnes was shaking her head incredulously. 'I can't believe you're not going to do anything!'

'I didn't say that,' he retorted sharply. 'I said I'd rather not accuse anyone yet. I didn't say I wouldn't be doing anything.'

After he left Agnes looked at Mouse and shrugged awkwardly. 'I don't know. Maybe he has a point.'

'Yeah,' growled Mouse again. 'His point is, Stuart Freyn has enough money to repair his church, and I'm a pretty good gardener.'

Agnes didn't believe that for a moment. But she could see how it must feel that way to the embattled boy. The boy ... She kept thinking of him as that, though he was only five years her junior. But then, parts of him seemed younger than his twenty years. The parts that didn't seem infinitely older. Also, she was auditioning for the rôle of his step-mother. It predisposed her to see him a certain way.

She said softly, 'You really don't know what to do with friends, do you? People who like you and want to help you. That man's hurting almost as much as you are, and he too would like someone to blame. He's tied himself in knots trying not to blame you. And you come out with a cheap shot like that.'

Mouse swallowed. For a moment he wouldn't look at her. When he did, his eyes were so open, the route to his soul so un-defended, that it took her breath away. 'Yeah,' he mumbled. 'I'm sorry. It's not that I don't appreciate his friendship. It's not that I don't appreciate yours. I really do. It's just ... I'm scared. And it's easier to be angry.'

If he'd been fifteen, or fifty, she'd have

hugged him and made them both feel better. But he was twenty, and she didn't want to be misunderstood. The best she could do was say, 'I know. I'm sorry too.' She cleared her throat, changed the subject. 'Robin will be here tomorrow night. Won't you reconsider? Get away for a couple of weeks, give things a chance to calm down?'

He shook his head fractionally, and behind his eyes the shutters fell with an almost audible clang. 'No.'

Fifteen

Agnes woke early. She lay listening to the birdsong and wondering what the day had in store. Wondering how Robin would react when she told him his stubborn son would rather face the threat of violence in his own house than leave it. Without much surprise, she suspected.

Birdsong? She hadn't heard the birds since...

She shot across the room to the window and peered past the corner of the ruined church to the field beyond. It looked the same. Tents and camper vans, and lines of impromptu washing. Just no people. All the people had gone.

She clambered into her clothes and hurried downstairs. She roused Mouse with a shake of the shoulder. 'Something's happening.'

When she threw open the front door she saw the tail of the long caravan of pilgrims heading up the road on sandaled feet. They moved in silence and without haste, but they moved as one.

'They're heading for The Nail!' Alarm barred her voice. 'You've got Freyn's number. Quickly – we have to warn them.'

She thought for a moment he was going to refuse. Then he dialled without consulting his diary. With all the things he'd forgotten, he remembered Stuart Freyn's phone number.

Frances answered. She sounded sleepy and resentful. Agnes wasted no time on apologies. 'The freak show's heading your way. Call the police. You're going to need some help.'

'I'm not calling the police...!'

'You have to,' said Agnes flatly. 'Or I will. But they'll come quicker for you.'

There was someone standing in the road, indecisive. He took a step or two in the pilgrims' wake, then stopped and looked towards the church. When he looked her way she saw it was Flanagan. Agnes raised her voice in challenge. 'Is this your doing?'

'No!' He sounded shocked. 'When I woke up they were already on the move.'

'They're heading for The Nail, aren't they? What are they going to do?'

'I don't know. I don't think they mean any harm. I think they just want to be close to it.'

'Freyn won't let them in. What will they do then?'

He shrugged helplessly. 'I don't know.'

'Get your car,' decided Agnes. 'We'll head them off at the pass. If they'll listen to anyone, it's you.'

She might have been suggesting he defend the Freyns with the last drop of his blood. His eyes flared whitely and his head made little spasms of denial that she thought he was unaware of. She added nastily, 'Or were all the guts in the family used up by the first six sons?'

He gawped at her, then turned on his heel. For a minute she thought she'd gone too far, he'd stormed off in umbrage and that was the last she'd see of him. Then she heard an engine, and a moment later the sports car pulled up at Ruth's gate.

She raced round the bonnet and climbed into the passenger side. She was still angry with him. 'Nice sound system. Bet that cost a couple of cancer cures.'

Flanagan didn't drive off. He sat there, turned in his seat, eying her speculatively. 'You really think I cheat sick people out of their money?'

Agnes shrugged negligently. 'I don't know you, Flanagan. It's not fraud if you think you're doing some good. What I think is immaterial.'

'But you think it's all smoke and mirrors. And if it's not actually fraud it is at least a cynical ploy to trade on people's fears when they're at their most vulnerable.'

She could have lied. He'd have known she was lying. 'Yes, that's pretty much what I think.'

'You're not the first.' But there was a hurt in his voice that suggested no one had said it for a while.

He put the car in gear. But before he could drive off they had company. There was no rear door: Mouse, with much huffing and grunting, hauled his battered body over the low side on to the back seat.

'What do you think you're doing?' demanded Agnes.

'I'm coming with you.'

'Why? Not to put too fine a point on it, Mouse, how much help are you going to be with a broken ankle?'

'I'm not coming to help,' he said as if she was being silly. 'I'm coming to watch.'

Flanagan gave a gruff little chuckle as he drove off. 'And you call me a cynic!'

Mouse knew a way to The Nail that didn't involve driving through the half-mile straggle of pilgrims. A farm lane cut off to the right and served as a back entrance to the big house. But there were no signs. You had to live here to know.

In the event, though, they never reached the lane. The closer they approached the Freyns' house, the denser the foot-traffic became in the narrow country road. At first people moved over to let the car pass, and waved when they saw who was at the wheel. Another hundred yards, though, and there was nowhere for them to move to. Flanagan drove a little further at walking pace, then pulled up. 'This is as close as we're going to get the car. We'll have to walk from here.'

'*We* will,' Agnes said pointedly. 'Mouse, you stay in the car. There's no room to use your crutches even if you could hobble that far. Look on the bright side: if they set fire to the house you'll see the smoke from here.'

Nothing changed. But outside the protective shell of steel, with the bodies of strangers pressed about her, she started to understand how threatening a crowd can be. No one was taking much notice of them, but even a benign crowd is an animal with a lot of limbs, a lot of power, a lot of momentum and not much sense. A crowd will do things that no individual member of it would countenance. People are largely aware of the effect of their actions and will temper their own desires to the reasonable needs of others. A crowd has no such empathy. It sees only that the people on every side are all heading the same way, doing the same things, and gets locked into a loop of positive reinforcement whereby the more people strive for the same ends, the more right those ends seem. With its inhibitions on hold the crowd becomes a mob.

It wasn't quite there yet. Agnes felt no animosity, only a kind of hunger. These people craved access to something they perceived as holy the way rational people crave food and drink, or sleep, or sex. They wanted it on a fundamental level, and could no more have explained why than Agnes could have explained her need for movement. It mattered. It mattered almost as much as things without which life cannot continue. It drew them like a magnet tugging at iron filings, and they responded because they felt to have no choice.

Though there was no hostility there, not yet, it was latent in the sheer numbers involved, in their singularity of purpose, in the strength of their wanting. They were walking down the road to The Nail towards the thing that called them. But the Freyns knew they were coming: when they reached the gates they'd find them barred. And the people at the back would keep pressing forward, and the people at the front would have nowhere to go. They had their children with them. They'd panic, they'd be angry and afraid, and they'd force the gates. Once they'd done that, nothing would stand in their way. Anyone who tried would get hurt.

Flanagan had known that when Agnes was taunting him. He'd come anyway. He rose a degree in her estimation.

Somehow they forced their way through to the gates. They weren't just closed but mightily padlocked against the pilgrim band.

For a moment Agnes thought Flanagan was trying to climb them. But he was just using the plinth to lift himself above the heads of the crowd. He needed to be seen to be heard. Agnes held her breath, wondering what on earth he could say to assuage their hunger.

He began with a joke. 'It's like the first thief said to Jesus on the way up the Via Dolorosa,' he drawled. 'I love a parade...'

Agnes was surprised that they shared his sense of humour. But shy grins appeared in the sea of faces around him. 'Listen,' said Flanagan, and he said it as if he was talking not to an out-of-control crowd but to a couple of friends, 'there's going to be a problem here if we don't get a bit more organized. The gates are locked. The gates are locked,' he said again, raising his voice so those at the back could hear, 'we can't get in this way. Some of the kids will get hurt if we try. Maybe this isn't what we should be doing. Not if we can come up with an alternative.'

Listening, for the first time Agnes understood why people found themselves drawn to him – believing in him. She had no idea if he was the seventh son of a seventh son. She was fairly sure he couldn't cure cancer by the laying-on of hands. But he could communicate. He had that magic touch shared by the best teachers and the best priests, of being able to find at any given time the right words to get through to the people before him. He was friendly without being condescending, humorous without being laboured. He talked as if he was one of the people he was talking to, but he did it without making any claims, any assumptions. People naturally warmed to him.

And the words always came. He never found himself using the wrong ones or struggling for the right ones. They were his servants, and they anticipated his needs and lined up to meet them. It made public speaking seem easy; more than that, it hardly seemed like public speaking at all. It seemed like a man talking to a friend about something that concerned him, and that's how they responded to him. They listened. They believed he had their interests at heart, and took his point even when it wasn't what they wanted to hear. They trusted him. Another minute and they would do as he asked – make their way back to the field for a sensible discussion on what they wanted and how to achieve it without anyone getting hurt or arrested. They'd been in the process of becoming a mob; now they were reverting to a number of individuals with individual thoughts, considerations and sensibilities.

And then some of the tail-enders spotted Mouse in the back of Flanagan's car.

He was doing nothing. Perhaps he was being Mouse rather more doggedly than was necessary – watching them with that oddly direct stare that might have hidden anything but seemed to conceal contempt. Or perhaps what happened next was in no way his fault. The pilgrims had seen enough and heard enough to know that Mouse was the closest the police had to a prime suspect. It didn't occur to them that if Mouse had started the fire, he was the one who brought the relic to their attention – that but for a little recreational arson it could have spent another forty years high up among the shadows and the spiders, and the pilgrims would have grown old and ordinary and moved into council flats without ever knowing it was there. They harboured no gratitude for that. They held him anathema.

About the time the crowd's progress was brought to a standstill by the Freyns' gates and Flanagan's oratory, frustrated in their purpose they found themselves seeking some lesser goal to score before turning round and heading back to camp. By now the tail of the dog had reached the point where Agnes and Flanagan had left the car to continue on foot.

The pilgrims knew the car, of course. If Flanagan wasn't exactly one of them, he was a companion, a fellow-traveller, someone they respected when it suited them, and they felt no urge to kick his mudguards even when they were having a bad day. But then they noticed the back-seat passenger.

The tail of the dog stopped wagging. It didn't even droop disconsolately. It stiffened with resentment, and it bristled. Late-comers who'd never got close to The Nail, who hadn't been close enough to hear what Flanagan had to say, now stopped even try-ing. Here was a focus for their frustrations. They drew one another's attention to it. They stopped shuffling past the car and gathered round it. They fell silent. Their eyes were like knives.

Instead of discreetly averting his gaze and slumping lower into the leather upholstery, Mouse stared back insolently.

By the time Agnes realized what was happening, the open car was rocking with the laying-on of hands. 'Flanagan!' She tugged urgently at his shirt sleeve.

'Oh, for pity's sake!'

But they couldn't get back there. The crowd – except now it was a mob for sure – had closed tight around the car, presenting a shield wall of backs. Flanagan tried to remain calm in the face of this threat to his paintwork. 'Come on, guys, there's no call for this – let me through and I'll get the damn thing out of your way.' Agnes had gone beyond calm, was red-faced and yelling obscenities that would have surprised the Covent Garden regulars.

And Mouse was responding to this crisis as he'd responded to all the others in his life: with a stony-faced refusal to give an inch. He could have dropped down between the seats, making it harder for them to reach him. He didn't even do that. He wouldn't give them the satisfaction of knowing they'd frightened him. He stayed where he was, awkwardly sideways to accommodate his plaster and his crutches, and waited for them to take him.

The mob was by now a single, multilimbed animal. There was no discussion about what it should do next. Instead, suddenly and simultaneously all the hands that could reach him were on him, clutching, grasping any part of the young man's clothes or body they could find. Almost, they defeated their purpose by pulling in opposite directions so Mouse stayed pretty well where he was, in the middle of the back seat, slapping at their thrusting heads with work-hardened hands.

Finally the mechanics of the situation occurred to the pilgrims and they organized themselves rather better. They yanked Mouse out of the car and he disappeared instantly into the press of bodies, the flailing arms and kicking feet. And Agnes, who was by now near enough to see the white face under the straw-coloured tangle of his fringe and the fear that he couldn't keep out of his eyes, thought she wouldn't see him again until they'd broken him like sticks.

She was wrong. He emerged from the pack where it washed against The Nail's garden wall, slammed against the stones with his arms flung wide as if they meant to crucify him. His face was bloody and his clothes torn, and desperation had turned the fear to fury so that his eyes blazed like green fire. If he'd had a weapon – if he'd even been able to hold on to one of his crutches – he'd have used it, and they'd have torn him apart.

Agnes heard the wail of sirens before any-one else; but then, she wasn't bellowing with bloodlust. The rampaging pilgrims heard nothing but their own roar. Close as they were, the crew of the police car couldn't have reached Mouse in time to save him.

Flanagan was closer. Agnes went on point, then jetéd up and down waving her arms to attract his attention. 'Help me!'

He saw her. He saw and understood the situation. His eyes met Agnes's for a furtive moment before sliding away, appalled and afraid. 'I ... can't. I can't get through...'

But he could have. He could have waded through the pack like God's scrum half, grabbing his friends by the scruff of the neck and throwing them aside one by one until he reached their victim. He was a big man, as big as Robin and younger, stronger; and these people knew and had an innate respect for him. If he'd put himself between them and Mouse they'd have hesitated, wondering what to do, just long enough for the police to take control.

Instead, he turned away.

For a moment Agnes was more stunned than angry. Then the adrenalin cut in – the old fight-or-flight hormone that had got her on to stages where angels feared to tread and through performances that, strictly speaking, her body should have been incapable of completing. The fury surged in her until she was nothing but rage poured into an Agnes-shaped mould. So the seventh son of a seventh son was nothing but a play-actor – a thing of smoke and mirrors. Well, she was an actor too. She could play brave; she could play dangerous. This angry, she could play dangerous well enough to make anyone think twice about tackling her.

She couldn't physically throw them aside. But she could dive between them, using her slender body and dancer's grace to slip through gaps where no gaps appeared to be. A couple of times she used her knees to pretty good effect as well. So she reached the stone wall, just as Mouse gave up and slipped down among the waiting feet.

She had no weapons either. She had her body. She hoped that those who were ready to trample Mouse to a bloody pulp would somehow recognize that her slender body and largely unclad limbs were not those of a jobbing gardener and back off. If they didn't they could kill her. If they only broke her leg, they would end her career. It wasn't worth it. She couldn't save Mouse, she could only share his fate.

She didn't care. And it wasn't because Mouse was Robin's son, and it wasn't because she'd been looking after him for a week and had grown grudgingly fond of him. It was simply because he was another human being at the end of his ability to withstand what life was throwing at him, and she wouldn't, she couldn't, leave him. It made no sense. His death would do her less harm than the boots of just one of these miracle-junkies. But she was human too, and sometimes humans do what they have to rather than what they want to because that's the price, and also the definition, of humanity.

She crouched, spreading herself over him as best she could. She took the boots in her thighs, her buttocks and her ribs. They knocked the air out of her. She felt them crash against her bones, and gritted her teeth and waited for a bone to give way.

The policemen arrived first. There were four of them, and while they were still vastly outnumbered they had more idea how to deal with the situation than Agnes had. In just a few seconds the small phalanx had tunnelled through the pack of bodies to reach the focus of their hatred and were pointing CS-gas sprays at the faces of the mob.

Sixteen

There were certainly miracles in the air: neither Agnes nor Mouse was seriously hurt. Which is not to say they weren't hurting, only that there was nothing broken – or in Mouse's case, nothing that wasn't broken before – and no cuts and bruises beyond the therapeutic range of iodine and sticking plaster.

The doctor brought in by the police wanted to send them for X-rays anyway, just to be sure. Mouse refused point-blank to leave his house, and Agnes knew from a professional familiarity with her own body that she'd be sore tomorrow, mending after that. 'I'll call you if either of us has any problems, how's that?'

It wasn't good enough. The doctor left grumbling, but he left.

The policemen stayed, and within half an hour reinforcements had arrived. The pilgrims were shepherded back to the camping field and kept there while efforts were made to identify those responsible for the riot. But it wasn't that sort of band. They didn't take instructions from anyone. Each was following a voice inside his own head: if they acted in concert it was because they responded to the same stimuli, scores of Pavlovian dogs jumping in unison.

Inspector Bleakley suspected he'd end up arresting either all of them or none of them. He settled today for gathering information and taking statements. 'I don't suppose you could identify your assailants, miss?'

Still angry, Agnes would have done if she could. But she shook her head. 'They barely looked like people, let alone people I'd recognize. I'll look at an ID parade if you like, but I doubt it'll be much help. All I can remember is open mouths yelling, and unless you're a dentist one set of teeth looks very much like another.'

'What about Mr Flanagan? Would you say he was making things better or worse?'

For a moment she toyed with lying – with blaming him for the riot. But she wouldn't dignify his performance with anything but the truth. Her lip curled. 'He didn't start it. He tried to stop it. He just didn't try very hard. He was as close to Mouse as I was, and could have done a better job of helping him. But he was scared of getting hurt.'

The policeman, who was both tall and broad-shouldered, was looking down at

Agnes who was neither with a kind of secret smile. 'And you weren't?'

'Of course I was!' snorted Agnes. 'Seen many ballerinas in wheelchairs, have you? Sometimes it doesn't have to matter. Being scared – even being hurt. You do what needs doing. They'd have killed Mouse. They wouldn't have meant to. Every one of them would have been horrified that it went that far. But they'd have killed him just the same if your guys hadn't turned up when they did. Because the one man who just might have been able to stop them was afraid to try.' Scorn dripped from her tongue like venom.

Inspector Bleakley would never see the little ballerina in his wife's jewellery box in the same light again. 'We'll do all we can to bring someone to book for this. Just don't hold your breath. And find somewhere to stay for a few nights. Somewhere out of Malleton. You know – just in case.'

She rounded on him as if he'd dropped her in the middle of a pas de deux. 'No, Inspector. This didn't happen because I did something I shouldn't. It didn't even happen because Mouse did something he shouldn't. It happened because there's a bunch of lunatics camping in the field behind the church. Well, lunatics are your business – if somebody has to move to keep the peace, move *them*. This is Mouse's home, and we

211

have more right to be here than a Lost Tribe who followed a diversion sign on the road to Damascus. I don't care if you arrest them, charge them, evict them or post sentries between them and me. But one way or another, I expect you to protect me, Mouse and Mouse's house from any further attack.'

Inspector Bleakley cleared his throat to cover his confusion. Of course she was right. That didn't necessarily mean he could do as she asked.

In fact it happened without him lifting a finger. He was leaving the cottage, wondering what the hell to do next, when one of his constables approached with a bemused expression. 'They're going.'

Bleakley frowned. 'Who's going?'

'The ... er...' Unable to come up with an appropriate term the constable pointed. 'Them. They're packing up and leaving. Do you want us to stop them?'

Bleakley looked. There were maybe a hundred of them, in forty-odd vehicles. The vehicles, like the people, were as curious a combination of shapes and colours as you'd find outside a circus. These were not folk who were going to blend into any background. 'I don't see why. We can find them again if we want them. And there's a lot to be said for getting them out of Malleton and away from that ... thing.'

Agnes thought he meant the banner. He just might have meant Mouse.

'No, let them go. Tell them they haven't heard the last of this. Even if it isn't true, it'll do them good to worry a bit.' As the constable headed back to the field Bleakley turned again to Agnes. 'Who'd have thought a scrap of cloth could cause so much trouble? *What* is it, again?'

Agnes shrugged. 'I don't think anybody really knows. It was supposed to be a Crusader banner. I think it's just a bit of old cloth. Freyn told people it was something special to earn himself Brownie points. The pilgrims want to believe it's something special because chasing miracles is more fun than providing for your family in such a way that they don't get dripped on when it rains. It's just a bit of cloth. The sooner all the fuss dies down and it can be quietly lost in an attic, the better.'

When the pilgrims had gone and the policemen had gone, the eighteenth century stole back into Malleton as if it was a product – like oxygen – of summer sun on all the trees. After a week in which the village's population was almost doubled, and Agnes and all of them had grown accustomed to the background hum of voices and children playing and car doors and car engines, the quiet was almost uncanny. Agnes stood in

Mouse's front garden and listened for ten minutes, and all she heard was the birds.

She shook herself. Robin would be here tonight – earlier, if he'd rescheduled some of his Friday meetings – and she had things to do. One was pack her own scant belongings and some essentials for Mouse. Another was persuade him that, now there was no longer any threat to him in Malleton, he could afford to leave for long enough to build some bridges with his father.

She'd made a start on the former, hadn't even decided how to approach the latter, when she heard a car in the lane outside. She thought it was Robin, that he'd rescheduled *all* his Friday meetings and got on the road first thing, and she skipped down the narrow stairs and threw the door wide in anticipation.

It was Flanagan.

She'd had time to calm down since this morning. That only meant that the anger inside her had turned from hot to cold. But cold burns too, and it lasts longer.

He saw her face change as if she'd bitten into something sour. A dull flush spread up his cheeks. His voice was low. 'I thought I should say goodbye.'

'Yes? Goodbye.' She turned to go back into the house.

'Agnes ... Don't let's part like this.'

'Like this?' He was going to regret calling her back. 'This is great. I'm black and blue, I feel like the football at the end of the Cup Final, I've about as much flexibility in my joints as a Chippendale sideboard, but I'm still standing. It could have been worse. We could have been saying goodbye in a hospital. You could have been saying goodbye in a morgue!'

'I ... I'm sorry.' He couldn't stand the fire in her eyes. 'I couldn't ... I didn't know...' He sucked in a breath and tried again. 'I suppose I was scared.'

'Scared? Really?' she hooted. 'Guess what, Flanagan? I was scared too. I'm pretty sure Mouse was scared. Well, he didn't have a choice about what happened; and I didn't feel to have a choice about it; and you did. That's the difference between us. Oh yes – and the fact that you're bigger than I am. And stronger. And you said those people were friends of yours. But apart from all that, the only real difference between us is that when someone shouts *Overture and beginners* I go on stage whether I'm ready or not, and you hide in the broom cupboard.'

He'd known she'd be angry with him. He knew he'd given her cause. He'd expected to feel the sharp end of her tongue, and decided this was something he had to do anyway. Only, right now, he couldn't for the life of him remember why. He hadn't been made to feel this small since his first miracle cure turned out to be Me Too! Morrison, a well-known local eccentric who couldn't see a bandwagon rolling past without scrambling on. For a couple of hours that day – it was in some little town in the industrial north-east – he'd thought, he'd really thought, he had a genuine gift. That it was more than just a bit of family mythology and a way to make a living without getting blisters. He hadn't thought so since.

And he hadn't felt like this since, either. This ... despised. And he didn't like it, and he didn't fully understand why he was putting himself through it when he could have made a brief apology and left. He didn't expect that even a fulsome apology would serve. Somehow, this was less about appeasing Agnes and more about penance. So he struggled on.

'I haven't any excuses. Everything you say is true. I froze. I'm sorry. I know that doesn't make it all right. I know it won't make any difference to how you think of me. I'm hoping it'll make a small difference to how *I* think of me. An apology may not be worth much, but it's all I have to offer.'

'You'd have let him die.'

Mumbled to his toecaps: 'Yes.'

'You'd have let him *die*. Mouse. You'd have

watched them kill him!'

'What do you want me to say? That I'm a coward? Yes, it rather seems I am.' Bitter as she was, Agnes could hear the pain in his voice that said her barbs were going all the way in. 'I didn't actually know that before. Never had occasion to find out, I suppose.'

She could have left it at that. She could have shut the door in his face, and never thought of him again. It would have cost her nothing. She knew her disgust was like a knife in his side. She didn't have to twist it just to check.

She said, 'Do you have any children, Flanagan?' He shook his head mutely. 'Well, make some. Get yourself a proper life. What you're doing is a sham, and it's made a sham of you too. Get yourself a family to care about, and a proper job to support them, and you never know, you might end up a man. Right now you're just a cardboard copy. Like one of those advertising cut-outs they put outside cinemas – good image, great smile, but entirely two dimensional. The least bit of a breeze and they always fall over.

'That's you, Flanagan. Any breeze at all and you blow away.' And with that she quietly shut the door between them, leaving him numb with shame under the arch of roses, dull red from his hairline to his collar, quite incapable of knowing what he should do next. It was five minutes before Agnes heard the car move away.

If she hadn't, if she'd thought he was still there, she probably wouldn't have answered the door to the urgent rapping that came there shortly afterwards. It still wasn't Robin. This time it was Peter Parsons, and he looked as if he'd won the lottery and had his dog die on the same day.

'Peter? Are you all right?'

'Me? Yes. Are *you*?'

'We're fine,' Agnes reassured him. 'Give or take the odd bruise. Where've you been? You missed all the excitement.'

'I went to Oxford. Talked to some people, looked at some books.' He sounded shell-shocked. It was dawning on Agnes that the drama at The Nail wasn't the only reason.

She steered him into the living room and dropped him in a chair. 'You have two choices. You can tell me what's happened to make you look like someone you buried a month ago. Or I'll make you a cup of hot sweet tea and *then* you can tell me what's happened.'

The threat was enough to loosen his tongue. 'I think I know what the banner is. It isn't a Crusader flag. It isn't a worthless rag either. I think – I *think* – it's the Monsanto Veronica.'

Seventeen

Agnes thought for a moment. Then she shook her head. 'Nope. Lost me already.'

'Veronica's Veil?' Another shake of the head. Parsons took a deep breath. 'OK. Religious mythology for beginners.

'Hauling his cross up the Via Dolorosa, Jesus meets a nicely brought-up woman called Veronica, who thinks not *I must do all within my power to stop this barbarity, you don't treat people like this whether or not they claim to be the Messiah*, but *The poor chap'll feel better if I graciously wipe the sweat from his brow.* Sorry,' he said then, casting Agnes a contrite glance. 'The whole crucifixion business still rattles my chain.'

'You should mention it to the bishop sometime,' murmured Agnes, and he managed a wry grin.

'OK. So history takes its course. Christ continues up the hill to Calvary, Veronica goes home for a clean hanky. At which point she notices that the face of the doomed man has somehow imprinted itself on to the fabric.'

Agnes put her hand up. 'Does head office like you calling it mythology?'

'None of this appears in the Bible,' said Parsons firmly. 'There's a reference in the Acts of Pilate – fourth century, strictly apocryphal – that may refer to the same episode, but this is pretty much left-field Christianity, at least for the Church of England.

'Veneration of the veil began in eighth-century Rome, but until the thirteenth century it was considered a work of art rather than a true relic. It's described as a diaphanous white cloth showing a man's face with a beard, long hair and open eyes. It was displayed to pilgrims in 1300. But during rebuilding at the Vatican Basilica in 1506 it disappeared. For more than a hundred years there was steady work for local artists making copies of it. Pope Urban VIII put a stop to that, and ordered the destruction of all existing copies under threat of excommunication.'

'I'm guessing,' said Agnes, 'that there were people who thought he didn't really mean it. Not really.'

'Apparently not. There are at least four places claiming to have the thing – St Peter's in Rome, Sacré Cœur in Paris, Jaén Cathedral and the Monastery of the Holy Face in Alicante. Of course, in the Spanish tradition that's all right because the veil was folded when Veronica used it so the image was printed on to four layers of fabric. Are you with me so far?'

'Ye-e-es.' She didn't sound entirely confident.

'Good. Because this is where it gets complicated.

'There was another copy of the veil. Or maybe the original, who knows? It was kept in a small monastery in the British Protectorate of Aden until the place was overrun during the Arab insurgency of the 1960s. The monks were murdered, their possessions were looted and the veil vanished. It was assumed it had been destroyed – the locals, backed by Yemeni and Egyptian money, wanted rid of the infidels so they probably weren't too bothered about preserving their relics. When it became clear the Protectorate was no longer defensible Britain withdrew, leaving Aden to become the capital of Yemen.'

'Stuart Freyn was in Aden,' remembered Agnes.

'Indeed he was,' said Parsons. 'At a time when the place was in chaos. When everyone knew the British would have to withdraw sooner or later, and those for whom the day couldn't come soon enough thought they could act with impunity and those who were going to be stranded without protection in a

221

hostile country were desperate to find the means to escape with as much as they could carry. All sorts of reprehensible things were going on. Think of Iraq or Afghanistan to-day.'

'So the Turkish merchant was one of those desperate to get himself and his ill-gotten gains out of the country,' Agnes supposed. 'But if he'd somehow got hold of a valuable relic, why would he give it away, even as a bribe? If he'd sold it he could have bought his way out and still had change.'

'I suppose it depends on what he wanted Freyn to do for him. The British army was still the most powerful force in Aden. It had trucks, ships, aircraft, and the manpower to go pretty much where it needed to. As a British officer, Stuart Freyn would have been an invaluable ally to someone who might otherwise be lucky to escape with his life.'

'He gave Freyn the Monsanto Veronica for helping him move house?'

Parsons snorted a gruff little chuckle. 'Pretty much. If I'm right. Freyn pulled strings to get the merchant to the head of the evacuation queue, and he took the Veronica in payment – believing that it was valuable, that once he got home he could turn it into serious cash, but with no idea what it really was, how much blood was on it and how many people were going to notice when it reappeared. It was like being bribed with a stolen Van Gogh – what could he possibly do with it that wouldn't bring the authorities down on his head?

'When he realized he couldn't sell it he did the only thing left – he gave it away. Just as the merchant had. He couldn't return it to the monks because they were all dead. If he tried to return it to the Catholic Church there'd be way too many questions to answer, but some impulse of decency was telling him it belonged in a church. So he invented a new identity for it and lied about how he came by it so that Dr Pyke would take the thing and mount it high enough on his wall that no one would ever see it. And for forty years it stayed there, and Freyn felt safe.'

'And then it had to come down,' said Agnes slowly, taking up the story, 'and he no longer felt very safe at all. He wanted it where he could keep people away from it – pilgrims and experts alike. After the fire it was only a matter of time before someone turned up who knew what a Crusader banner should look like. While it was in his house he could fend them off while he figured out a Plan B.'

'Like what?' demanded Parsons. 'How do you fend off a respectable academic without making it obvious you've got something to hide?'

'Another fire?' hazarded Agnes lamely.

'How about a car crash?'

They'd done it again: forgotten Mouse's uncanny ability to turn up where he wasn't expected, where he wasn't wanted, and to make sense of conversations when he'd only heard a few words he hadn't been meant to. Either very stupid or very smart – and sometimes both.

'Mouse? I thought you were asleep.'

He dismissed that with a curl of his lip. 'Fat chance, all the comings and goings.' There'd been Flanagan and now there was the vicar: Mouse made it sound as if she'd been entertaining a brigade of paratroopers. 'So? How about another car crash?'

Parsons shook his head bemusedly. 'Sorry, Mouse. How would that help?'

'The first one did.'

Agnes was getting a glimmer of his reasoning. 'Are you saying that Stuart Freyn was responsible for your accident?'

'Why not? You think he set fire to the church.'

She hadn't an answer to that. A theory she'd put together mainly as a diversionary tactic had hardened into a genuine suspicion. She *did* think the Freyns could have burned the church in order to destroy the banner. But murder?

Parsons said quietly, 'Mouse – we know why you crashed the van. You'd been drinking.'

'No.'

'The evidence is there.'

'Evidence can be faked.'

'You're suggesting – what? That Colonel Freyn murdered your mother and tried to kill you? What possible reason could he have? Even if we're right about what the banner is and how the fire started, why on earth would he want to hurt you and Ruth?'

'I don't know,' growled Mouse. 'Because I can't remember. But someone who's prepared to burn a church to cover his back wouldn't draw the line at faking an accident.'

'But why?' asked Agnes. 'Why would he feel threatened by you?'

'I don't *know*! I just know it didn't happen the way it's supposed to have. I wasn't drinking.'

'You ran off the road, Mouse,' said Parsons, clinging on to his patience.

'I wasn't drinking!'

Agnes was all out of patience. Risking her life for him was one thing; protecting him from the truth was another. 'You're half right. You were drinking. But you didn't run off the road. You drove off it.'

The angry confusion twisting his broad

face turned of a sudden to a watchful stillness. 'What?'

Parsons flashed her a warning glance. But
the cat was out of the bag now, and even if
she'd been able to shove it back she might
not have tried. 'You heard me,' she said
roughly. 'You don't think it was an accident?
Me neither. I think you tried to kill yourself.'

Only the wires kept his jaw from falling.
'You think ... you think...' He was almost
stammering in his effort to get his head
round it. *'You think I tried to kill myself and
killed Ma instead?'*

Agnes shrugged unkindly. 'You keep telling
us you don't remember what happened.
Maybe that's why. Maybe you don't want to
remember.'

'How can you even think that?'

They stared at one another in an angry
stand-off. Four hours ago Agnes had saved
Mouse's life: now they were trading glares
like enemies.

Peter Parsons forced a metaphorical shoulder between them. 'OK, guys, let's calm
down for a minute. Mouse – are you serious?
Do you really think Stuart Freyn had something to do with your crash?'

For a moment he was unable to put together a coherent reply. Parsons didn't think
it was just fury, although there was un-
doubtedly that too. He thought Mouse was

226

genuinely astonished.

Then with a last venomous look at Agnes he organized his thoughts enough to answer the question. 'Someone set fire to the church. Everyone else thinks it was me, but I know it wasn't. If Freyn's going to lose his army pension over it, he has a reason to destroy the banner. She' – he wouldn't dignify her with her name – 'said as much.'

'It's possible,' agreed Parson. 'But it's a lot easier to burn a bit of cloth – even a whole building – than to make someone's car crash. He's an old man. Maybe he could splash a bit of paraffin around and light a match. But even if he wanted to, how could he make you drive on to the railway?'

Mouse had no answer. His heavy eyelids flickered uncertainly. 'I don't know. But you've got to admit, it was pretty convenient for him.'

'Why? Sorry, Mouse, but why should he care enough about you and Ruth to want to hurt you?'

'Ma had a book on medieval textiles, and I'd been up dusting the thing. If we talked about it, maybe we realized there was something wrong with it. That he'd lied. Maybe I asked him about it. And he knew his secret was out unless he shut us up.'

'*Were* you talking about it?' asked Agnes.

'I don't *know*,' whined Mouse, childish in

his frustration. 'Amnesia, remember? It's possible.'

'That bit is,' agreed Agnes coldly. 'Just about. But then what? What do you think happened next? That a man in his seventies force-fed a fit twenty-year-old gardener with whisky and persuaded him to drive on to a railway line? And somehow convinced his mother to go along for the ride? Is that what you're suggesting, Mouse? Because if it is, I've got that psychiatrist's number on speed-dial.'

'Of course not,' growled Mouse. But he had been, until he heard it spoken aloud and realized how absurd it was. 'But doesn't that big a coincidence bother you? That nobody in the whole country could make trouble for him except me and Ma? Because I'd seen the thing close up, and she was one of a handful of people who had a book on the subject!'

'I understand how much this matters to you,' said Peter Parsons quietly. 'You need to know what happened, and if at all possible you want to think someone else was to blame. But, Mouse, you need to keep a grip on reality. Lots of things could have happened, but there aren't very many that are likely to have happened. Slinging wild accusations around isn't going to help.'

'What you mean is, I make a better scape-goat than Stuart Freyn!' For just a moment

Mouse had glimpsed a way out – a version of events that didn't leave him responsible for his mother's death. Of course he'd wanted desperately to pursue it. Finding it was after all just another dead end was a bitter disappointment. 'He's rich and respected, an officer and a gentleman, and I'm that crazy guy that does the gardens. No one's going to care if they lock me up. Someone else will mow the lawns. But Peter, I didn't do it! I *know* I didn't. I didn't drive the van while I was drunk because I don't drink. And if I didn't do that, none of the rest of it makes sense.

'OK, maybe it wasn't Freyn,' he conceded unsteadily. 'You're right, he's an old man. But he has a son. Nick Freyn put up serious money to prevent the truth about the banner coming out. He works in the Middle East, doesn't he? Maybe he'd lose a lot of business if he became known as the man whose father smuggled the Monsanto Veronica out of Aden. It was in Nick's interests too to keep the thing out of sight.

'And he thought he'd managed it. He wrote his anonymous cheque for the roof fund, and he thought the Freyn name was safe for another generation. Until I asked the Colonel why the thing didn't look like the other Crusader banners in Ma's book, and Nick realized they weren't safe after all. But they'd *be* safe if they could shut up Ma and me. Not just one of us. It had to be both.

'Is no one else puzzled by the fact that I'm supposed to have gone out on a night's blinder with my mother? Doesn't that strike you as odd? Like someone was trying to make it look like something it wasn't?'

Agnes was reeling from the force of his appeal, amazed at how fluent his speech became when he needed to express himself. Not stupid, not stupid at all...

Clever enough to find a plausible alternative to an unpalatable truth?

She tried to organize her thoughts. 'Yes, that did strike me as odd. But your mother didn't drive, did she? Maybe she needed to go out at short notice, and turned a blind eye to the fact that you'd had a few drinks.'

'Where the hell would she be going at that time of night?' Mouse demanded savagely.

Agnes gave a negligent shrug. 'Maybe she felt unwell and you were taking her to hospital.'

'The scenic way?' he snarled. 'Only, halfway there I thought it would be easier just to kill us both?'

He was right: it made no sense. And the reason was that they didn't have all the pieces of the puzzle. Some of them were still locked up in the strong room of Mouse's amnesia. 'If only you could remember,' murmured the vicar.

'But I can't!' yelled Mouse, tormented beyond endurance. 'I can't remember. How often do I have to say it?' His broad hands made fists that shook by his sides.

For the first time Agnes felt afraid of him. Of the depths of his anger; of his irrational convictions; of the fact that, if he put the crutches aside, he could lift her with one hand. She'd been pleased at how much stronger he'd grown under her care. Until right now she hadn't realized that his recovery could pose a threat.

Peter Parsons seemed to be thinking the same thing. He put one of his own broad hands on Mouse's shoulder in a gesture that was not solely compassionate. 'Calm down, Mouse. If people are struggling to believe what you're saying, shouting almost never convinces them.'

'But I don't know what else to do!' he cried. 'I can't tell you what happened because I don't know. I can't tell you we were set up by Stuart Freyn, or Nick Freyn, or anyone else because I don't remember. Maybe I'll never remember. Maybe someone's going to get away with murder because the truth seeped away through the holes in my brain! And nobody cares. I can't make anyone *care*.'

Agnes felt his pain almost physically. She'd

thought he'd forfeited her compassion, but she was wrong. 'Maybe we could find out whether Nick was in Malleton a fortnight ago. Robin's done business with Nick, his secretary will know Nick's secretary – she could probably find out where he was that Saturday.'

Mouse's voice was a thick plaint. 'This is Nick Freyn we're talking about, yes? Rich Nick Freyn? If he decided to get rid of some inconvenient peasants, he wouldn't do it himself. And he'd make sure he was somewhere else while it was happening.'

'Mouse.' Parsons's voice was low and deliberate. 'This is a fantasy. You must know this is a fantasy. I'm sorry, I wish I could give you some answers about your mother's death, but I can't and I don't think anyone else can either. If you don't remember, I think you have to believe that you had good reason for what you did that night. That it was the least worst option, and you were unlucky not to get away with it. People drink and drive every day, and a lot of them never kill anyone.'

'But I don't,' insisted Mouse. *'I don't.'*

'This time you did.' He turned to go; but at the door he paused. 'You're wrong about one thing. People *do* care. I care, and Agnes cares. Your father cares. Stop thinking the world's a conspiracy against you. On the

232

whole, Mouse, it has more time for you than you have for it.' And with that Thought For The Day he was gone.

Eighteen

The next knock at the door was finally Robin. He and Agnes looked at one another across the threshold and for a moment it was a toss up whether they started with hugs or recriminations. Robin waited, unaccustomedly diffident, to see what Agnes would do.

But Agnes had been angry with a lot of people since she'd last been angry with Robin. 'I am *so* glad to see you!' she said fervently, and her long arms went round his neck. He felt the tension running out of him.

For a couple of minutes they said nothing more. They went inside and sat down, and held hands like a couple of teenagers, and grinned ruefully at one another.

At last Robin pulled himself together. He looked round the little living room. 'Well – are you packed?'

'Ah.' Only then did Agnes remember he wasn't up to date. She hadn't called him after this morning's developments, and she was pretty sure Mouse wouldn't have. 'You don't know about the riot, do you?'

'*Riot?*' His eyebrows disappeared into his front hair.

She looked for a better word but there wasn't one. 'Yes, riot's pretty well what it was. The pilgrims marched on The Nail, trying to get at the banner. Flanagan tried to talk some sense into them, and Mouse and I went with him because I didn't trust either of them on his own. When they couldn't get into The Nail, the pilgrims turned on Mouse.'

Robin paled. 'Is he all right?'

'Yes. Yes, Robin, he's fine. A few more bruises, nothing worse. You can see for yourself. He's upstairs.' She went into the tiny hall and called him. 'Anyway...' she went on, returning to the living room. 'The upshot of all this is, the pilgrims have moved on. All of them. Folded their tents like the Arabs and ... something or other. Which removes a lot of the urgency. Mouse is probably safe enough staying here now.'

Robin stared at her. 'I've just driven a hundred miles!'

Agnes wound her arm around him again. 'And very glad I am to see you,' she assured him. 'You'll stay for the weekend?'

'I haven't brought anything. I thought we'd

be home tonight.'

'We can buy you a toothbrush.'

'Agnes...' He swayed on the brink of bitter words that would drive a wedge between them again. He sucked in a deep breath, and with it patience. 'How long do you think you'll be here?'

Agnes gave a wry shrug. Even her shrugs were graceful. 'Until he's all right.'

'But what does that *mean*? Until he can walk without crutches? Until after the court case? Or until he gets out of Pentonville?'

He'd succeeded in shocking her. 'You don't really think he's going to jail?'

Robin's shrug was less elegant, more ominous. 'I don't know. But the charge will be causing death by drunken driving. That's not a trivial matter. The fact that he can't remember doing it won't save him from the consequences.' He frowned. 'Where is he, anyway?'

She started to say, 'He must have nodded off...' Before the words were out, though, she knew they were wrong. This was Mouse. Mouse didn't do anything as normal as nodding off and not hearing his name called. He hadn't come downstairs, or even called a greeting, because he wasn't there.

A couple of quick steps and Agnes threw the front door wide. She stared both ways up the lane but there was no sign of him. And there should have been. Crutches are not a rapid means of transport.

Peering around anxiously, she spotted Peter Parsons, at his front door across the lane, also peering round. He scratched his head bemusedly. 'You haven't seen my car?'

Agnes may have resisted the idea that Mouse Firth was going to prison for the death of his mother, but Mouse believed in it absolutely. He knew it was what everyone thought. He knew that sometimes the weight of belief is enough to set flimsy evidence like concrete.

And the possibility that the Freyns knew what had happened waved before him like a lifeline, just out of reach. He wasn't blind to the possibility – the likelihood, even – that a lifeline that tenuous would break if he grabbed it. But it was the only one that had come his way, so he had to try.

Alone in his room he'd been thinking desperately about what Parsons had said, and what Agnes had said, and how the pieces might fit together. Then he'd heard Robin's car at the gate, and as surely as if he lived through time backwards he knew what was coming. Robin would ask him to go back to London. If he went he'd never get back here; if he refused, his father wouldn't ask again. He'd already lost his mother. Maybe she hadn't been right up there with the great mothers of all time, but he owed her his life twice over. And he was going to lose years of his life paying for something he didn't believe he'd done. He didn't want to lose anything more. Not his home, and not his father. But if they argued one more time, he knew he was going to.

If he wasn't here they couldn't argue. Robin would curse him roundly, but that was par for the course – Mouse behaving like Mouse, Robin behaving like Robin. They could get past that. He stole down the stairs on feather-footed crutches and let himself quietly out into the lane.

Until that moment he had no idea where he was going. His only plan was to keep out of his father's way and hope Agnes could pacify him. Go home with him if necessary, Mouse could manage alone now if he had to, but somehow paper over the rift once more. But when he found himself in the lane with two cars and no onlookers, the next step seemed blindingly obvious.

Cotswold villages aren't like cities, or even suburbs. People habitually leave their front doors unlocked and the keys in their parked cars. What Robin would never have done in London he did automatically in Malleton; and Peter Parsons would no more have locked his car than locked his church. Lurching past at speed, Mouse took the keys from Robin's and hauled himself into the vicar's. He did it that way round in the rather sad belief that Parsons would forgive him his trespasses before his own father would.

Last time he came this way he got hurt. Again. Even if Mouse could shut his mind to the memory, his body couldn't forget: as the 4 x 4 approached the spot where Flanagan's car had ground to a halt and the pilgrims had poured in on him, of its own accord Mouse's right foot eased up on the accelerator. The road ahead of him was empty now, and still he was slowing.

He set his jaw – a hollow gesture since it was still wired – and forced his foot down, pushing down on his knee with his right hand. The big car stuttered and picked up speed again. Mouse looked neither left nor right until he reached the gates of The Nail.

They were still locked. In other circumstances that wouldn't have stopped him – he was the gardener here, he knew ways in that the pilgrims wouldn't have found if they'd had twice as long to look. But it was a tough scramble followed by a long walk for a man on crutches. And there was a way to get the car closer to the house. He headed back to the farm lane that skirted the two acres of ground that was Stuart Freyn's garden.

He couldn't get the car through the back gate. He pulled as far off the lane as he could and hoped no one would need to open the field gate he was blocking until he got back. He didn't expect to be long. He thought there was a good chance he wouldn't get a hearing at all.

In fact he was lucky. When he let himself into the garden, the first thing he saw was Stuart Freyn, clad in angling waders and above his knees in the pond. Which saved Mouse both the trek up to the house and the possibility of being sent packing by Frances before he could talk to her father. He changed direction with a sigh that combined relief with trepidation.

Freyn saw him coming and raised a hand in greeting. Steadying himself with the pond rake, he climbed out of the water and stood dripping on the bank. 'Mouse. How good to see you. Are you feeling any better?'

Mouse spared a hand from his crutches and rocked it. 'Was doing. Till this morning.'

Freyn looked concerned. 'You were there? Were you hurt? You look a bit battered. Come and sit on the bench before you fall over.' Despite his age and the waders, he had to slow his pace to Mouse's.

They sat together on the long Victorian bench beneath the willow. 'What can I do for you?' asked Freyn. 'Whatever it is, you didn't have to come here. You should have phoned – I could have come down to you.'

'My da's there,' said Mouse gruffly.

'Yes?' Freyn didn't understand his tone. 'A visit, or...?'

'He wants to take me back to London.'

'Ah.' The Colonel considered. 'Well, perhaps, in the circumstances...?'

This wasn't the conversation Mouse had expected to have with Stuart Freyn. 'It's not what I want,' he said stubbornly. 'I need to sort things out. I can't do that in London.'

'Yes. Well...' Freyn crossed his long legs at the ankles. 'Sort out what?'

Mouse had acted so much on the spur of the moment that he hadn't worked out what he wanted to say. He had no strategies prepared for when the old man stone-walled him, as – if he genuinely had secrets to protect – he surely would. And language wasn't Mouse's strong point anyway. So he came straight out and said it. 'I need you to tell me about the banner.'

'The banner.' There was a world of ambivalence in the words. 'What do you want to know?'

'What it is,' growled Mouse. 'Not what it's supposed to be – what it is. Why people die for it.'

That shocked Stuart Freyn to the core. He fought to keep his voice calm. 'Mouse, I've no idea what you're talking about. You know what it is. You've heard the story – damn it, you've dusted the plaque! It's a Christian banner from the time of the Crusades. At least, that's what I was told. I suppose it could be a fake. I've no way of knowing for sure.'

'But Ma had,' insisted Mouse. 'She had a book on medieval textiles. If it isn't what the plaque says, she'd have known. But she can't tell anyone now, can she? And neither can I. Is that why I'm still alive? Because I can't remember what happened?'

He made himself look Colonel Freyn in the face. The old man's cheek had gone to ash. But he'd spent all his professional life as a soldier: he wasn't going to turn and run at the first shot. His lips tightened and his voice was cold. 'You're not making any sense, Mouse. You've been ill, concussed – I think your mind's playing tricks. You were hurt, and your mother was killed, because you were silly enough to drive your van after you'd been drinking. I'm sorry to put it so bluntly, but that's the truth. As to the banner ... all I know about it is what I was told. And whatever it is, it had nothing to do with your accident. How could it have had?'

Mouse had no idea. He only knew what he needed for his absolution. He tried to remember what Agnes and Peter Parsons had been saying. Even that, that only happened an hour ago, was jumping around in his mind like sheep that don't want to be counted.

He grabbed one as it passed. 'Because it's the Monsanto Veronica?'

'Why would he steal my keys and not my car?'

'Why would he steal *my* car when he knows he only has to ask for it?'

'Why would either of you call it stealing,' demanded Agnes tersely, 'when it's *your* son and *your* friend, and you both know the state he's in?'

She didn't like this rôle that was being wished on her, of finger-wagging mother-substitute to every man she met. She was younger than all of them except Mouse; and between the lot of them – Robin, Peter Parsons, Flanagan and Mouse – they hadn't the sense of a ten-year-old girl. She wondered if she'd left it too late to become a lesbian.

The two men blinked at her and took a step back. 'OK,' said Robin carefully. 'So what do *you* think he's up to?'

'Isn't it obvious?' Then she realized that Robin had no idea what they'd been talking about while he was still on the motorway. She swivelled towards Parsons. 'He's gone to The Nail. It's the only place he could possibly want to go that he'd need a car.'

'He could just be avoiding me,' murmured

Robin, who'd known Mouse longer than any of them.

Agnes shook her head. 'He took your keys to stop anyone following him. And the only place we could guess he'd go is The Nail.'

Robin frowned. 'Why would he go to the Freyns' place? I know he's their gardener, but surely to God he isn't *that* desperate to prune an azalea?'

Agnes ran frantic fingers through her hair. 'I'll fill you in as soon as we have a minute. But right now we have to catch up with Mouse. Peter, where can we borrow a car?'

He peered down the lane into Malleton, trying to work out who was in and who was out. 'I suppose...'

Robin was looking the other way. 'I don't know about lending us his car, but I dare say Nick Freyn would give us a lift.'

The big silver saloon was coming down the road from The Nail. Agnes's heart leapt and turned over. She couldn't think quickly enough to work out if it was better to stop him or to let him pass.

Robin didn't know there was a dilemma. He stepped into the road with a hand raised in friendly greeting. 'Nick! Hang on a minute, Nick. You haven't seen my idiot boy, have you? Driving the vicar's jeep?'

Nick Freyn lowered his window with the self-satisfied hum of good machinery. He looked at Robin with cool recognition, at Parsons with guarded politeness, at Agnes as if he'd never seen her before. He shook his grey head. 'No. You've lost him?'

Agnes spoke up before anyone else could. 'A misunderstanding. We were supposed to meet here. Now Robin's mislaid his keys so we can't go looking for him. What we were hoping, Mr Freyn, is that you'd give him a lift into Gloucester. If you're heading that way.' He might just have come out for a pint of milk, but there was a good chance that he was heading for the motorway.

'Gloucester?' Freyn looked at Robin in surprise. 'Why do you want to go to Gloucester?'

If Mouse had taken Robin's car and the vicar's keys, Parsons would have understood why she thought it important to keep the truth from Nick Freyn. He was probably a terrible liar – you'd expect it of a man in his profession – but at least he'd have known to try. Robin had no idea what was going on.

Two things saved them. Robin trusted Agnes. And he operated in a forum where telling God's honest truth was not always the best policy. He winged it. 'I stayed there last night. That's where I left my keys. The spare got me this far but it's an old one and now it's bent. Thank God the cleaners found my bunch. So if Gloucester isn't too far out of

244

your way...'

Nick Freyn looked like a man who'd never lost a key in his life. He gave a bemused shrug. 'Sure. Get in. Can you make your own way back?'

'I'll get a taxi,' said Robin expansively. 'Good of you...' He was still thanking Freyn for taking him somewhere he didn't want to go to get something that wasn't there as they pulled away.

'And then there were two,' said Agnes.

'Yes,' agreed Parsons. 'Why?'

'Because if Mouse *has* gone to The Nail, keeping Nick Freyn away from there is the best help we can give him. Until we get there and drag him away, kicking and screaming if needs be.'

'Do you think Nick knows he's there?'

Agnes shook her head. 'If he'd known the banner was getting another visitor, he wouldn't have left the house.'

'So there's only Stuart to deal with.'

'And Frances.'

Parsons chuckled. 'An old man and a middle-aged woman. We should manage.'

'He was a soldier, remember.'

'And she's a hospital visitor and organizes the church flowers roster. We can take them.'

Nineteen

They didn't actually call it a war. They called it a police action, on the basis that a bunch of bandits in headscarves couldn't be considered an enemy worthy of the British army. To those serving in Aden during the 1960s, it felt pretty much like a war. The bandits in headscarves were armed by the neighbouring states of Yemen and Egypt, and they were fighting for their independence. They *were* bandits, and also freedom fighters. They ambushed British military convoys. They occupied mountain villages. They bombed military married quarters, blew up cinemas and shot at schools. To the people on the ground, on both sides, it felt exactly like a war.

And war is a melting pot. It changes people. Good people do bad things and bad people become heroes in the adrenalin-charged atmosphere of the battlefield.

Aden was a British colony surrounded by Yemen which was itself all but surrounded by Saudi Arabia. Monsanto was an Italian

246

monastery manned by Christian Arabs, set on a rock promontory in the northern mountains surrounded by increasingly nationalistic Radfan tribesmen.

All that remain are photographs and some stones on a hill. The photographs show a grim stone edifice, more like a fortress than a religious house, built atop cliffs a thousand feet high and approached by a spine of rock that could be held by one determined monk swinging a censer. The men who built it, Italian Crusaders taking the scenic route home from Jerusalem, had not expected to be welcome in this wilderness.

It must have seemed like a good idea at the time. But the difficulties of getting food and water to such a place, and of finding monks sufficiently sick of the world to stay there, would have given the monastic community of Monsanto a limited lifespan but for one thing.

One day in the late thirteenth century a cloaked pilgrim, walking down the stony mule track with a package under his arm, craved shelter for the night. He was given food and a place to sleep, but in the morning when they went to wake him for prayers the pilgrim was gone. The monks couldn't understand how he could have left un-observed. They looked nervously at the thousand-foot cliff under his window and wondered if their hospitality had been so poor he'd jumped rather than stay. One of the more devout of them suggested he might have been an angel and flown away.

Apparently angels can't fly with a package tucked under one wing, because he'd left it on the plank bed. The monks resolved to keep it for his return. But, like all good resolutions, it wore thin after a while and the abbot decided that (a) the angel wasn't coming back, and (b) he'd left the package because he wanted them to have it. So he opened it.

A few centuries earlier or later the puzzled monks would have sent it to the laundry then put it at the back of a linen closet in case someone some day had a use for a lawn handkerchief. But this was the end of the thirteenth century, when interest in relics was at its height, when even Pope Boniface VIII kept a Veronica's Veil in the Vatican Basilica and displayed it on important occasions. Of all the things that might have injected new life into a grim and uncomfortable monastery on the edge of the then-known world, only an authenticated Second Coming would have served better than a really convincing Veronica's Veil. A fact not lost on the world's cynics, then or later.

When word of the Monsanto Veronica spread, increasing numbers of pilgrims found their way down the Red Sea coast, bringing the fourteenth-century equivalent of tourist dollars and taking away tales of miracles and little glass phials containing a few fibres which no one with the technology of the day could prove were not combed from the frayed edges of the cloth.

So the monastery continued to eke out a living among the high rocks of north Aden until midway through the twentieth century; and if that isn't a miracle, what is? By 1964, when the Quteibi, Bakri and Ibdali tribesmen suddenly realized that, little as they liked one another, they all hated the British more, the community was shrunk to a hard core of sixteen very old or very young monks and the pilgrim trade had all but dried up in the harsh climate of the desert mountains. But the Veronica was still where it had been for almost seven hundred years, in a reliquary in a shrine in the heart of the grim Crusader fortress.

Three years later it was not. The decision was taken to bring British rule in Aden to an end and the British army marched out towards the end of 1967. The massacre at Monsanto was discovered the following spring, by which time the fate of a small enclave of Christian Arabs and the disappearance of a Christian relic was not the highest priority of a new government suddenly discovering that the Quteibi, Bakri and Ibdali tribesmen didn't like them much more than they'd liked the British.

'You can't begin to understand the chaos of a state in revolution,' said Colonel Stuart Freyn pensively. 'All vestiges of civilization vanish. We sent the families home - it wasn't possible to protect them, even on our own bases. You never knew where the attacks were coming from. I felt sorry for the locals. We had a date to look forward to, we only had to survive till then and we were going home. They had no idea what would happen to them, and the only homes they had were in the middle of a war zone. After we pulled out, no one was going to care. If their own people killed them as collaborators, or if the whole region descended into a bloody civil war, no one would lift a finger to help them. The Arab nations would be broadly content that they were back to killing one another instead of being protected by foreigners, and the rest of the world would just shake their heads sadly and thank God it wasn't their problem.'

They were still sitting on the bench beneath the willow, forty years and four thousand miles and a huge body of human experience away from a war over a rocky desert. Freyn was right: a twenty-year-old gardener could have no idea what it had been like. He himself, looking back down the years, struggled to make sense of the memories. Had it really been like that? Had it *felt* like that? The things he'd seen...

'Who killed the monks?' asked Mouse.

Freyn gave an elegant shrug. 'Who knows? We don't even know when it happened. We pulled out at the end of November, the atrocity was discovered the following May. Six months in which rival bands, deprived now of both an enemy army to fight and any travellers to raid, swarmed back and forth across those mountains. One month it was one tribe holding the passes, the next another. Even if we knew when the monastery was overrun, it would be impossible to pin down which band held the area at the time. And after so long, what good would it do anyway? The bandits turned into freedom fighters and then into government ministers. Monsanto was...' He spread a fatalistic hand. 'A casualty of war.'

'Why did you give the Veronica to Grampa?' asked Mouse. 'Why not return it?'

Freyn had to do a quick gear-shift to think of the austere, bookish Dr Pyke, late vicar of St Bride's-in-Malleton, as Mouse's grampa. 'Return it to whom? The monks were dead and the monastery in ruins, dynamited to cover the evidence. The new government of

South Yemen needed a Christian relic with Christian blood on it like it needed a hole in the head. And I didn't want to be answering a whole lot of questions. I just wanted to be rid of the thing.'

'And the Turkish merchant?'

'I don't know what became of him. Maybe he died – a lot of people did. Or maybe he found some other city on the edge of the abyss where internationally important artefacts could be bought for a berth on the next ship out. There were a lot of cities like that then. There are still some now.'

Mouse said nothing. He was thinking. In fact, he was doing mental arithmetic.

Freyn looked up. 'Here comes Frances. Mouse – don't tell people about this. It'll make things difficult for Nick. He does a lot of business in the Gulf states – I wouldn't like to think that his father's foolishness forty years ago would be an embarrassment to him now. Come to that, I'd rather not have to justify myself to the gutter press.'

'Did you burn the church?'

'No!' So far as Mouse could tell he was genuinely startled. 'No, Mouse, of course I didn't. To be honest, I thought you...'

'And Ma?'

'What about her?'

'Do you know what she was doing in my van?'

There was compassion in the old man's eyes. 'I'm sorry, Mouse, I don't. Maybe one day you'll remember.'

'One day's too late! They're going to lock me up, Colonel. I'm going to prison, for killing my mother!' Freyn had no answer for him. Mouse looked away, fighting to regain control. 'What happens to it now? The Veronica.'

'Well, there's no St Bride's to return it to, nor likely to be for a while. Perhaps I should keep it at home.' He gave Mouse a conspiratorial grin. 'High on a wall. Get you to dust it for me, when you can.' He stood up as his daughter reached them. 'Look, Fran, it's Mouse. Look how well he's doing.'

Frances regarded the visitor with a small tight smile that said he only had business here if he was pushing a mower. 'You didn't walk all this way, did you?'

Mouse shook his head. 'I've got Peter's car.' It wasn't a lie: he didn't say he also had the vicar's permission. 'In the back lane.'

'Ah. Well, lunch is ready, Dad. You get out of your waders and I'll help Mouse with the gate.' She parted them with an ushering arm.

She had to adapt her long stride to Mouse's hobbled one. She filled the time with an effort at conversation. 'Has my father been regaling you with his war stories?'

'It's interesting,' mumbled Mouse, aware that he couldn't leave quickly enough for her. 'Aden and all that. It's just history till you talk to someone who was there.'

'Yes.' The terse smile again. She was a woman who was easier to admire than to like. 'The Colonel will have been glad to see you. He says you're good company. I think it's because you listen more than you talk.'

Mouse wasn't sure it was meant as a compliment. He plugged on towards the gate.

'Was he telling you about the Veronica?' Mouse nodded. 'Quite a story, isn't it? I first heard it when I was twelve. I *so* longed to join the army too, and go the places he'd been and do the things he'd done. But it wasn't considered a suitable career for a young lady then.'

Mouse was slowly grinding to a halt, his brow corrugated by a frown. 'It doesn't work,' he said. 'If it was bandits after we pulled out...'

'Hm. Sorry?' Frances wasn't listening. She was struggling with the gate. It didn't get enough use, and because of that it didn't get enough maintenance. Mouse saw her fighting the rusty bolt and made a mental note to replace it. If there was time between getting back to work and going to court.

He negotiated the rutted lane to where he'd parked the vicar's car. Frances was still muttering behind him. 'Stupid thing! Mouse, is there a tool kit in there some-where? A spanner, a wrench, something like that?'

It was in a canvas bag in the back. 'What size?'

'The biggest.' She came for it. And when Mouse turned towards the car she smashed it across the back of his skull with as much force as her long, wiry body could muster.

Twenty

'You've done *what*?'

If Frances could have managed alone she wouldn't have involved her father. But Mouse, though shorter than she, was sturdy and she couldn't lift him. Ruth had been much lighter.

She dismissed the appalled tone in the Colonel's voice, the wide-eyed shock in his face, with a peremptory sniff. 'You heard me. Now hurry. If he wakes up before the situation's sorted we're going to be talking to policemen. That's the kind of trouble even Nick's chequebook won't get us out of.'

He followed her down the slope of the

lawn with a kind of reluctant haste. 'But Fran, I don't *understand*,' he whined fractiously.

She broke her stride just long enough to fix him with a fierce gaze. 'Yes, Dad, you do. You understand perfectly. Forty years ago you did something that, if it had come out, would have wrecked your career and ruined your name. Which also happens to be my name and Nick's. So forty years later I had to do something even worse to protect us all from the consequences of your ... misjudgement. Don't pretend this is nothing to do with you.'

She never spoke to him like that. One advantage to being a career officer was that your children held in awe the distinguished stranger who maybe saw them twice a year. It was like being Father Christmas: coming home after months abroad, laden with presents and stories, to a family unnaturally respectful of a man whom in many ways they hardly knew. And this relationship had endured beyond the end of childhood.

But there wasn't much respect in Fran's voice now, or in her eyes. Of course, he hadn't brought her a Costumes of the World doll this time. He'd brought disaster. 'It's only Mouse,' he mumbled. 'Mouse was never going to hurt us. Whatever he thought he knew. Even if he told someone, who's going to believe him? The boy's an idiot.'

Fran's gaze was scornful. 'And that's exactly why we're in trouble right now. Because you talk to him the way other men talk to their dogs, thinking nothing they say will ever get passed on. He's not an idiot. His mother wasn't an idiot. And things you said to Mouse, for no better reason than to pass the time while he was trimming the hedge, didn't go in one ear and out the other. He thought about them, he knew they didn't make sense, and he talked to his mother. Between them they worked it out.'

'They didn't work it out,' objected Freyn. 'Maybe they guessed what the cloth is, but that's all. I asked Mouse not to talk about it and he agreed.' Actually he hadn't. But Colonel Freyn was so used to people doing as he wanted that the possibility of disobedience didn't occur to him.

Fran shook her head in disbelief. 'You're a foolish old man! This isn't the army – Mouse isn't a raw recruit you can intimidate. When he realized you'd lied about the cloth he wanted to know why. Ruth waded through her eclectic library, and she got at the truth. And she understood what it meant, that you'd brought the thing out of Aden. No one could have bribed you with an artefact he couldn't have got hold of until three months after you left the country!'

257

There were of course other cars in the village. But finding their owners would have taken time. A dancer and a skier: two fit young people, they set off to run.

They just hoped they were running in the right direction. They couldn't think where else Mouse would have gone, but it was odd that Nick Freyn had seen neither him nor the vicar's distinctive car. Unless Robin had been right, and Mouse's only object had been to avoid his father. In which case he was probably safe enough, but only until Robin caught up with him.

When they reached the gates of the big house without any sight of car or driver, Parsons dragged a sleeve across his sweaty face. 'What do we do now?'

'I'm going to ask at the house,' decided Agnes. She was hardly out of breath.

'Ask *what*?' demanded Parsons. 'Have you seen our friend, he was coming here to accuse you of murdering his mother?'

Agnes cast him a withering glance. 'Don't be silly. Forget what he said. Mouse knows who's responsible for Ruth's death. He's always known. That's what the amnesia is about. When he faces up to what he did, he'll remember well enough.'

'You don't think there's anything in it, then? That Nick Freyn killed her to stop

Ruth reporting what she'd discovered?'

'Honest to God?' She gave an apologetic little grin. 'No. I think Mouse would give anything to be able to blame someone else. And I do think the Freyns have something to hide, or at least that Stuart Freyn does. Because what he's been telling people all these years isn't true. If someone gave him the Monsanto Veronica, it wasn't as a little backhander. Only someone very desperate, or very grateful, would...'

Parsons waited, but the sentence had tailed away into silence. 'Agnes?'

She flicked a finger at him. 'Just a minute.' She was doing the same mental sums Mouse had done. 'This doesn't make sense.'

'Well, he lied,' Parsons said reasonably. 'It was never a Crusader banner.'

'Not that. The timings. It's not just that the thing isn't what he said it was. He couldn't have got it the way he said either. He said a merchant gave it to him to help him get out of Aden, yes? So the merchant must have left before Freyn did, and Freyn left in November 1967 at the latest. But the Monsanto Veronica was still safe in its monastery until it was overrun by the nationalists after the British withdrew.'

Parsons frowned. All the authorities were agreed on the point. He'd read four different accounts in the process of identifying the cloth. But he hadn't realized there was a problem with the chronology. 'What are you saying? That he got it later than he says? And therefore not from a Turkish merchant but from a Yemeni bandit?'

But that wasn't what Agnes was thinking. She wished it was. If that was what Stuart Freyn had to hide, all that was at stake was his reputation. He might lie to protect it, but that was probably all.

'No,' she said slowly. Her eyes were filling up with fear. 'I think that's the one thing he told the truth about – that he brought it out of Aden when the army left in '67. Peter, don't you see what that means? It means the atrocity occurred while the country was still under British rule. And it was covered up. If Yemeni tribesmen had killed the monks of Monsanto and stolen their treasure, the British government would have said so. I don't think it was tribesmen. I think it was British soldiers.'

'You're telling me...' Colonel Freyn had trouble getting the words out. 'You *killed* her? Mouse's mother?'

'No, I didn't kill her,' said Frances dismissively. 'It was an accident. But in a way it made things easier. When there were two of them, it didn't occur to me I could do anything but plead for their help. When it was only Mouse ... well. Everyone knows what he's like. Everyone would be sorry. if he ended killing the pair of them, but nobody'd be surprised.'

'Fran – tell me what you did.'

They'd reached the garden gate. Outside, in the lane, Mouse still lay crumpled in the dried-up ruts of the tractor tyres. He looked smaller than usual, like a broken child, and there was blood in his straw-coloured hair. Stuart Freyn stared at him in horror and pity.

Fran opened the back of the 4x4, then bent and picked up Mouse's feet. 'Once he's out of sight,' she promised.

She'd gone into St Bride's on the Saturday evening to do the flowers for the Sunday service. It should have been Mrs Roslyn, but Mrs Roslyn's daughter was having a baby and altering the flower roster was a mine-field. Fran found it easier to fill any gaps herself.

She expected the church to be empty. Instead she found Mouse and Ruth standing in the aisle, staring up at the cabinet with binoculars.

She didn't know what to do, what to say. Another moment and she'd have tiptoed away, and history would have taken another course. But Mouse, who always heard more

261

than was convenient, heard her and turned round, and then it was too late to run.

'You know, don't you?' Ruth said quietly.

'Know what?' stammered Fran. Which was as good as an admission. Normally it took dynamite to disturb Frances Freyn's composure.

'Oh yes, you know.' Ruth's voice was soft, but at its core – as at hers – was a grain of adamant. She couldn't know everything from a book, a trawl of the Internet and a pair of binoculars, but she knew enough. She knew what it meant, that the Monsanto Veronica had been hidden away in an English church for forty years.

Frances did what she never did: she bowed to the situation. Eyes lowered, she asked them – begged them – to sit with her and talk about this. What had happened, what it meant, what happened next. Because it was too late for the truth to do anything but destroy an honourable man.

Ruth couldn't see how anyone who had been involved in the murder of sixteen monks could be considered an honourable man.

'He wasn't at the monastery,' insisted Fran. 'When he learned what one of his patrols had done, he was horrified. He confiscated the valuables and reported the incident to his superiors. It was them – the generals and the politicians – who decided to cover it up. Ten days later British involvement in Aden would end. Telling the truth wouldn't bring the monks back, it would only spoil a dignified withdrawal and bring the whole operation into disrepute. A lot of good men would pay for the actions of a few thugs.

'He was told to go to Monsanto and destroy the evidence. He took one sergeant and a box of dynamite, and made sure there was nothing left to implicate the British forces. That's when he took the Veronica. It was lying on the altar of the monastery church. The soldiers were looking for jewels and precious metals: they didn't know that the rather grubby-looking cloth they'd discarded was more precious than the reliquary that held it.'

She looked at Ruth, desperately seeking a hint of sympathy in her gaze. 'That was his mistake. If he'd done as he was told and destroyed it, there'd have been nothing to link him or any British soldier to the Monsanto atrocity. But he couldn't bring himself to. A lot of people thought it was a holy thing – that it had touched the face of Christ. How could he destroy it? He brought it away so it wouldn't be haggled over by profiteers, and ten days later he left Aden with it in his kitbag. When the atrocity was discovered early in '68, the world assumed it was local tribesmen eradicating the last vestiges of Christian occupation.

'But he didn't know what to do with it. If he'd sent it to his superiors they'd have known he hadn't done what he'd been told to. The same if he'd returned it to the monks' order. Yet he felt in his heart that it needed to be on consecrated ground. After Monsanto was destroyed, St Bride's seemed as good as anywhere else.'

'It's forty years ago,' Ruth said quietly. 'Don't you think it's time the truth was known?'

'My father is seventy-three,' said Frances in a low voice. 'He won't live forever. Please, can't we wait until it can't hurt him any more?'

And in truth, it could have waited. But Ruth was impatient for her moment of glory. She'd discovered something no one else in the world suspected. She knew where the Monsanto Veronica was, and how it had come to be there. For fifteen years she'd toiled at a keyboard, turning pages of academic scrawl into books that publishers might look at and readers want to buy, and all she'd got in return was a small income and the occasional compliment on her typing. Researchers earned more money than typists; for one thing, they earned respect. She craved respect. She didn't want to grow old waiting for Stuart Freyn to die.

'I'm sorry.' She stood abruptly, headed briskly up the aisle.

Frances rose too, launched from her pew by an explosion of fear and anger and frustration. Who was Ruth Pyke to refuse her request? Her gardener's mother, for God's sake! The strange, scarred, private woman you saw sometimes in church and sometimes in the shop, and from whom you never got more than a quick nod before she was gone. Of course, she was ashamed of her face. The story in the village was that Mouse had done that. They should be grateful, both of them, that the Freyns or anyone like the Freyns would admit to knowing them.

And in that moment of anger Frances grabbed Ruth's arm. That surprised the pair of them: Mouse, who was hovering round them like an anxious Quasimodo, unsure what to do about a violent argument between his mother and his client, and Ruth, swung off balance by the strength of Frances's fury, who staggered and stumbled and fell among the pews.

They waited for her to get up. When she didn't, Mouse gave Frances a worried look and Frances knelt down. 'Ruth?'

As soon as she moved the spilt hair away from Ruth's cheek she knew the other woman was dead. Her eyes were open but there was nothing in them. There was a depression in her temple where she'd fallen against the edge of a pew, and though the skin was torn there was hardly any blood. It wasn't enough for a doctor, had one been present, to certify death, and any professional would have attempted resuscitation. But even the professionals wouldn't have expected to succeed. Death has a look of its own, and Frances Freyn – who was a hospital volunteer, who'd seen dead people before – recognized it in the scarred face of Ruth Pyke.

Time had slowed right down. There seemed to be as much as Fran needed to figure out what to do next. She hadn't meant to hurt Ruth, but the fact remained that she had. It had been an accident, but the police mightn't see it that way. And they'd want to know what the argument had been about. Frances could lie, but Mouse wouldn't.

Mouse.

If it had been the other way round, if he was the one with the broken skull and Ruth had been the only witness, in all probability the thing would have ended there. Fran would never have asked herself what she needed to do to silence Ruth. She was a respectable, law-abiding woman, had been all her life.

But it was possible to think of Mouse as

not quite another human being. His slightly odd way of speaking, of looking at you, of looking at the world, made it just possible to think of removing him from the equation without resorting to the word *murder*. Like a big clumsy dog that no one could find room for, that filled the house with muddy paw prints and knocked people over. You didn't like having to put it down, but it was an option if the need arose.

With the Freyn family facing catastrophe, Fran considered the need pressing. But ... *that* pressing? Ruth's death was an accident, something no one could have predicted. Mouse could attest to that. But Mouse was the only one who even knew they'd been here together. Who even knew they had something to talk about. With Mouse gone...

Gone? *Killed?* Was it even possible? He was stronger than her, and it would have to look like another accident.

No ... it should look like the same accident. That wasn't beyond the bounds of ingenuity.

And morality? Was she really thinking of ending someone's life?

It was only Mouse. He was a gardener, for God's sake, and three stakes short of a trellis. It wasn't that much of a sacrifice. Not to protect her family.

And all this thinking, this internal arguing, took place inside Frances Freyn's head in just a few seconds, stretched by the disaster to provide all the time necessary. All the time she wanted. If she was going to do this, she didn't want to think too much about it first.

Like a big clumsy dog, confused and anxious and scared of doing the wrong thing, Mouse leaned over them, getting in the way. Frances shooed him back, and shrugging off her cardigan pillowed it under the dead woman's head. 'Go and get my phone. It's in the car, outside.'

She was still thinking in terms of: You know, what I *could* do is ... She wasn't committing herself to any particular action – to any action at all. It was just a thought. She was keeping her options open.

He couldn't find her phone. He hunted desperately for three minutes, then raced back. 'I can't...'

Frances was talking on the thing, rang off as he arrived. 'Sorry, Mouse – it was in my pocket. I called for an ambulance. They've nothing closer than Gloucester. They said we should bring her in ourselves. Bring your van to the door so we can keep her flat.' None of it, of course, was true. But she sounded convincing, even to herself.

Mouse hesitated. 'Won't we hurt her? I could get Peter...'

Frances shook her head decisively. 'Time matters. We can lift her between us – we'll be

268

careful, we won't hurt her. I'll ride in the back to support her.'

And that's what they did. They left Malleton without anyone else knowing what had happened. Frances sat in the back of the van with the dead woman's head cradled in her lap, and thought, and thought.

Still keeping her options open she said, 'Take the old road, Mouse. It'll be quicker.' If he'd queried that she'd have come up with a plausible lie, but in fact he was too worried to. He was just glad to have someone telling him what to do.

The obvious solution was a crash, the obvious spot for it the bend at the Mile End Cut. How she could persuade Mouse to stop, let her out, and then drive on to the railway tracks was less clear. Until, moving some of his gear to make herself more comfortable, she found a bottle of single-malt whisky, still in the plastic bag from the off-licence.

'Whisky, Mouse?' she said lightly. 'I thought you didn't drink.'

'What?' Distractedly: it was the last thing on his mind. 'Oh, yes. For Da's birthday.'

'Ah.'

The bend was coming up. It was now or never. If never, all she had to explain was an accidental death. And what one of the premier relics of Christendom was doing on the wall of her parish church.

'Mouse.' Her voice quavered. 'Pull over, Mouse. I think she's stopped breathing.'

He did as he was told. He twisted in his seat, his broad face distraught. And met a bottle of single-malt whisky coming the other way.

With the woman dead and the boy slumped unconscious behind the wheel, Fran had time to arrange things to her satisfaction. First priority was to get the van on to the bank and pointing down the slope, held by the handbrake. She squeezed herself between Mouse and the wheel in order to reach the pedals. Slim as she was, the wheel dug into her ribcage – if it had been more than just a few metres she couldn't have managed. But the need drove, and she put off breathing until she was able to crawl out on to the grass.

Next thing. The idiot boy wasn't stirring, so at least she wouldn't have to hit him again. The seat belt had held him in place. Ruth could stay in the back, the other seat belt parked on the passenger side testimony to the carelessness that had led to her tumbling round inside the van. Now there was just *why* the accident had happened. Frances opened the bottle carefully. Some of its contents she got down Mouse's throat, some spilled down his front, but that was all right too. As long as there was enough inside him to raise his blood levels. When she was satisfied she wiped her prints off the bottle, clasped it in his slack hand for a moment then let it fall into the well of the van.

'OK,' she said to herself shakily. She ran through the checklist again. She reclaimed her cardigan. She wiped over any surfaces she thought she'd touched. The engine was still running. The gearstick would be in neutral when the van was found, but the police would suppose the driver was wrestling with it when he passed the point of no return. There was nothing more she could do, and anyway no way back. Gloving her hand in her handkerchief, she reached across Mouse to release the handbrake.

She waited long enough to see the van pick up speed and nosedive on to the track, landing in a shatter of glass and steel. She saw the first flickerings of flame under the crumpled bonnet. She checked her watch. Only minutes to the next train. At this time of night, on a back road through the countryside, what were the odds of him being found first – or being alive, even if he was? Frances backed away from the scene, noted with approval that nothing was visible from the road, and walked home. By the time she got there it all seemed like a dream.

Twenty-One

'Oh Fran,' whispered Stuart Freyn brokenly.
'Oh Fran.' He couldn't think of anything else
to say.

'Listen,' she said fiercely. They were back
in the house now, with Mouse – roped and
half conscious – on the hall floor between
them. 'This is where we are. Of course we
never wanted this, but we need to deal with
it. If we don't, I'm going to prison, Nick's
going to lose everything he's worked for and
God knows what'll happen to you. And
maybe you and I deserve it, but Nicky
doesn't. None of this was his doing.

'And even if you and I deserve it, I'm not
going to let it happen. Not for *that*.' The
glance she cast at the boy at her feet was
purest hatred. As if he'd purposed her
family's destruction.

'We can't *kill* him!'

'Dad, you were a soldier for thirty years.
You fought wars. You killed a lot of people.
Not all of them were bad people – they were
just in the wrong place at the wrong time.
You killed them because it was your job and

there were higher priorities. Like achieving objectives. Like keeping your men safe. That's where we are right now. It's Mouse or us. There is no third way.'

And a weasel worm in his brain was saying she was right. That everyone puts their own needs first. That a man with children to worry about hasn't the luxury of always doing the right thing. He was sorry about Mouse. But the boy had become an unacceptable danger.

They were talking about *killing* him. About killing someone they knew. And he wasn't even the first.

Stuart Freyn was widely considered a brave man. A man who'd shown courage under fire, who'd enjoyed his generals' confidence and his soldiers' regard. On good days, when he could forget the things he'd done, he still thought of himself that way. But he no longer really believed it. 'Nobody's going to believe in *another* accident.'

'No? They thought it was an accident when he pulled his IV apart, didn't they?'

Freyn stared at her. 'That was you?'

'He was supposed to die on the railway line,' said Fran angrily. 'He could have died in surgery. But no: he was recovering, getting stronger. He was going to wake up and talk. I had no choice, Dad. People were used to seeing me around the hospital – good old

Fran, pushing the library cart, visiting the infirm. No one saw me go into Mouse's room. It was the work of a moment. I thought that was the end of it.

'Of course, I didn't know then that he'd lost his memory.' She gave a mirthless chuckle. 'They say whisky will do that to a man.'

'And the church? Was that you too?'

'Of course it was me,' she said impatiently. 'Me and a watering can full of paraffin. Good old Fran, tending to the church flowers. I know for a fact that people saw me coming out after eleven o'clock. And not one of them remembers. Not one of them said to the police, *Talk to Frances Freyn, she was in the church quite late*. I might as well be invisible. Being a middle-aged spinster is just like being invisible.'

'But ... why?'

Fran ground the heels of her hands into her eyes. 'Isn't it obvious? To get rid of it. To destroy it once and for all. Once it's ashes, no one will ever be able to say for sure what it was. If I'd succeeded we'd be safe now. It wouldn't matter what Mouse Firth said, or thought, or even what he remembered. He'd be forever that crazy kid who sets fire to things, and he'd be locked away where people just nod and smile when you claim to be the victim of a conspiracy.'

274

'Why didn't you *tell* me?'

'Because you'd have tried to stop me!' she cried. 'Because it needed doing, and everybody thinks that you're tough and Nick's ruthless but both of you would have shrunk from doing this. Wrung your hands and let the moment pass. And that's as true now as it ever was. We're in this mess today because forty years ago you hadn't the resolve necessary to destroy the Veronica. It's the only evidence of what was done at Monsanto. The monks are dead, the soldiers are scattered, nothing else that was taken has ever been identified. Only that.' She turned on her heel and glared at it, still parked in its heavy case on the hall table, with the same hatred she bore Mouse. 'As long as it's here – as long as it's *anywhere* – it's a threat to us all.'

She frightened him. What she had become – what his actions had forced her to become – appalled him. 'My poor girl,' he murmured. He wanted to put his arms around her, and somehow didn't dare to. He didn't know her well enough to know if she'd welcome it. 'How did we come to this?'

'You *know* how,' she spat. 'I love you. You, and Nicky, are the only things that matter to me. You're my family – my *only* family. I have nothing else. No children, no career, not even a home of my own. This is it – you're it. Everything in my life. And *anything* is worth doing to keep you safe. Kill for you? I'd *die* for you. You know that.'

Freyn swallowed. He could no more have tried to stay her than stand in front of a tornado. 'So what do we do now?'

'You know that too. We finish what we started.'

'Shouldn't we call the police?'

Peter Parsons looked totally out of his depth, desperate for someone to take over and tell him later what was true and what wasn't. Agnes too was facing a situation she'd never expected, was equally unprepared for. But she was used to having to think on her feet, and she didn't think he was. The respective natures of their jobs, perhaps. It's not uncommon for a dancer to hit a problem in the middle of a performance and have to improvise. She suspected that chucking the book away and improvising wasn't encouraged by the Church.

'Of course we should,' she agreed. 'But they'll tell us to stay put and do nothing more till they get here. And that's going to be – what, twenty minutes, half an hour? Mouse may not have half an hour.'

'Before *what*?' demanded Parsons. 'What are you expecting to happen? I'm not breaking into someone's house in order to save Mouse from the rough side of Frances

Freyn's tongue. If you think he could get hurt in there, that's different. But *why* do you think that?'

She didn't know how to answer him. Honesty seemed as good as anything else. 'Peter, I don't know what's going on. I don't even know if we're right about the banner – that it really is the Monsanto Veronica, and that means it was British troops who murdered the monks. I don't know. But *if* we're right, Mouse is sure as hell in danger, and he doesn't even know how much. People have died for that cloth already. I don't want Stuart Freyn thinking one idiot gardener is all that stands between him and safety.'

'You'd rather him think there are three of us?'

Agnes grinned, entirely without humour. 'You said it already. We can take them.'

'And if he has a gun?'

She considered. 'Then this would be a really good time for you to get on to head office.' She didn't mean the bishop, and he knew she didn't.

In the end she called the police. She told them there was more trouble at The Nail and that someone – she didn't tell them who, in case it compromised the speed of their response – was in imminent danger, then she hung up before they could tell her what to do. She knew what she had to do. She hoped Peter Parsons, and his boss, would help.

Perhaps both of them did. Parsons gave her a leg-up on to the high wrought-iron gate; and when she was just about as exposed as you can be without floodlighting, Frances Freyn drove up in Parsons's car. She stopped and looked at Agnes on top of her gate, and Parsons looked at his car. 'Er...'

'What are you doing up there?' asked Frances, with a kind of polite restraint.

'What are you doing in my car?' countered Parsons.

Slightly shame-faced, Agnes climbed down. 'Mouse?' It served for both question and answer.

Frances shrugged. 'Yes? I found it in my back lane. It is yours, isn't it, Vicar?'

'Mouse borrowed it. Have you seen him?'

Frances shook her head. 'Why would he come here? He's not fit to work yet, is he?' As if the only thing the Freyns and someone like Mouse could have in common was the garden. Agnes bridled her tongue.

'I think he was looking for your father,' said Parsons.

'My father's in the house.' The unspoken rider: And we don't let Mouse over the threshold. 'I had to move the car out of the lane and I didn't know what to do with it.

You can take it with you.'

'But where's Mouse?' insisted Agnes.

'I've no idea, Miss Amory,' said Frances calmly. 'But if you want to search the gardens for him, I'll open the gate. There's really no need for acrobatics.'

She was as good as her word, unlocking the padlock with keys from her pocket. Agnes thought she was meant to demur, to get in the car with Peter Parsons and quietly drive away. But all her life she'd tried not to do what was expected of her. 'Thanks. I will.' She slipped past the older woman and angled right across the lawn. 'I'll check the pond. Peter, you go the other way and I'll meet you behind the house.'

Frances watched them for a moment with a kind of offended disbelief. Then she stalked back to The Nail.

Now what do we do?' demanded Colonel Freyn.

His daughter glared imperiously at him. 'We keep our nerve, that's what. This isn't a problem. They're not going to find anything in the garden. When the police are working out what happened, they'll be useful as witnesses. They know it was Mouse who came here, not us who went looking for him. Whatever happens is his responsibility.'

'Whatever happens?' echoed Freyn faintly.

'Don't start with me, Dad,' said Fran crisply. 'You know what needs doing. After this we'll be safe. He'll be gone, and that damned relic will be gone, and everyone'll shake their heads sadly and say they saw it coming. Sooner or later, playing with matches was going to get him killed.'

Twenty-Two

By the time Agnes reached the pond reality was intervening. She was never going to find Mouse this way. Perhaps he'd thought better of confronting the Colonel, and was even now hobbling home because Frances had moved the car he came in.

But she was already at the back of the house – she might as well keep going and meet Parsons as agreed. She turned at the willow, keeping parallel to the boundary hedge.

The summer sun was high above. At another time of day she mightn't have seen it. But across the Freyns' perfect lawn were faint silver tracks where the grass had been pressed flat and the blades reflected the light. Someone had driven across the lawn.

Between – Agnes looked left and right – the house and the gate on to the back lane. And not just once: someone had driven across the lawn and then driven back.

Who the hell, she asked herself in awe, would have the nerve to drive across the Freyns' lawn? Not Mouse – Agnes was pretty sure of that. He might have driven up the back lane, because it wasn't as far to hobble from the garden gate to the house as from the front gate and up the drive. But never in a hundred years could she see him driving across the grass.

If it wasn't Mouse, was it one of the Freyns?

Frances had been driving the vicar's car. She said she'd found it in the back lane, and that could have been where she was coming from. But what on earth would make her drive back and forth across her own lawn first?

Perhaps, having something heavy to transport between the back lane and the house?

Peter Parsons appeared round the far side of The Nail. He semaphored an exaggerated shrug. 'Any luck?'

'No,' she shouted back. But she ran to meet him.

Close enough to keep the words between themselves, she rattled out urgently: 'Mouse is here. Somewhere in the house. I think he's

281

hurt.' She told him about the tyre tracks, and the only explanation she could find for them.

From where the vicar was standing, it was more a feasible explanation than a plausible one. 'Fran?' he said, as if he might have misunderstood. 'You think *Fran*'s kidnapped *Mouse*?'

'If we're lucky,' said Agnes, her voice flat. She'd passed through alarm and come out the other side. 'But he wasn't walking. She needed the car to carry him.'

If she'd provided him with proof that St Mark's Gospel had been written in 1905 by an unemployed boiler-maker in Luton, Peter Parsons could hardly have looked more shocked. The mere idea hacked at the foundations of his world. The spinster daughters of prosperous middle-class England didn't do things like that. She was a hospital visitor, for God's sake! She arranged the flowers in his church – when he had a church. 'Why?' was all he could manage.

'Because Mouse was right. Not everything he's been blamed for was his fault. And somewhere deep down he knows it, and Frances knows he knows it, and he's only got to remember what happened that Saturday night and her whole bloody family's up shit creek without a paddle.'

Parsons winced. He still couldn't reconcile the delicate creature he could see with some of the things that came out of her mouth. 'This is all because the bit of cloth that was on my transverse wall for forty years wasn't the bit of the cloth it was supposed to be?'

Agnes's expression was scathing. 'Peter, try to keep up! It's not the cloth that's important. It's that Stuart Freyn could only have got hold of it if the Monsanto monks were killed by British troops rather than Yemeni tribesmen. There was a cover-up, and that cloth proves it. While nobody knew what it was, it didn't matter. But then Mouse got curious, and Ruth got curious, and they worked it out. And someone killed Ruth and tried to kill Mouse – twice, I don't believe that the incident with his IV was an accident, not now – to protect the secret. They burned your church trying to protect it.

'And now someone's taken Mouse inside The Nail, and Frances is telling us she hasn't seen him. I don't believe her, Peter. I think she knows where he is. I think she knows what happens next.'

The vicar's strong, honest face was pale. 'What happens next?'

'Peter, they k—'

She never got to finish the sentence. From inside the house came a sound like a karaoke singer blowing on his microphone. Agnes and Parsons exchanged a startled look. They didn't know what it was, but they were fairly sure it wasn't good news. Uncertainly at first, then with increased urgency, they headed up the lawn towards The Nail.

Before they got there the back door opened and Frances Freyn staggered down the kitchen steps and collapsed in a heap on the gravel. Smoke billowed from the open door.

Agnes and the vicar reached her in a moment. 'Frances, what's happened? Where's the smoke coming from?'

'I don't know,' she stammered. There were smuts on her face. 'The cellar, I think. It was Mouse. He took the banner off the hall table and down the cellar steps. He locked himself in. And then ... And then...'

It didn't take a leap of imagination to guess what she was going to say next. 'He set fire to the place?' whispered Agnes.

'I ... I think so. My father!' Her eyes were vast with fear. 'He's still inside! Find him, get him out...'

'Oh yeah,' muttered Agnes. 'That's my first priority.' She plucked at the vicar's sleeve and headed for the back door at a run. 'Come on.'

Frances was in no danger sitting on the gravel. Parsons left her and hurried after Agnes. His voice was a plaint. 'What the hell's going *on*?'

She wouldn't wait for him. 'I told you what's going on! They're disposing of the evidence. They've locked Mouse and the cloth in the cellar, they've started a fire, and they think that by the time anyone gets in there they'll both be past causing any more trouble. It'll be just one more bizarre incident to blame on Mouse. He didn't do any of it, Peter! The Freyns were behind it all. They used him as a scapegoat.'

'You think that's where he is? In the cellar?'

'I'm sure he is.' She crossed the kitchen in a couple of strides, following the smoke trail to the cellar door. 'That's where his body will be found. With the ashes of the cloth that for some reason he started obsessing about. He burned the church trying to destroy it; when that didn't work he followed it here to have another go.

'Only none of it's true.' She reached for the handle more in hope than expectation, but it turned and the door opened on to steep stone steps. At the bottom was another door. Flames flickered lurid in the gap beneath it and the stairwell was acrid with smoke.

'Mouse is in there?' Parsons's voice cracked.

For the first time Agnes hesitated. 'Peter – he may already be dead. Maybe this is as far as we should go.'

He took a deep breath – a little like before preaching his first sermon, more like before tackling his first black run. He gave her a

285

smile filled with fear and trepidation and dogged determination. 'This is as far as *you* go. There's nothing you can do in there, Agnes. If he's hurt, I can carry him. You can't. Get back on the phone. Police, fire service, ambulance. And ... maybe you should call Robin too.'

He tried the knob, snatched his hand back with a hiss. He tried again through the folds of a handkerchief but the door was locked.

Agnes was thinking at the speed of adrenalin. 'She pushed it under the door. The key – she locked the door and pushed the key through the gap. It has to be found in the cellar after the fire or it's not suicide, it's murder.' She raced back up the cellar steps, returned with the longest knife she could find.

It was where it had to be. It took a matter of seconds to locate the key and coax it back under the door. They were the longest seconds of her life. If she let it slip away ... Then it was on the flags in front of them. 'Careful,' she cautioned, 'it'll be...'

Too late: another hiss and he dropped it ringing on the stone floor, shaking his hand and cursing like a navvy.

Lacking a big enough handkerchief, Agnes used the hem of her dress. She hoped the vicar was too much of a gentleman to enjoy her déshabillé – or, failing that, that he was too preoccupied with his burnt fingers. The lock turned and the door opened.

Flames erupted at them through the doorway. Agnes dived one way, Parsons the other. By the time they'd picked themselves up the gout of fire had been sucked back into the room.

It was a big room, piled as cellars are with generations of junk no one would ever find a use for. Smoke wreathed blackly between the stacks like smog among skyscrapers, and they couldn't see Mouse from the door. But – like the key – Agnes knew where he had to be. If he was alive he'd have crawled away from where the fire started, where the flames were thickest. And if he wasn't it didn't matter. She pointed to the far corner of the room. 'There.'

'You can see him?'

'No.' They were both struggling to breathe now in the choking fumes. 'Must be.'

Ultimately it became a matter of faith. Peter Parsons believed absolutely in the goodness of God, though the evidence was often sketchy and sometimes contradictory. And he thought he was going to have to trust Agnes on the same basis. She'd been right before. She'd been right much more often than she'd been wrong, and she'd been right when he couldn't see what she was basing her guesses on. He'd nothing better to offer.

Either he went with Agnes's hunch or he hovered here in the doorway, filling his lungs with the murderous smoke, until he had neither the moral nor physical strength left to plunge into the fire.

He took one last breath, and wished it had more oxygen in it. Piece of cake, he told himself, unconvincingly. Compared with walking on water? – piece of cake. He waited a second longer, for one of the random gaps to appear in the flame curtain, then he threw himself through it.

Agnes would have done as he said. She intended to do as he said. But when she pulled her phone out again, here in the brick bowels of the Victorian house it couldn't get a signal. She stared at it aghast, then turned quickly and headed back up the steps.

Then she stopped and looked back. Peter Parsons was gone, swallowed up by the smoke and the flame, groping through the skin-crackling heat and the blinding glare, risking pain and injury and death to save someone who might already be beyond saving. Did she really mean to leave him to it? To trot outside into the clean fresh air and make some phone calls while he battled time and the smell of burning flesh, and the knowledge that some of it was his? Malleton was a long way from anywhere. The police were already on their way; the fire engines and the ambulance couldn't arrive for another twenty minutes. If Mouse was somehow still alive, his best chance lay not in a phone call but in being found and hauled out of there in the shortest possible time. Two of them looking would be quicker than one.

She left her phone on the step. She'd want it again, hopefully just a couple of minutes from now. She looked at the doorway. The room beyond seemed full of flames. But logic told her it wasn't, it was the stacks of old deckchairs and forgotten toys and battered suitcases full of clothes nobody could remember wearing that were alight. There would be ways for someone who was both swift and careful to pass between them unscathed. Or only slightly scathed...

But she had to do this if she was to live with herself afterwards. It wasn't the first time she'd embarked on something that terrified her, and with luck it wouldn't be the last. The difference was, if Covent Garden didn't like your Sugar Plum Fairy they didn't take a flame-thrower to you.

Green Berets yell 'Geronimo!' as they go into action. Agnes Amory snarled, 'Buggery-buggery-buggery...' and launched herself into the burning room.

The God of righteous causes, the God of innocent victims – Peter Parsons's God –

was on the job. She barely had time to register the incredible heat that had built up between the brick walls like an oven before she bumped into the stooped figure of the vicar, staggering backwards and half carrying, half dragging something behind him.

"This way.' She grabbed his belt and tugged him towards the door. When she could she reached past and got a hand on his burden, and together they hauled it to the foot of the cellar steps.

There Parsons sank to his knees, whooping in great draughts of air. But Agnes wouldn't let him rest. 'If that flashes over, we'll have a fireball coming out the door behind us.' Stumbling, helping one another, dragging Mouse like a sack of coal, they somehow reached the kitchen and slammed the door behind them.

'Outside,' gasped Agnes. She thought the door would hold back the fire for a while, but once Parsons sat down there'd be no shifting him. Safety was only a few paces away. She kept them moving until the kitchen floor turned to steps and then to gravel, and the smoke cleared and the sky was blue above. Finally she looked at Mouse.

Until now she hadn't dared to. If he was dead – worse, if he was still alive with the flesh burned from his bones – all her resolve would vanish in a moment. Now she could afford hysterics.

He *was* burned, but not to cinders. His hair was singed, his clothes were charred rags, and there were big dark shiny areas of skin where the flames had licked his cheek and one arm. It looked angry and unpleasant but it didn't look life-threatening. He was in for a lot of pain, maybe for skin-grafts, certainly more scars, but he should walk away from this. Or at least hobble.

Except that he wasn't breathing.

Twenty-Three

In her preoccupation with Mouse's injuries, Agnes had overlooked the fact that – though there are an almost infinite number of contributory factors – there are a comparatively small number of things which actually kill you. One of the biggies is not breathing, and smoke will do that, silently, without much drama, while fire is still warming up for its big scene.

From before Frances Freyn had staggered out of her kitchen door to raise the alarm,

Mouse had been breathing smoke. Though he was still barely conscious his body knew it was a bad idea and it shook him awake to tell him so.

If he'd recovered all his wits at once – which you tend not to do when someone's hit you behind the ear with a wrench – and thought as swiftly as Agnes, he'd have crawled to the door and groped round for the key. Instead he found himself in a place he didn't know, in a situation he knew all too well, where the only light came from the mounting flames and the only air was filling with gases that would soon kill him. He'd scrambled backwards away from the seat of the fire until a wall stopped him. He had no idea where the door was, and by now there were sheets of flame between him and it. And he still had only a vague idea of which way was up. He thought, he believed – he knew – that fire was going to be his unmaking after all.

Even so he did what he could to delay its victory. He kicked the junk-room detritus, ablaze and otherwise, as far from him as he could, hoping to preserve a space where there was just the stone walls, the stone flags and him. And he found a scrap of fabric, only a little singed, which he cupped to his face like a mask, breathing through it, hoping it would hold back the choking particles. It helped, but only for a little while. As the flames consumed his oxygen and spat out fumes that poisoned him, as his lungs sobbed and heaved and the coughing turned him inside out, he felt the strength leaching unstoppably from his muscles as his fragile consciousness spiralled once more towards the pit. His last thought that was recognizably his own was the old terror. He was going to burn. He was going to die burning. He'd thought he'd escaped it, but it was only waiting for him, waiting its chance ... Then even that faded, and his scorched eyes closed and his hand slumped nerveless to his side, still laxly clutching the singed cloth.

It was still bundled in his burnt hand when Agnes and Peter Parsons dragged him outside and dumped him on the gravel.

'Peter – help me. He isn't breathing!'

But Agnes was alone with this. Parsons had already given all he was capable of and probably more. He was burnt too, on his hands and arms, and he sprawled on his back with his chest pumping like a bellows to replenish his oxygen. She turned back to Mouse. All she knew was that if people weren't breathing, you breathed for them. She closed her lips over his, and blew unsteadily into his lungs.

Three or four times she did it, and then rocked back on her heels to observe the results. For a moment, watching Mouse's chest fall, she thought it had worked. But he drew no breath of his own to replace the ones she'd fed him. She felt for his heartbeat and there was nothing. She did what she'd seen them do on the telly and thumped his chest. Still nothing. She thought he was dead. She thought he was probably dead when Parsons found him.

'Oh Mouse,' she whispered brokenly.

Parsons groaned and rolled on to his front, looking at the weeping girl and the white-faced youth. 'Is he...?'

Agnes only nodded.

But the vicar of St Bride's-in-Malleton hadn't walked through fire to recover a corpse. He hauled himself over to where Mouse lay and took over where Agnes had given up. 'This ... isn't how ... it ends,' he declared grimly between breaths.

Then he saw the cloth. It took a moment to register what it was. Then he shot a startled glance at Agnes. 'Isn't that...?'

'Is it?'

Parsons breathed again, once for himself, once for Mouse, and thumped the bare chest where the shirt had burned away. Then he took the thing from Mouse's unresisting fingers.

'All right,' he said shakily. (Another breath; another breath.) 'This is where we are, this is what we have.' (Breathe, breathe, thump.) 'I don't know what it is. Maybe nothing.' (Breathe.) 'And I may not be the seventh son of a seventh son.' (Breathe.) 'But they say faith can move mountains, and I have faith aplenty. And I don't need a mountain moving. I just need *this*' – (thump) – 'to start up again. It's not an awful lot to ask.'

Agnes grew aware that he was no longer talking to her. 'I've done my best. I've tried to do what you wanted. And I tried not to put a price on that. But this is it – this is the bill. This is what I'm asking in return. Not a miracle – just a small adjustment in reality. It happens all the time. People's hearts stop, then they start again. Make it happen this time. He's a child – he's got all his life ahead of him. He shouldn't die like this. Not because it took me a few seconds longer to find him than there was air for him to breathe. A few seconds! You can turn the clock back a few seconds.'

Perhaps unconsciously his spare hand, the one that wasn't holding Mouse's nose, was bunching the dirty cloth between his palm and the boy's chest. Next time he brought his knotted fist down on Mouse's sternum the thing spread across his heart like the wing of a broken bird.

And nothing happened.

Except that's not quite true. What happened is that the police car which had had to come nearly all the way from Gloucester, which should have taken twenty minutes to get here, arrived in fifteen because the journey had taken less time than always. Because every junction had been empty when they got to it, and the motorway had been unaccountably quiet, and all the tractors that usually clogged the country lanes were in the fields today. Not a miracle, of course; but curious in its way.

And what this police car was carrying as part of its first-aid kit was a small canister of oxygen. That wasn't a miracle either. It just meant that a bit of thought had been given to the kinds of incidents an Immediate Response Vehicle might have to deal with, and how many of them might involve trauma victims and heart-attack victims who could be kept going till the ambulance arrived by a few whiffs of oxygen.

Parsons stayed where he was, pumping Mouse's chest with the cloth wadded in his hand, as the policemen put the mask to his face. Agnes too, desperate to help, knelt beside him and took his limp hand in hers. Nothing happened; nothing happened.

And then it did. They both saw the first hint of colour seep back into the pallor of Mouse's face.

Policemen are harder to impress. The one

who wasn't wielding the oxygen mask straightened up with a grunt of mild satisfaction. 'OK. Who's next?'

The tall man in the dog collar – it was true, vicars looked younger every year – was going to need treatment for some burns, but it clearly wasn't an emergency. Shock, and having other things to think about, were so far proving an adequate anaesthetic. And the slender girl in the black – shift? – appeared unhurt though tears were coursing down her elfin face.

But they looked at one another, and then around the gravel square behind the house, and the girl said, 'Fran?'

'Who's Fran?' asked Constable Gilbert.

'Frances Freyn,' explained the vicar distractedly, 'she lives here. She was right here. I didn't see where she went.'

'She's looking for the Colonel,' said the girl in a small voice.

The vicar nodded. 'Her father should be around here somewhere as well. Stuart Freyn. Constable.' Something in his tone of voice made Gilbert turn back. 'The pair of them are responsible for this' – he jerked his head first at the blaze now spread to the kitchen behind them, then to the boy on the ground – 'and this. Don't put yourself in danger.'

Constable Gilbert knew what he was being

297

told. He appreciated the thought, but it didn't make any difference. The job was what it was: he didn't get to say who deserved help and who didn't.

It was obvious from here that there was no longer a way into the house through the kitchen door. He headed round the front of The Nail at a run.

The front door was open. So someone had either come in or gone out that way, apparently in a hurry, probably since the fire started. He swept the gardens with his eyes but there was no one on the grass. He went up the steps into the front hall.

At least he didn't have to hunt for them. They were both there, the man with his arm around his daughter's shoulders, the woman with her arm around her father's waist, backs to the door, watching the progress of the flames from a minimal safe distance.

'All right,' said Constable Gilbert firmly. 'Let's get outside and wait for the fire service.'

The old man turned his head with a smile. An odd smile, both sad and contented. He said, 'None of this was supposed to happen. No one was supposed to get hurt. I thought I'd fixed things so that no one else would get hurt.'

Constable Gilbert was looking uneasily at the growing momentum of the fire. 'Yes?

Well – can you tell me about it outside?'

'It is getting rather close in here,' admitted Stuart Freyn. The three of them backed towards the door, and Constable Gilbert breathed a little more freely. 'And there are a couple of things I must tell you. The first is that my son was involved in none of this. It wasn't a family enterprise – it was me trying to protect myself, then my daughter trying to protect me. And the boy – the gardener – did nothing wrong either. We just made it look that way.'

None of this was making any sense to the constable. But it would, after CID interviewed Peter Parsons and Agnes Amory and all the pieces were on the table.

'There's one thing more I have to say. Not even to you – to Fran. I'm sorry I put you in this position. Knowing who you are, the sheer indomitable strength of your loyalty, you were always going to do whatever it took to keep me safe.'

'It wasn't your fault,' she murmured into the shield of his body.

He hugged her. 'Actually, it was. What I told you was mostly the truth, but the worst of it I didn't want to confess even to you. Do you know why? Because you're the strongest person I know. I didn't want to disappoint you.

'I told you about the cover-up. I said the

order came down from above. That was a lie. General Staff never knew there was anything to cover up, because I didn't tell them what had happened. And I didn't report it because the Monsanto atrocity wasn't something I learned about later. I was there. It was my patrol.'

The end was already in sight. British troops were soon going to be marching out of Aden. And if it was not a military defeat, none of those involved could feel it was a victory. It made it harder to maintain morale, and discipline.

Some of the men had heard of the treasure of Monsanto. No one knew what it was. A sergeant under Major Freyn suggested they go and look for themselves, before the opportunity was gone. It was risky – Freyn was thinking of the tribesmen in the hills, not the tired frustrated men in his trucks – but he too was tempted. And it wasn't much of a diversion, to take the dirt road up into the hills and see if there was any truth to the gossip.

The monks of Monsanto had survived for a thousand years in a hostile environment, and kept their treasure safe, by knowing when to slam the door in visitors' faces. The monastery was built like a fortress, and the desert beyond made it impractical to besiege it.

But their aeons-old strategies took no account of modern explosives. While Freyn was trying to swallow his anger and get his troops back on the transport, the sergeant was breaking out the dynamite.

He could have stopped it. But the devil on his shoulder whispered that it was no more than they deserved. British troops had died to hold the line between these Christian monks and the Arab world – but they weren't good enough to see the treasure? Serve them right if their front door was turned to matchwood!

But of course it didn't stop there, and Freyn should have known it wouldn't. The first casualty was the brother porter who was checking through the spyhole to see if the soldiers were leaving. It was more bad luck than an act of murder, but it meant it was no longer possible just to shoulder their way into the treasury, gawp at the wealth of a millennium, liberate a few souvenirs and leave. The death meant repercussions.

There were, it turned out, sixteen monks. Perhaps if there had been thirty, certainly if there had been a hundred, they would have been safe. No one would have contemplated the murder of dozens of innocent men to keep the wormwood secret of an honourable regiment momentarily out of control. But sixteen – fifteen, now ... And there were eight of them in the patrol. And a man might consider that two lives, the lives of two odd brown-skinned little monks holed up in a desert fortress, wasn't too high a price for his own freedom.

It took twenty minutes, no more, to render Monsanto uninhabited. Twenty minutes for eight men to search every room and kill everyone they found. They used knives, for fear that bullets might be identified. The last five they found huddled together in a corner of the high-vaulted church, praying aloud. Freyn couldn't understand the words, but the urgent rhythms remained fresh in his head after all these years. One by one, methodically, the soldiers slit their throats. The last, the very last of them, was a boy no older than Mouse Firth, who died with terror in his eyes and entreaties on his lips, and his blood spilt on Stuart Freyn's boots and turned the red dust there to clay.

It took half an hour to gather the bodies together beneath their altar and have the church dynamited ready to blow. Only after that were the killers allowed to choose their spoils. They were surprisingly responsible, Freyn thought bemusedly. They didn't load themselves down with a whole load of jewelled crosses and church plate they couldn't sell without announcing their guilt. They filled their pockets with small, precious but largely unidentifiable items they could realize one at a time, via discreet jewellers in Istanbul, Riyadh or Amsterdam. And they chose well and sold carefully, because Freyn never heard that any of the Monsanto treasure was recovered.

He himself, both excited and appalled by what had happened, took the reliquary that he recognized as the true treasure of Monsanto. But before he even got out of the church he knew it was a mistake. There was nowhere he could sell it, no way he could keep it. He put it back on the altar and took out the cloth. It was just a cloth, painted by time and the eye of hope into the vague likeness of a bearded face. Away from here it would never be recognized. He had no idea what he might do with it, but he somehow expected that a solution would present itself.

He spent the next forty years waiting. And in the end he was proved right.

Constable Gilbert wasn't sure what he was hearing. An explanation, a confession – a boast? But Frances Freyn knew. He was setting the record straight, because there wouldn't be another chance. Her arm tightened round his waist. 'It doesn't matter, you know,' she said softly.

Stuart Freyn smiled. 'Good.' Then he looked at the policeman. 'Sorry to keep you. Probably time we got out of here now, do you think? That' – he indicated the ravening flame – 'seems to be getting worse.'

The constable gave a relieved nod and headed for the door. 'Come on then. Let's get this sorted out.'

He had a fraction of a second to realize he was doing it wrong. Whatever the Freyns had done, forty years ago and in the last few days, it was his job to protect them. Anxious as he was to leave the burning building, he should have seen them to safety first. He thought they were right behind him. And they were. He was barely across the threshold when Stuart Freyn shut the door behind him and turned the key.

Don't believe what you see in films: you cannot break down a Victorian front door with just your shoulder and determination. Constable Gilbert hammered with his fists at the solid wood and yelled through the letterbox, but no one answered.

Beside the door were two narrow panes of etched glass. By craning his neck the policeman could see into the hall.

Looking back over his shoulder, Stuart Freyn saw him and smiled again. Then he and his daughter, the woman who was so much like him in every way, still with their arms about one another in that affectionate, understanding embrace, walked into the flames and vanished.

Twenty-Four

Soon after they parted in Gloucester, Nick Freyn continuing towards London, Robin Firth to look for a ride back to Malleton, they were intercepted by policemen and escorted to the same police station.

It was better news for Robin than for Freyn. His son was safe. Singed and suffering from smoke inhalation – again – back on the same hospital ward but fully conscious, sitting up and complaining that everyone knew what had happened except him. He was clearly going to be fine. Also, he was off the hook as far as any charges were concerned. When Robin was up to date on events in Malleton the area car took him to the hospital.

Agnes had travelled in with Mouse; and the vicar of St Bride's was being treated for his own burns further down the same ward. It was as if Malleton had opened a consulate

305

in the district hospital.

Before he had time to talk to Mouse, his doctor arrived with more tests to run and displaced the visitors into the corridor. Robin and his fiancée regarded one another gravely. There was such a lot to say, so difficult to know where to start. 'Are *you* all right?'

'Fine.' She was dirty, her odd little dress ragged, and now the adrenalin had subsided she looked tired. But he believed her.

'It was the Freyns? It was all the Freyns?'

'Yes,' said Agnes.

'Even Ruth...'

'Yes,' said Agnes; and there was an inflection there warning him this was something they had to talk about. That *even* and what it signified. That a part of him was still in love with his ex-wife. He'd almost lost his son to these people. Three times they'd come close to killing him. But it was *Even Ruth...*

Robin shook his head in weary self-recrimination. 'I know I've made a mess of this. But for you, and Peter, I'd have lost him. Mouse would be dead now, but for you. He'd be dead because I didn't believe him. He knew, even if he couldn't say how he knew, that he'd nothing to feel guilty about. And Peter, who knows him a little, and you who didn't know him at all were ready to give him the benefit of the doubt. And I

306

wasn't. He's my child. You're supposed to love them regardless. Even if they've done something terrible, you go on loving them. But I didn't.

'Mouse'll forgive me. I don't know how, but I know he will. Because he's better at loving than I am. When Mouse loves, it's unconditional. Which makes him a better man than I am.' He swallowed and glanced nervously at her. 'What about you? Can you forgive me?'

She had to think about it. If he was hoping for instant absolution he was disappointed. Finally she said carefully, 'Robin, it would be easy to say, Let's forget everything that happened – let's start afresh. But it would be a mistake. Maybe, a fatal mistake. We've all been traumatized, whether we realize it or not. It's going to take time, and work, and maybe some outside help, to get through it.

'But if you're asking me whether I think it's worth the effort, whether I want to put in that much time and work when I could just walk away and leave you and your crazy son to sort things out as best you can, then the answer is yes. I don't love unconditionally either. Not like Mouse and spaniels. But I believe in working for what I want. And I believe we'll come through this.'

She had to stop then. Tears were coursing down Robin Firth's cheeks into his beard.

He took her to the train station. All at once she wanted to be home, sleeping in her own bed, surrounded by familiar things; with time to think about all that had happened and what it meant for the future. She didn't even collect her things from Mouse's house. She washed her face in a hospital bathroom, borrowed money from Robin to buy a dress from the nearest chain store, then had him take her to the station. He waited with her until the London train was ready to leave. It was hard to be sure, but he thought they were going to be all right.

He intended to stay in Malleton until Mouse was back on his feet, in every sense. He hoped they could help heal one another.

As he was leaving the station he found himself in traffic behind a long silver car that was immediately familiar. He'd known Nick Freyn for ten years. It was a business relationship – sometimes they'd been allies, sometimes competitors. He'd have hesitated to call Freyn a friend but he'd never thought of him as an enemy. Actually, he still didn't.

By now Robin had heard most of the facts, from the police and Agnes and especially Mouse who'd been present in body and increasingly in spirit when Frances Freyn told her father what had happened. What she'd done, and how. And Nick had been no part of it, nor had he known or had any reason to suspect what was going on. None of us, Robin thought ruefully, can choose our families. If we could, surely to God Mouse would have come up with one decent parent...

Sooner or later, Robin was aware, he and Nick Freyn would have to deal with one another. With the grief that was between them. If they weren't going to spend the next ten years avoiding one another at City functions, they'd have to talk. And it would get harder the longer they left it.

Even so, the chance came sooner than he expected. Traffic lights changed ahead of them but the silver car didn't move off. Robin waited patiently. Cars behind him started hooting. After a minute he got out of his car and walked forward.

Nick Freyn was sitting rigid behind the wheel, staring past the empty junction with fixed, appalled eyes. Whatever he was seeing, it wasn't the green light; whatever he was hearing, it wasn't the impatient honking behind him.

Robin opened his door. He had to touch his sleeve to get Freyn's attention. 'Nick, you're holding up the traffic. Pull over there. Let's talk.'

Given a direct instruction he could obey. The traffic started moving again. 'OK,' said

Robin, 'you're in no fit state to be driving. We're going to leave your car here for an hour and go somewhere quiet. OK?' Again, Freyn did as he was told.

Robin found a park, and bought hot dogs from a kiosk mainly to give them something to do with their hands. They sat in the evening sunshine, surrounded by people walking their dogs and children playing football, and the events of the day could have been an age and a continent away. Except for the shock still drawing Freyn's cheeks – and actually, if he'd looked in a mirror, Robin's too.

Now he'd got them here he couldn't think how to start. So he dived right in and said what he needed Freyn to hear. 'No one blames you for any of this. I don't, and no one else will.'

Freyn cast him a quick glance that was half grateful, half tormented. 'She killed your wife! She tried to kill your son.'

'Yes, she did,' agreed Robin softly. 'Nick – I don't think Frances was entirely sane when she did that. She was so consumed by the need to protect your father that any price seemed worth paying.'

'And he killed those monks.' He knew it was true. He'd been told by people he had no choice but to believe. But all his instincts rebelled against it. They were his father and his sister. He thought of family meals round the long table heavy with the good china, and drinks on the lawn watching impromptu games of tennis. Now when he thought of them he couldn't even grieve for all the blood getting in the way.

Robin gave a helpless shrug. 'It was a war situation. Under that much stress, people do crazy things. Sometimes they make heroes of themselves, sometimes the opposite. It's hard to sit in judgement when we're not facing the same kind of danger.

'Nick, there's one thing you should know. Mouse told me and he told the police, but maybe they didn't tell you. Ruth's death was an accident. And though Fran meant to kill Mouse, she didn't succeed. And she paid for what she did. Both of them did.'

Nick's grey eyes were bright with tears. 'That helps. Thank you.' He blinked. 'Does that mean Mouse has got his memory back?'

Robin shook his head. 'No – he heard them talking.' In fact, they'd been doing exactly what had got them into trouble in the first place: talking in front of Mouse as if he wasn't entirely there. And this time he wasn't. He was barely conscious, tied up with washing line and lying at their feet like a roll of carpet. But he'd heard every word, and this time he remembered.

'Is he...?' He had to swallow and try again. But somewhere he found the courage to look

311

Robin Firth in the face as he asked. 'Is he going to be all right?'

'Yes,' nodded Robin. 'Yes, he's going to be fine. He'll be out of hospital tomorrow, maybe the day after. No lasting damage. Well – a few missing weeks, still. They may come back in due course, or they may not. Maybe it'll be better if they don't. He knows what happened, now – maybe he'll be better not remembering it as well.'

'Robin, I'm so, so sorry...'

'I know.' Robin smiled. 'I know you are. Don't worry about Mouse. My son is made of stout stuff.' The amount of pride he heard in his own voice pleased him.

'Listen.' He wrapped the remains of the hot dog in its paper and binned it. 'Go home. There'll be things for you to sort out here, but they don't have to be done today. Go home, spend a few days with your wife and children, come back when you've got your head together. I'll be at Ruth's – no, Mouse's – cottage. If I can help, call me.'

The offer, which he would never take up, nonetheless meant more to Nick Freyn than he could say. All he could do was shake his head in a kind of agonized wonder. 'I can't help missing them. Is that insane? After what they did – what they tried to do. To still love them? I can't help still loving them.'

'I'll let you into a secret,' said Robin

gruffly. 'When I thought Mouse was responsible for his mother's death, I stopped loving him. I wasn't just angry and bitter and disappointed and shocked – I stopped loving him. I would give *anything* to have those few days over again, and do them better. Don't apologize for loving your family, Nick. They never hurt you the way I hurt Mouse.'

They walked back to the cars then, slowly, in no hurry to part. Hot dogs in the park had begun the reconciliation.

Nick said, 'What about the cloth? Whatever it is. What happens to it now – what's left of it?'

'It's on its way to Rome,' said Robin. 'Peter took it with him to the hospital, and would not let it out of his sight until his bishop picked it up. As for what it is, who knows? It's the reason nineteen people died, and maybe why one lived. Does that make it a good thing or a bad thing?

'Or is it just a thing – an object, a curiosity? From where I'm standing, it was Peter Parsons who saved Mouse's life, and he'd have acted exactly the same way if he'd never heard of the Monsanto Veronica. Would his actions have had the same results? There's no way of knowing. Those who believe in miracles would say not; pragmatists would say they would.'

'And you?' asked Freyn, watching his face.

'I don't care,' Robin Firth said honestly. 'My son's alive when he could so easily have been dead. He's alive because a brave man risked his own life diving into a fire to save him. That's miracle enough for me. I don't know if there's a God. But I do know what decent people are sometimes capable of, and it astonishes me.'

He smiled then and clapped the smaller man on the shoulder. 'Go home, Nick. Kiss your wife. Tell her ... Tell her to buy a new dress. I think she's going to an engagement party.'